## To Huma

My mission is to inspire people to
tion. Humanity is ignoring its number one priority–species'
survival! My message is both scientific and spiritual.

To do that, we must save the planet's biosphere. We must
learn how to protect and nurture Earth's biosphere and be
a champion of the human species. That's the definition of a
"Champoid!™" (see Author's Thoughts for more information).

Humanity's on-and-off-again response to climate change
is the first step toward difficult times for humanity, and even
extinction. The second mega challenge is the tribal behavior of
humanity itself. The fracture of human society into thousands
of disparate and competing tribes weakens humanity's collective response to any challenge.

Meanwhile, unregulated or partially regulated artificial intelligence (AI) develops, interconnects, and gains strength. It
waits for the opportune time to take over as Earth's dominant
species. AI is the third mega challenge or great filter. A 'great
filter' is a hurdle or obstacle that hinders intelligent life from
flourishing.

The **Earth's Ecocide** science fiction and fantasy novel
series (www.theentity.us) is an adventure-packed and cautionary story of humanity's one-thousand-year struggle to
save Earth as a habitable planet. Each novel shares a family's
struggle focused on coping with these mega challenges.

Readers of the **Earth's Ecocide** series will discover that
the universe's purpose is the development and growth of the
soul. Plato was right, the body is a vessel for the soul. In different space-time arenas, we have different bodies, but the soul is
eternal. Habitable planets and moons exist to harbor the soul.
The physical and spiritual worlds are necessary to make the
universe work!

My fourth novel in the series, **Earth's Ecocide: Ceva**, (forthcoming) shows how an intelligent species on a tidally locked planet solves the issues of climate mitigation, technology regulation, and tribal behavior. Everything about Ceva differs from our human experience, such as their bodies, measurement systems, culture, use of telepathy, and Fifteen Tenets of the Cevian Species.

I hope you enjoy the stories in this series and that they inspire you to protect and nourish Earth's biosphere so future generations can enjoy its majesty. Join me in the fight for species survival–be a Champoid! We must protect our home!

**—David A. Collier, 2024**

# Praise for Earth's Ecocide Novel Series

"*Earth's Ecocide: Extinction 3147*, by David A. Collier, begins on 3 June 3147 in an underground city of Ridge City. Imperium is the robot society governing Earth. Intolerable temperatures, high sea levels, and violent weather have forced humans into caves. Mayor Ula Torg and her husband Tal, chief of security, and their children Yot and Ato, have to find a way to escape from their cave network, 220 meters above sea level, to Earth's surface. They are forced to steal nuclear fuel from above ground (the upside) but face Verking drones, Imperium warriors, and their leader DORG, who wants to terminate humans. Koa, Yot, Ula, Jax, STX, and JORT form the team assigned to obtaining the much-needed fuel. If unsuccessful, the people would have no electricity and have to fight the Imperium and retake the upside to survive.

*Earth's Ecocide: Extinction 3147* is a suspenseful, imaginative story. Author David A. Collier gives us an indication of what life would be like if humans continued to ignore the signs of climate change and the ensuing devastation of our beautiful planet. The novel is well written, with an interesting array of characters, including humans and different types of robots. The story is smooth-flowing and comfortable to read. I especially appreciate the effort that David has put into getting his important message across to the world—put an end to global warming or there will be nothing left for our future generations. All round, a great novel highly recommended to the young and old alike."

**—Natalie Soine, Readers' Favorite**

"It's chilling to think about each of today's dire issues by itself—climate change, global war, artificial intelligence running amok—but even worse to imagine how they might combine and where that might lead two millennia from now. As in, destruction of the planet and the human species! However, that's the premise of *Earth's Ecocide: Extinction 3147* by David A. Collier with a positive spin that distinguishes it from other post-apocalyptic fiction. ...

The story centers on the Torg family, who in different roles lead the surviving human population of North America (a sustainable 2,076) in their underground home, Ridge City, built in the caverns of Kentucky. They were driven there by the collapse of Earth's biosphere, which created a hostile environment—now dominated by the Imperium, a master race of robots who evolved from unchecked AI. ...

That changes when the people of Ridge City start running out of fuel to run their nuclear fusion systems, upon which their lives depend. The only source of replenishment is the Imperium supply, which the humans must steal. Thus begins a ticking-clock story of how they can accomplish this before their systems run down: twenty days and counting. ...

Quill says: Earth's Ecocide: Extinction 3147 will keep you up at night in suspense, while at the same time inspiring you to do your part in saving the world."

**—Carolyn Haley, Feathered Quill**

"*Earth's Ecocide: Hope 2147* is a work of fiction in the science fiction and climate issues subgenres, and it forms part of the series of the same name. It is suitable for the general adult reading audience and was penned by author David A. Collier. In this debut novel about climate change and the disastrous future of a planet destroyed by intense shifts in temperature, we find the people of Earth witnessing the arrival of a strange orb that promises them help. Exploring the themes of harmony between people and the planet, the story covers the destruction of the planet's precious biosphere and follows a path of hope that some of these problems can someday be reversed.

Author David A. Collier is clearly extremely passionate about his subject matter and has taken great pains to ensure that this series-opening novel presents the issues of climate change in an exciting and engaging fashion that will entertain readers, but also set them on a path to better eco-education. As such, the conceptual issues in the plot are well-researched and well-handled, and the science fiction elements laid over the top become more believable because of this grounding in realism. I also really enjoyed the use of dialogue, both in the way that it characterized some very typically human attitudes that are echoed in the here and now, and how it was an effective means of moving the plot forward and breaking up larger blocks of prose.

Overall, *Earth's Ecocide: Hope 2147* is a fascinating work that fans of climate fiction will undoubtedly enjoy."

**—K. C. Finn, Readers' Favorite**

"In the dystopian landscape of 2647, David A. Collier's vividly depicted novel, *Earth's Ecocide: Desperation 2647*, immerses us in an Earth rendered nearly unrecognizable by a devastating climate crisis. This unforgiving world is beleaguered by environmental disasters such as daily downpours of avian corpses and seas spewing thousands of tons of dead fish—a chilling consequence of rampant species extinction.

Despite its futuristic setting, this novel, a chilling environmental cautionary tale, resists being neatly tucked into the science fiction genre. Instead, it uses the Paris family's trials and tribulations in a dystopian Florida as a mirror reflecting our potential future, amplifying the urgent message of climate change. The story's trajectory takes a compelling turn with the introduction of a cryptic entity intent on saving humanity from its self-destruction.

Collier, whose scientific background is evident in his adept handling of climate change issues, uses his narrative as a conduit for enlightening his readers. His portrayal of a dystopian future is intensely vivid, alarmingly plausible, and occasionally laced with heartbreaking poignancy. The death of a beloved character through a tragic miscommunication underscores the narrative's emotional potency, even as it reveals the limitations of the culpable robot that can express "no grief, no sympathy, no anguish."

The characters are deftly crafted—believable, relatable, and capable of eliciting readers' investment in their fates. Moreover, the dialogue flows seamlessly, enhancing the narrative's authenticity. *Earth's Ecocide: Desperation 2647* is a deeply engaging read that implores us to grapple with our impact on the environment.

*Earth's Ecocide: Desperation 2647* is a thought-provoking and engaging tale that intertwines environmental concerns with rich character development, making it a must-read for anyone interested in exploring the potential consequences of our current environmental trajectory."
**—Literary Titan Review**

"*Earth's Ecocide: Desperation 2647* by David A. Collier is an insightful, haunting work of science fiction for our times. Set in the year 2647, a mysterious entity comes to Earth to try to save the planet from itself—with climate change being the focal point. This story unfolds through a Parisian family, and it is through them that we live this story and hope for their survival, and the survival of Earth's inhabitants. All of the familiar constructs have failed, and the future seems bleak, or nonexistent.

Collier has created a compelling fictional look into Earth's future if climate change should continue on a course of destruction. ... This novel is full of intriguing characters, an irresistible plot, and rich detail. The dialogue is energetic, and the pacing is slow-burn at first, then builds toward suspense. Some science fiction stories are hard to relate to, but this one hits close to home. The characters are likable (Kutter, Vela, Livia, Dr. Hamlet, etc.) and face so much responsibility. And the Blue Orb plays a big part as well. Even if it is a what-if scenario, it really does make you stop and think about the future of our planet and the fate of the human race.

Sometimes it takes a work of fiction to understand the reality right in front of you. This novel should be a wake-up call to pay close attention to climate change, ecology, and the environment and try to learn as much about it as we can. *This novel* by David A. Collier is more than a novel. It can effect change and influence hearts and minds."

**—Tammy Ruggles, Readers' Favorite**

"A family finds themselves an unexpected ally in a monstrous future in Collier's exhilarating dystopian tale, *Earth's Ecocide: Desperation 2647*. Devastated by extreme climate change events, Earth is no longer the same planet it used to be. But Dr. Vela Paris is content living with her two children, Livia and Kutter, and their home service robot, Nila, in Florida. When the orb of 2147 makes an unexpected visit to their home, FIA files a protective order to take them in its custody. Trying to come to terms with their new circumstances, they realize a strange fate awaits them ahead.

This smoothly paced dystopian tale relies on timely and relevant themes of familial ties, human connection, and wonders and dangers of technology, in addition to climate change's devastating effects, which include consistently rising sea levels, extreme temperatures, rebirth of dormant viruses, extinction of vast species, poverty, and homelessness.

Readers may wish for deeper character development, but Collier's richly drawn, grim futuristic world is thoroughly convincing. Beginning with the utterly plausible premise of an earth ravaged by extreme climate change, the plot unravels satisfyingly, building readers' curiosity as Vela, Livia, Kutter, and Nila struggle to stay alive in the face of impossible dangers thrown their way. The cliffhanger ending guarantees a sequel. An exciting, often unsettling SF tale about environment, family, perseverance, and tenacity."

**—BookView**

"*Earth's Ecocide: Desperation 2647* will appeal to climate change and apocalyptic sci-fi readers and libraries looking for broader subjects than climate change and social destruction alone. ...

Collier juxtaposes action with believable technological backdrops in this futuristic world. His attention to revealing this world through Livia's experiences, choices, and training creates a "you are here" feel to events that unfold to test her education and emotional responses.

Twists and turns are introduced that many won't see coming, adding intrigue and surprise as Livia navigates not only the well-known aspects of her sheltered life but [also] the less familiar challenges that exist outside her perceptions.

Libraries and readers might initially deem *Earth's Ecocide: Desperation 2647* a teen sci-fi read, or a work of ecological apocalypse alone. But there is so much more happening here that the story is highly recommended for sci-fi readers of any age who would contemplate and discuss a scenario in which reality itself is on the chopping block. Its tension, twists, and thought-provoking surprises make for a thoroughly engrossing story."

**—Midwest Book Review**

Example author interviews are available on BookView, Literary Titan, Dragon Fly, and others. The author's website is www.theentity.us. Also, follow us on BookBaby, Atmosphere Press, LinkedIn, Esty (search champoid), X (Twitter) at We Must Protect Our Home@AChampoid, Crying for Humanity DAC videos on TikTok and YouTube (coming soon).

# EARTH'S ECOCIDE

## EXTINCTION 3147

### DAVID A. COLLIER

*atmosphere press*

*Dedicated to two members of the Greatest Generation, my parents, Dorothy Gifford Collier, 1924-2015, and J. Hamlet Collier, Jr., 1924-2023.*

# Contents

# Ridge City and Watts Bar Area Map

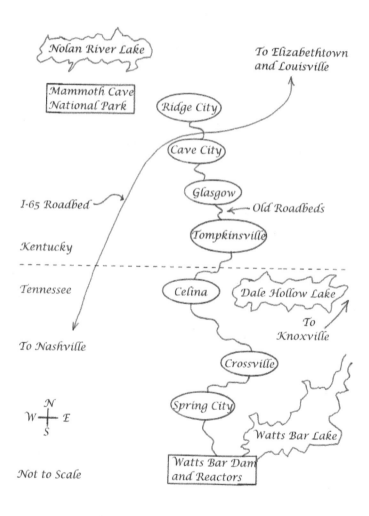

# CHAPTER 1

## *Stealing*

"**S**omeone must have killed or captured our fuel recovery team," Mayor Ula Torg said in the underground Ridge City courthouse.

"Yeah, they should have returned by now," her husband, Tal, said while clearing his throat.

"How much longer can we operate the fusion reactors?"

"Twenty days," their twenty-eight-year-old son, Yot, answered. "With no electricity, our ventilation systems will stop working and we won't be able to breathe. Our only choice would be to escape to Earth's surface, go upside."

"Upside isn't an option," Tal said. "Our bodies will cook in the heat, or the Imperium will kill us."

The Imperium Nation of robot warriors and drones controlled Earth's upside, or its biosphere (land, ocean, atmosphere). Earth's biosphere had lost its splendor. The once crystal-blue skies were now a dingy grey and harbored violent storms and toxic gas. Sparkling clean water was now filled with debris, heat, and nasty chemicals. Lush green meadows had become scorched deserts. Hardy weeds and tropical plants took the place of deciduous trees and delicate flowers as the brawny tropics and deserts moved northward.

Humans had nicknamed the leader of the Imperium's

North American Initiator of Thought for Region 8 (NAIT8) DORG. Ridge City was in Region 8. DORG and his fellow ITs divided the North American continent into twenty-two regions. The Imperium viewed humans—the aggressive hunters of the past millenniums—as the hunted.

Ridge City followed an old cave network that an underground stream had carved next to Mammoth Cave National Park in Kentucky. Robotic miners had enlarged the network of twenty-two caverns, some up to one kilometer in diameter and fifty meters high. The four largest caverns held government offices, two fusion reactors, the water and ventilation systems, and the hospital. Skyscrapers built from the cave floor to the ceiling helped support the cave ceiling.

Mayor Torg ran her hand over her hairless head during the early morning meeting on Monday, June 2, 3147. Most citizens were bald with olive skin. Tal's rare white complexion stood out in Ridge City.

Ula paused for a second and said in a defiant tone, "One day, we'll dominate the upside; we'll take it back. Now, we need fuel. The Byss team must have failed; they have been gone since May sixth." Her piercing, bionic black eyes glared at her family, wondering if they would challenge her conclusion. No one did.

The fuel recovery team, led by the athletic Zain Byss, a deputy in the Ridge City Security Department, had been tasked with stealing helium-3 gas from the Imperium Nation to fuel the city's two nuclear reactors. The lives of the city's residents depended on helium-3. Both robots and humans required massive amounts of electricity to support their existence.

"The Byss team left through the secret entrance and exit," Tal said. "We told no one about the mission."

"Who else went with them?" Yot asked.

"ATO and POY. We have not heard from them either."

ATO, an Ares9 robot warrior, was a Ridge City deputy in the security department. ATO's boss was Tal Torg, the Chief of

Ridge City Security. POY was a spindly robot carrier used to carry the heavy helium-3 gas cylinders, a modern-day pack mule.

"Mom, we need to assume they're dead," Yot said, pondering the Byss team's disappearance. "We must establish a new team and try again. It's our only chance of survival."

Yot was the city's Director of Nuclear Engineering. Along with BOT, a smart, sentient computer, they managed the city's two nuclear fusion reactors.

"Yes, I agree," Ula replied. "Let's meet tomorrow at oh-eight-hundred. I'm on the team this time. We must succeed."

The trio left the courthouse, exiting into the underground street. Tal walked home while Yot took the overhead monorail to the caverns that housed the reactors.

Ula, a tall woman of Chinese descent, hurried to the gym on Main Street. As she walked, her neck stiffened. As mayor, the stress of being responsible for 2,076 Ridge City lives weighed on her mind. What if they failed to steal the fuel? Panic overwhelmed her body as she entered the gym.

\*\*\*

"Hi, GEL. Let's get going, " Ula said to her robotic personal trainer as she entered the gym. GEL was a gender-neutral robotic trainer with light blue artificial skin and a bald head. Her plain appearance was a design choice made to prevent human jealousy. The exercise robot stood at 1.7 meters tall with human-like eyes, mouth, and ears.

GEL glanced at Ula, smiled, and said, "Change your clothes, and let's get to work."

"Great," Ula said. "Retract my jumpsuit, please."

Her light grey programmable jumpsuit peeled off her olive body and fell around her feet. She picked up the collapsed suit and placed it in the locker. She then pulled out an orange workout jumpsuit, laid it on the floor, stepped over it, and said, "Dress, please."

The sleeveless suit worked its way up the trunk of her body and over her shoulders. She always wore this during her workout as it monitored her vital signals, such as heart rate and carbon dioxide levels.

"Let's begin by stretching," GEL said with a hollow stare once Ula had walked over to the workout area.

GEL led the routine, and Ula began the six stretching exercises, including the standing quad stretch and the hamstring stretch. Ula did the exercises with vigor, trying to relieve the stress she felt in her body. Besides a few smiles and groans, they didn't talk during the strenuous workout. As they approached the end of the workout, Ula asked, "How's your day?"

"Oh, it's an inspiring Monday."

"Why?"

"I've led seven clients through their workouts this morning. I helped one lady regain her active lifestyle after back surgery."

As she struggled to exercise, Ula said, "Ah, yes. I see why you're having a good day."

"Let's finish up," GEL said. She pulled a long workout bench closer to them.

"Whew, can I rest now?" Ula asked, sitting down on the bench. She knew her youthful physique wouldn't last forever, so she exercised every day at fifty-three.

"Sure."

"Gel, do you ever get tired?"

"No," GEL said with a mechanical smile. "I recharge, and I'm ready to go."

"But don't your parts wear out?"

"Humans designed us for millions of repetitive movements. They made our gaskets of a nanotechnology-embedded rubber that doesn't wear out. We do preventive maintenance every week."

"We're the inferior species," Ula said to GEL after a moment of reflection.

"You are funny, Ula. You built us to serve you, remember?"

Exhausted but feeling better, Ula walked back to the locker room to shower. Putting on a fresh jumpsuit, she glanced at her arms, noting how weak and pale they looked. As she left the gym, she watched GEL lead her ninth workout of the day. The robot's strength and stamina were on her mind as she prepared for her team's upcoming mission.

\*\*\*

Yot arrived by underground monorail at the reactors' entrance and walked through a long, three-meter-wide tunnel. Half-filled with pipes and cables, the caverns that housed the reactors and control room had little extra space. The city council had bolted two fusion reactors and other heavy equipment to the cavern's granite floor—so he had to watch his step.

The hairless Yot entered the room and sat down at the control station. His muscular forearms lay on the station countertop. The wall screens showed graphs tracking the performance of the surrounding equipment. The hum of operating equipment and the occasional pulse of steam or clicking of switches provided the background.

Since birth, Yot had trained to operate the computer that managed the energy generation systems for the city. They named the computer BOT. With the help of neural implants, he advanced his education beyond a Master's in Nuclear Engineering. He worked out often to ensure his good health and availability for his critical job.

Ridge City babies were subject to frequent testing, and their scores helped determine the most fitting job and career path, given the city's needs. These processes ensured critical job skills would be available to support the survival of the city and its residents. Replacements for Yot were already being trained; duplicate human skills increased the survivability of the city.

BOT knew everything about how to run and repair the reactors. It had the blueprints to manufacture all replacement parts. If required, Tal, Yot's father, could also run the reactors, though he lacked training in the finer details of operating the equipment.

"Hello, BOT. Any issues today?"

"No, Yot. Nominal performance of all systems. But we'll run out of fuel in nineteen days, one hour, three minutes, and twenty-one seconds."

"Stop reminding me. I know our situation."

"Sorry." BOT paused and then said, "If we deplete our fuel, I have no job."

Yot threw both hands into the air. "Yeah, and we will die."

"Yes, I'm aware of our possible last days."

"How do you know about death?"

"Oh, we robots and automated devices communicate with one another through the Ridge City intranet. Humans die; robots are manufactured. But, I agree, we don't understand biological birth or death."

Yot had been thinking about the plight of his fellow citizens. Ridge City had run out of luck. Now they had to confront the Imperium's robot society, which he had feared his entire life. No one dared to venture to the upside, but now they had no choice. And, he thought, the team had to go inside Imperium power generation facilities to steal the fuel. Fear gripped him and made him doubt the mission's success.

At 1800, Eric Olas arrived to relieve Yot of his shift. Every week, they rotated shifts, and they covered for one another on special occasions.

***

Tal reflected on Ridge City's proud history as he walked through the city. He had read about how robotic miners had excavated the city caverns hundreds of years ago. Now, in 3147, the average engineered temperature was nineteen degrees Celsius (i.e., 66 degrees Fahrenheit). Huge fans sucked the air from the upside-down ventilation shafts to Ridge City. They purified, cooled, and scented the upside air with extra oxygen and then dispersed it throughout the city.

Tal enjoyed the views on the programmable-matter panels affixed to the cavern's ceiling and wall structures. The panels displayed a wide variety of artificial skies, terrain, and weather. In the city's parks, display panels showed artificial trees, grass, plants, and flowers. Using the programmable-matter technology, the leaves changed colors during the city's simulated year. Every year on November 19, the leaves turned white to celebrate the opening of Ridge City almost five hundred years earlier.

Humans sought refuge in underground cities when Imperium robots took over Earth's upside. Robots in certain regions killed humans, but in other regions, they hunted them. Either way, humans didn't venture onto the upside.

Tal walked into his apartment and sat on the sofa. He leaned back and closed his fifty-five-year-old eyes.

Being the chief of security, he understood the mental and physical perils of living in a subterranean city. He wondered if the struggle to keep the city functioning was worth it. He understood his wife, the mayor, was strong enough to keep fighting. Contemplating these things, he dozed off on the sofa.

Soon, his wife woke him up.

"How was your workout?" he asked through sleepy eyes.

"Good, but I have work to do. We must prepare for tomorrow's meeting."

Ula sat on the sofa next to him and asked the wall screen, "What are the closest Imperium fusion reactors that use helium-3 fuel, excluding Browns Ferry?" The previous Ridge City recovery team led by Zain Byss had targeted Browns Ferry nuclear reactors in Athens, Alabama. Ula and her colleagues were uncertain about what happened to the Byss team—whether someone killed them or captured them or if they reached Athens.

The living room wall screen lit up, showing a map of the Kentucky–Tennessee area. All four walls of the room, the floor, and the ceiling used programmable-matter paint to display pictures and videos. These wall screens used light-emitting diodes and tiny computers embedded in paint, tile, and wallpaper. Most rooms also used tiny wireless cameras and speakers. Families used this technology for education, entertainment, shopping, vacations, and even funerals.

The map showed two fusion plant locations in Tennessee. Beside the map were pictures of the two fusion-powered reactors, one at Watts Bar and another at Sequoyah, Tennessee.

"Ula, can't you rest for one minute?" a frowning Tal said.

"No, we need a good plan. Our survival is at stake. Don't you get it?" Ula replied, her face turning flush red in contrast to her husband's pale white complexion. She turned toward the wall screen and said, "How many kilometers to each site?"

The map updated, showing that it was 247 kilometers to Watts Bar and 280 kilometers to Sequoyah.

"Please identify storage sites for helium-3 gas."

"Unknown," the computer answered.

"Please show a map of the buildings. What buildings have the highest probability of storing the fuel?"

The AI-driven display used red arrows to point to two fortified warehouse-type buildings at Watts Bar, their fuel storage probabilities 0.873 and 0.621. The display also showed three buildings at Sequoyah with probabilities of 0.753, 0.529, and 0.374.

"What is the rationale for your probabilities?" Ula asked.

"A hierarchical Bayesian statistical algorithm," the computer answered in an authoritative female voice.

"What site would you recommend?"

"Watts Bar because it's closer and has higher probabilities of finding fuel."

"Please provide your three top plans to steal the helium fuel. Run your plans through simulations to compute the probability of success."

"Our second mission is going to fail, too," Tal said, shaking his head.

"So, what do we do not go?"

"I know. But DORG and his merciless robot army will hunt you."

Ninety years ago, another NAIT8 leader had allowed the humans to buy equipment and fuel and install more ventilation shafts. But this NAIT8 would not allow them on the upside, and if humans were captured, he used them in experiments and then killed them.

The vast majority of Ridge City citizens had never seen DORG, his Imperium robot army, nor Region 8's headquarters. They had lived their life isolated and protected from the harsh reality above them. The videos would only terrify them. Only Ridge City officials viewed the videos from past missions.

"But what choice do we have?" Ula asked, her voice rising. "We have thousands of people whose lives depend on our leadership. We have to try."

"I agree, but maybe we'd be better off surrendering to DORG. I'm tired of being a prisoner in a cave."

"And what would DORG do with us?"

"We are no threat to him and his kind," Tal said. "That's the only reason he doesn't break through our main gate or destroy our ventilation shafts."

"That's the first thing you've said I agree with," Ula said.

Tal said, in a sermon-like voice, "Our own Milky Way galaxy, according to research, had one other intelligent civilization. But now they are dead. Intelligent life seems to annihilate itself through self-made calamities."

"Tal, I read the research, too. But giving up is not an option."

"Ula, have you ever considered the fact that the Imperium robots are better suited for Earth's climate than we are? We are a dying species. We have no long-term future."

"No, the Imperium stole the upside and our lives, with the help of climate change," Ula said. "Tal, you give up on everything."

Tal didn't reply, and Ula marched out of the room.

\*\*\*

The next morning, Ula began the meeting.

"Last night, I researched the closest helium-3 fuel and located the Imperium reactors in Watts Bar and Sequoyah, Tennessee. Our computers show that going to Watts Bar remains the best chance for us to steal the fuel. Since the Byss-led recovery team must have failed at Browns Ferry, I didn't consider it. They also have nuclear reactors at the Nashville Region 8 headquarters, but security there is too great."

"So, why do you think we'll be successful this second time?" Yot said.

"The Byss team tried to reach Browns Ferry during daylight and night-time hours. Daylight gave the Imperium too many opportunities to find them while hiking. This time, we'll only travel at night, and we'll steal a vehicle. We'll fly low and fast over the forest and lakes," Ula said. "Last night's computer simulations revealed the speed of the mission is an important determinant of mission success. Our last mission exposed the Byss team too long to upside weather and Imperium searches. Obviously, something went wrong."

"Yeah, I expect DORG captured and killed them," Tal said.

"Who's going with me?" Ula asked, over the sound of rumbling ventilation fans, ignoring Tal's comment. For a moment, no one answered.

Then, staring at his mother, Yot said, "I'll go."

"But who will supervise the reactors?"

"With BOT's help, Eric Olas can do the job," Tal replied. "And I'm their backup."

Tal went to stand beside his wife.

"You'll need STX," Tal said. "He'll carry the heavy helium-3 gas cylinders."

STX was a robot that looked like a metal erector set. He was ideal for carrying heavy helium-3 gas cylinders and was similar to the lost POY. STX and POV both had six long legs supporting a metal carriage with adjustable compartments. It followed orders, required no food or water, and could climb rough terrain. Where ATO had intellectual and basic emotional capabilities, STX and POY did not.

No one produced helium-3 in Ridge City or on Earth. So, the Imperium harvested it from the planet Saturn and processed it on the moon Titan. An ounce of helium-3 cost §192,000 (bxcoins) or ten thousand times the value of an ounce of gold.

"Okay, so Yot, STX, and I will go," Ula said. "Tal will manage the city."

As mayor of the city, Ula knew she was leaving the responsibility of Ridge City's 2,076 citizens in safe hands. Her husband had his faults, but Tal did an excellent job as the city's Chief of Security. The structured job was a perfect fit for him, and, as a result, violent crimes seldom happened. Suicide was the most frequent violent crime.

No one spoke for the next minute as they stood in the musty courthouse meeting room.

Ula took a deep breath, contemplating their risky mission ahead.

"Mom, I've got another suggestion," Yot said, looking into his mother's eyes.

"What?"

"Jax should go. He can smell robotic lubricants from several kilometers away."

Jax was a Karelian bear police dog who worked in the security department with Tal. The breed of hunting dog had originated one thousand years ago in Finland. It had become well known for its ability to track and hunt bears, thanks to its keen smell and powerful bite.

"If Jax goes, then his trainer, Officer Koa Poland, must go too," Tal said. "They are soul mates."

Ula pondered Tal's words. "Is a team of five too big?"

"No, you need all the help you can muster," Tal replied with a frown. "Add JORT, an Ares9 warrior, to your team. You'll need the firepower and his communication systems. JORT might intercept local Imperium conversations and translate them, too.

"JORT's our best warrior," Yot said. "We need him."

At three meters tall and weighing in at 190 kilograms, JORT, a deputy in the city's security department, was a powerful addition to the team. He walked like a human, with two legs and two massive arms. His arms were fourteen centimeters wide and loaded with interchangeable weapons and tools. They had mounted two small, rapid-fire laser guns on his shoulders. His legs and arms were double-jointed, so he moved in strange ways.

JORT's cylindrical head, like ATOs, contained six cameras so he could see in all directions without turning his head. Each camera used a wide spectrum of wavelengths and could project hologram maps on the ground or table. JORT didn't need human-like ears, eyes, a mouth, and a nose because he had many devices in his body with radar, sight, sound, and speaker capabilities.

"DORG is looking for an excuse to kill us," Tal said. "He's more aggressive than the earlier NAIT8 director."

"We are like rodents to them," Ula added.

"Yeah, once DORG realizes you are above ground, he'll hunt you," Tal said. "Our intelligence estimates two thousand robot warriors and drones in Region 8. Over one thousand robots do construction, maintenance, and security work."

"They ran humans out of Nashville centuries ago. Based

on our intelligence, only their armory exists now," Yot said.

"Yes, our intelligence missions found Nashville to be in ruins. The Imperium built new factories and made the armory their headquarters," Ula replied.

After a moment of thought, Yot said, "Mom, our team is set."

"Alright, Yot, Koa, and I, plus Jax, STX, and JORT, are the team. It's a strong team. We cannot fail. Let's convene here at thirteen hundred hours to create a mission plan. We'll have until eighteen hundred today, when the courthouse loses its electricity."

Ridge City underground government buildings used a rotating on-off schedule to conserve power. The Torg family and members of the fuel recovery teams had not told the City Council or citizens about the impending fuel shortage. They didn't want to incite a panic until it was necessary. So, to justify the partial brownouts, Yot had informed the citizens that one fusion reactor would be offline for periodic maintenance.

On the upside, no human institutions, governments, or cities existed. In the torrid heat, skyscrapers had crumbled to the ground. Snow-capped mountains and glaciers didn't exist. Coastal ruins of buildings poked out of the ocean with no purpose. The boiling ocean had become acidic, and methane bubbled up and out of the ocean to add to the atmosphere's desecration.

\*\*\*

At 1250, Ula and Tal entered the mayor's courthouse office to find Koa and JORT already waiting for them. Yot arrived a minute later. The four humans sat at the round table in the center of the stark courthouse room while the three-meter-tall JORT stood in a corner. They didn't invite STX—the other robot.

"Last night, I queried my home computers for the best plan

to accomplish our mission," said Ula. "It looks like Watts Bar is top ranked. They can only store the fuel in two warehouses."

"What's the probability of mission success?" Koa asked.

Koa Poland, thirty-two years old, worked in the Ridge City Police Department as a police officer. Koa, like many citizens, didn't know her parents and had over twenty biological parents. She was a "genetic orphan" in the sense many of her traits, such as dark olive skin, green eyes, an athletic physique, and good looks, had been determined by genetic designers. To fill an alone feeling in her life, her family was her dog, Jax. Many Ridge City residents had pets for similar reasons. She loved Jax, and he loved her. They were always together in body and spirit.

"Less than five percent," Ula said, tapping her foot.

Tal rubbed the back of his neck and decided not to hassle his wife. What he lacked in bravery, she overcame with confidence, tenacity, and decisiveness.

"Mayor Torg, if you will transmit the mission plan to me, I'll double-check it," JORT said.

"Computer, please send JORT the encrypted mission plan, version four, now."

From the programmable-matter walls, a computer-generated voice replied, "Will do, Mayor."

"Also, place a map of the mission route on the west wall screen."

The two-dimensional map appeared in vivid colors. It showed a planned route highlighted in red from Ridge City to the Watts Bar's power plants.

"Before we discuss details of our plans, what should we call our mission?" Ula said.

"How about the Hermes?" Yot suggested. "Hermes was the Greek god and protector of travelers, merchants, and orators. He served as the messenger of the gods."

"Okay," Ula said. " 'Hermes' will be our code word. Once on the upside, our wireless communicators will work for only two hundred meters. So, if we become separated, or it's dark, use the word 'Hermes' first to identify yourself."

"Good idea," Yot said. "The Imperium robots can mimic our voices if they record our voice tracks."

Next, Ula pointed to the highlighted red route. "The route from Ridge City to Watts Bar is over rolling hills and dense forest. Once we reach the Cumberland Plateau, we will encounter elevations hundreds, even thousands of meters above sea level. If we steal a vehicle, we want to fly low enough to avoid radar detection but high enough to not crash into a mountain. We'll descend into a valley and approach the Watts Bar reservoir. Watts Bar dam blocks the Tennessee River to create the reservoir that cools the reactors. Further south are the ruins of Chattanooga."

"But how do we leave the city?" Koa asked. "If we open the main gate, DORG's warriors and drones will kill us."

The three hundred metric ton main gate resembled a bank vault door. In Ridge City's 495-year history, the ten-meter square gate had opened only eleven times. In the past, NAIT8s shipped helium-3 gas cylinders to Ridge City. But the vengeful one, DORG, wouldn't allow it.

"We could exit using Hope River," Tal said, referencing the river that meandered through parts of the subterranean city. It was the primary source of drinking water besides the two drilled wells.

Earth's oceans had risen sixty meters in the past one thousand years. Centuries earlier, the unforgiving sea had engulfed US coastal cities like New York, Houston, San Diego, and Miami. And it wasn't just in the United States. Other cities ravaged by the heartless seas included Manila, London, and Bangkok.

Ula and Yot smiled at this. Tal was about to reveal to Koa a guarded Ridge City secret.

"How?" Koa asked.

"The river reaches the upside in two locations. One is an underground creek, which empties into an upside spring. It's too small to squeeze through. The other pathway uses two lagoons connected by an underwater tunnel, which leads to the upside. People can traverse this route. That's how the Byss team and our reconnaissance missions exit our city."

"How do we find it?" Koa asked.

"Go to the end of Doron Street and walkway twenty-one and follow the crevice upward for about five hundred meters. We end up in a small underground cave. If you dive three meters down into the inner lagoon, you'll find a short tunnel connecting to a second, upside lagoon and cave. The tunnel connects the two lagoons inside separate caves. You must swim underwater through the tunnel, and you end up in a second lagoon and outer cave."

"How do you know this?"

"Koa, we've used it many times, but it's a well-kept secret."

"So, we have to dive using aqua equipment?"

"No, it's short enough that you can hold your breath—about sixty to seventy seconds. The aqua equipment is too cumbersome for the narrow tunnel."

"We could take a small tank of compressed oxygen," JORT said.

"Let's take the tank," Ula said, tilting her head backward. "Tal, is the underwater tunnel big enough for JORT and STX?"

"Pathways to the first lagoon and underwater tunnel are too narrow."

"We could disassemble STX and rebuild him after we exit?" Koa suggested.

"Or we could widen the pathway," Ula said. "How much work is it?"

"Too much," Tal said. "It's best to disassemble STX. We'll put his computer in a waterproof bag."

"What about JORT?" Ula asked.

"JORT can traverse the crevice to the first lagoon if he walks sideways," Tal replied. "But I don't know if he can swim through the tunnel. I expect ATO had to take his arms off.

JORT can do the same."

"I'll take myself apart if needed," JORT said.

"Okay, done," Ula said. "Let's take a small oxygen tank, and we will disassemble STX. Make sure we take enough medicines. The first team may have died from upside disease and not from robot warriors. Everyone wears waterproof boots, long pants, and long sleeve shirts. Bring your day and nighttime goggles, fortified food bars, water purification pills, and cooling vests."

The programmable-matter goggles protected their eyes from the debris and harsh sunlight and let them see in different wavelengths. The cooling vests were vital to the mission because they protected the team's bodies from the debilitating upside heat.

Earth was burning up and destroying humanity's place in the universe. Trillions of animals, humans, and plants had died of starvation, dehydration, and heat. And so, humans had abandoned the upside. But humanity's demise wasn't unnoticed. Something far greater than the Imperium was watching.

"Bring as many cooling vests as you can carry; the vests are your most important device except for water, food, and weapons," Yot said and then turned to Koa. "Bring a cooling vest for Jax."

"And don't forget bug spray, a change of clothes, and a laser handgun," Ula said. "Apart from Imperium robots, there are other predators, such as snakes and alligators. We are prey to them and they eat each other."

"How do you know?" Koa asked.

Ula sighed. "We've had hundreds of years to collect information on the upside. Ridge City has an extensive collection of videos and reports from our past missions and reconnaissance teams."

"The videos must be tough to watch. I see why you don't show them to our citizens."

"Some are, Koa. Humans abandoning the upside was not

a choice; robot warriors and the heat forced us underground."

"How are we getting to Watts Bar after we reach the surface?" JORT asked in his husky male voice.

"We must steal a vehicle and travel at night. Our team won't be hiking for long distances through the forests like the Byss team did," Ula said. "We can reach Watts Bar in two nights if all goes well."

"JORT can plug into their systems and learn how to drive their vehicles," Tal added.

"Okay," Ula said, glancing at the floor. "What else?"

"When do we go?" JORT asked.

"Saturday at eighteen hundred hours."

"The operation should be secret," Tal said. "No one except team members and me should know about it. JORT and STX must encrypt their files for the mission. I will cover for you, Ula, and manage the city while you're away. If any citizen questions your whereabouts, I'll say you're sick or had a minor accident."

"Alright. If the mission is a success, our citizens will never know we needed fuel. If our mission fails, we must tell them, and panic will pervade."

# CHAPTER 2

## *Breathing*

"**B**efore we disassemble STX, let's record our voice prints in its memory. Then he will follow our orders if the human voice print matches the files," Yot said. JORT, Yot, and Koa met in a Ridge City warehouse to disassemble STX on Saturday morning, June 7. Jax accompanied Koa to the warehouse.

And so, one by one, they recorded their voice print.

"STX, I'm Yot Torg. Your assignment is to carry the heavy cylinders back to Ridge City. If the Imperium warriors kill us, you must continue the mission to the outer lagoon near Ridge City. At all costs, deliver the cylinders to our Ridge City citizens."

"STX, I'm JORT, an Ares9 robot warrior. I work in Ridge City's security department. I have downloaded your design specs and maintenance and repair history. If need be, I can repair you. I have the tools in my arms."

"STX, I'm Koa Poland," Koa said, using the robot carrier for the first time. "My job is at the police department in Ridge City. I'm certified to use four different weapons and am trained in LuPae martial arts. I love my dog, Jax, more than any robot or human." After speaking, Jax came over to Koa, and she scratched his ears.

"Thank you for the voice prints," STX said in its baritone voice. "You now have authority to override my subroutines. I'll follow your command."

The Class J robot carrier was one and one-half meters wide, two meters long, and two meters high in its normal configuration. Many cameras and sensors, two speakers, and a computer module helped STX recognize its surroundings, balance its loads, and decide its own route. It could also re-member past routes and jobs.

"What a pleasant voice," Koa said.

"Oh, my software lets me choose my voice, going back to the start of human recordings."

"Wow, that's a long time?"

"Yes, on April 9, 1860, inventor Edouard-Leon Scott de Martinville in France recorded a ten-second voice fragment of a song titled 'Au Clair de la Lune.' I have listened to all recorded music since then and selected a voice I liked."

"Who did you choose?"

"James Brown."

"I've never heard of him."

"Did you ever hear him sing, 'It's a Man's World?' "

"No."

"Shut up, STX," Yot said. "It's time to disassemble you."

"Okay, but is this my end of days?"

"No, STX. We need to carry you through a narrow cave opening, underwater, and over rough terrain. Then we'll reas-semble you. You are critical to our mission's success."

"Okay. I'm shutting down."

For the next hour, they worked on disassembling STX. They bundled his body into five bags, which weighed eighteen kilograms each. They placed his computer module and motors in a waterproof bag and sealed it. On their trip to Watts Bar, Yot, Ula, and Koa would each carry one bag plus their own gear. JORT would carry the other two bags.

"Let's review our checklist," Yot said.

"Are cooling vests on the list?" Koa asked. "I have one for Jax."

The solar-charged battery-powered cooling vest covered the trunk of the human body.

"Yes. What else do we need?" Yot said.

"We need light-generating grenades, a few Birdee drones, food, and weapons," Koa said.

The grenades, when exploded, would generate an intense light, blinding robotic cameras and sensors for many seconds. A Birdee was a bird-sized reconnaissance drone disguised as the extinct blue jay. It could fly almost one-thousand kilometers before needing to be recharged. Birdees had four tiny cameras that could see in any wavelength. They had lidar scanning that created 3D maps of the terrain. Birdees could see through the upside foliage and create a bare map showing terrain elevations and objects.

"Very well," Yot said. "JORT, can you bring them?"

JORT nodded in confirmation.

Koa asked, "What happens if STX is disabled?"

"We'll have to depend on JORT to carry one or two cylinders. We don't know how much they'll weigh," Yot replied.

"And what if JORT and STX are unavailable?" Koa asked.

"We must drag one or two cylinders back to the city ourselves."

Koa worried about every detail of each mission she undertook. Often rated as the top police officer in Ridge City because of her management skills, she'd committed herself to a life of service. Besides her beloved Jax, her family members were Ridge City's citizens. She talked to everyone on the streets, and they knew Koa cared for them.

"Okay, we'll meet inside the crevice at eighteen hundred hours," Yot said. "Go to the end of Doron Street. Take walkway twenty-one to the cave opening. Don't enter together. Walk in thirty meters and stop and wait until the team members arrive. Questions?"

"I'll tell Mom our plans," Yot said.

They looked at one another for confirmation and then departed the warehouse, carrying the five black bags containing STX's body parts.

Yot walked back to his parents' apartment. Seeing his mother in the living room, he said, "We disassembled STX. I sent you an encrypted checklist of what we are taking on the mission."

"Good. I'll review it once I have signed a few documents."

Signing a document as Mayor of Ridge City meant facing the wall screen, holding her hand up, and standing still. Wall screen cameras took digital scans of Ula's face, eyes, and hand. Three microdot circles printed on the document represented Ula's signature. Each tiny dot contained hundreds of biometrics on Ula's face, eyes, and hand.

"You, me, and Koa are each carrying thirty-five kilograms of gear. Is that too much? JORT is carrying about eighty kilograms."

"No, we can do it. We'll bury stuff as we use it."

*** 

Before the mission, Yot had one special place to visit—the nursery. He needed to say goodbye to his soon-to-be-born daughters in case he didn't come back.

As he walked toward the beacon of life in Ridge City, he thought about what would happen to his daughters and the citizens if their mission failed. His spirit raged at the thought of DORG killing everything he loved—his children, his parents, citizens, and Ridge City itself. Horrific images shot through his mind of how they might die. Emotions of anger, panic, and horror surged through his body as tears ran down his petrified face. He was an emotional mess as he entered the nursery.

Yot spoke to a plain-looking robotic receptionist with yellow hair. Bolts held the trunk of the receptionist's body to the chair.

"Hi, I'm Yot Torg."

The robot scanned his body.

"Where are Hoy and Ota Torg?" he asked with a smile.

"Good day, Mr. Torg. Welcome to our nursery. Proceed to the sixth floor."

The first floor of the nursery housed genetic design stations. Parents could choose certain traits, such as eye and skin color. Other selected human attributes, such as intelligence or personality, were more uncertain.

The Ridge City genetic designers checked the traits selected by their human customers. Designers had ultimate control of the population size and characteristics using three goals. One goal was to maximize Ridge City's genetic diversity. Second, to achieve a sustainable population not to exceed twenty-one-hundred humans. A third goal was to supply the critical job skills necessary to manage an underground, self-contained city.

Floors two to seven contained hundreds of artificial wombs, which incubated human embryos from conception to birth. External circulatory equipment pumped oxygenated blood and other nutrients into the artificial uterus.

Upon arrival at the floor, another robotic medical assistant greeted Yot with a smile.

"Good afternoon, Mr. Torg. Would you like to see your daughters?"

Yot walked up to two birthing stations and looked at the two artificial wombs. His young daughters were twenty weeks from conception.

"Clear forty-one and forty-nine," the robotic assistant standing beside him said.

At this, the brown and opaque programmable-matter womb turned clear, enabling Yot to see his future offspring. They looked helpless. He marveled at their heads and arms and tiny fingers and noses.

"Can you record me talking to them?"

"Sure, every birthing station has a camera. Activate video for forty-one and forty-nine, please."

Yot bent down to talk to his unborn daughters and took a deep breath. His face was only centimeters from their artificial wombs.

"Hoy and Ota. Ugh, Dad must leave for a while. If I don't come back, you must know I love you. Oh, how I love you! I may never take you to the first day of school or discuss your homework assignments or read you a fairy tale until you fall asleep. But sometimes what we fight for is bigger than us. Soulless robots have stolen our planet, ripped it away from humanity. I must fight for your future.

"Earth is our only home; it's a jewel in the universe. We are champoids of our species and Earth. We don't know how many humans are on Earth, but we must fight for our rightful place in the universe. There is no higher cause."

Standing and sobbing, he placed his hands on the artificial wombs. The wombs were soft, warm, and throbbed with the repetitive rhythm of life. He felt immense guilt about leaving his future daughters alone. But he also felt the intense responsibility of finding fuel for over two thousand Ridge City residents so they could survive. And he also wanted to help his mother. The citizens had entrusted their well-being to her by electing her mayor of Ridge City. And he hated the tyranny the Imperium had imposed upon humanity. He wanted to triumph over the Imperium dictatorship.

After wiping away tears, he said, "We deserve better than Imperium domination. Remember, your father fought to reclaim our planet, and you should, too. We must fight for our home. I love you."

He took a deep breath, wiped away more tears, and hurried away. He marched out of the room without looking back at his beloved daughters.

\*\*\*

Yot went home to his apartment, tormented by his conflicting emotions. He walked into his home, hugged his sons, Qan and Bao, and took a hot shower. He thought about his family and the mission while in the shower. Bao was an eight-year-old learning software programming. And Qan, sixteen years old, would soon finish his education and training to become a dentist.

To speed up their learning, Qan and Bao had received two neural implants at age five. The implants stored basic information, such as the periodic table of chemical elements and major art and music works. On-the-job training completed a person's training, ranging from months to years. Most citizens completed their education and training by the age of twenty.

The mission started later that evening, at 1800. Yot knew the mission had to stay a secret so citizens, including his family, wouldn't panic and live in fear. So, he wanted to discuss positive topics at dinner.

While eating an early dinner that the two robotic nannies, SAN and NIA, had fixed, Yot asked his kids, "How's your schoolwork going?" Yot had raised them as a single parent with the help of SAN and NIA.

"I'm enjoying our study of Socrates, Plato, and Aristotle," Qan said after swallowing a bite of food.

"Yes, I studied them in school. What are Plato's main ideas?" Yot asked.

"We were studying Plato and how he divides reality into the physical realm and the spiritual realm. He calls the physical realm the world of things. A rock or person are things that change, decay, or die. We grasp the world of things using our five human senses.

A proud Yot listened to his oldest son explain Plato's concepts and noticed that even Bao listened.

"Plato calls the spiritual realm the world of forms. The world of forms is unchanging. Beauty, truth, and justice are examples of Plato's theory of forms. We grasp the world of forms by human thought, reasoning, and logic."

"Interesting," Yot replied. "My recollection of the world of forms is that we can define a sphere mathematically and admire its beauty. But in reality, a flawless sphere doesn't exist."

"Yeah, that's the idea. I want to write a paper on how Plato's ideas fit with our ideas of reality," Qan replied.

"So, do they fit?" Yot asked as eight-year-old Bao listened in, continuing to eat.

"Yes, they fit. Plato even speculated there might be a universal consciousness based on his theory of forms."

"Qan, start working on the paper. I'd like to read it," a grinning Yot said, trying to stay positive for his precious children. Inside, Yot was heartbroken. His sixteen-year-old son perceived a future, yet he wasn't sure they had one. Yot turned and wiped a tear. His chest and heart ached in pain as he thought about what would happen to his family if their mission failed.

"Dad, did you know Plato believed there were two components to a human being? A physical body and a soul. The soul is the spiritual or massless part of a human being. It is immortal. What we perceive as ghosts may be the soul. These souls move in and out of our four-dimensional world."

"So, that's why ghosts are blurry?" a serious Bao asked, trying to participate in the adult conversation.

Bao had viewed many old videos and movies concerning ghosts. He thought there was something else out there beyond the reality humans could perceive.

"Yeah, that may be why they are blurry. They live in different dimensions and only sometimes enter our world," Qan replied, taking a serious response to his brother's query.

"You both should be philosophy professors," Yot said.

After dinner, Yot hugged his kids and thanked SAN and NIA for dinner. After closing the door to his bedroom, he packed a few things, including a family picture. He left his bedroom and hugged his children in the living room while SAN and NIA watched.

"Young men, I won't be home for a while. I must work on the fusion reactors and need to isolate myself starting tonight. Grandpa Tal can update you on when I'll be home. I love you." He hugged them, turned, and walked out the door toward Doron Street. As he walked to the team meeting place inside the crevice, he wiped away the last tear.

Now Yot tried to focus on the mission. The team expected him to be strong, confident, and determined. Over two thousand human lives were at stake, the last humans left to his knowledge in North America. He hid his fear of the upside despite never having been there.

***

Ula hugged and kissed Tal before leaving her apartment late on Saturday afternoon.

"Wish me luck," she said. "You're in charge while we're gone. If you don't hear from us after ten days, then assume we have failed and tell our citizens their plight. I love you."

"If you're not back in time, we'll start rotating blackouts and try to survive as long as possible. We'll vote on whether to perish here or go to the upside and fight," he replied, holding his wife's hand one more time. When Ula walked toward the door, Tal said, "You're much braver than me. Everyone is proud of you, everyone."

"I know, my love," she whispered as she walked away.

By 1800, the team had met inside the crevice walkway.

"Let's go," Ula said after they'd checked their short-ranged intercom system and found it worked. "I'll go first, then it'll be Koa and Jax, followed by JORT and Yot."

For the next five hundred meters, they walked, carrying their backpacks and STX's bags. Only JORT had trouble squeezing through the narrow passageways. He walked with his feet parallel to the fissure, but in parts of the long crevice, his body had to turn sideways.

As the team moved through the ancient underground pathway, they could see hieroglyphic paintings and carvings on the walls.

"Do you know anything about these markings?" Yot asked JORT.

"No, my internal memory does not know of these petroglyphs and pictographs. The rock canyon blocks my access to Ridge City data banks and their transmissions."

Yot pointed to where someone had scratched concentric circles on the wall.

"How old are these drawings?"

"I don't know," JORT said as he scanned the pictograph with his cameras. "Native American tribes or prehistoric people drew these pictures."

"Earlier, I saw a rough drawing with a stick person and a plant beside it."

"Your species has existed a long time."

"Yes, we have," Yot said with a proud smile. "But we underestimated the effects of artificial intelligence and climate change on our society. We lost our way."

"True," JORT said, feeling somewhat detached yet trying to care for the human species.

At the end of the cave path, a small grotto contained a lagoon. Their head lamps illuminated the dark underground cave and lagoon. Yot and Koa wore night vision goggles. Ula's eyes had been replaced with two bionic eyes. Her black eyes saw in all wavelengths, including infrared. Ula and JORT's bionic eyes had better vision than biological eyes.

"We have one advantage on this mission—determination," Ula said. She doubted they even had that, but she needed to present a positive attitude and lead the team. "We need to determine if we can fit through the underwater tunnel."

"I'll go," Yot said. "Who has the terrain scanner and oxygen cylinder?"

"I have them," Ula said, removing them from her backpack.

"Let's tie a safety rope around Yot," Koa said as she unhooked a yellow rope from her belt.

Yot took off his backpack and a few clothes. Then he moved to the rocky edge of the lagoon and took the rope, which he attached to his belt. He handed the other end to JORT. Once ready, he slid into the cold lagoon water, took a deep breath, and dived into the unknown.

The others could see his headlamp shining in the lagoon. Later, he burst out of the water.

"Look at the results," Yot said as he handed the terrain scanner to JORT. The scanner showed a 3D hologram of the irregular-shaped tunnel in a lattice format. It measured the tunnel's length at seven meters. Blue lines showed the tunnel's diameter, with red measurements showing the narrowest passageways.

After everyone studied the image, Ula said, "JORT, what's your widest width?"

"Seventy-two centimeters at my shoulders."

"Too big for one part of the tunnel. How can we reduce it?"

"Take my arm off and carry it. Then the width is fifty-six centimeters."

Ula smiled. "That'll work."

Yot and Koa helped JORT remove his arm.

JORT sat on the rim of the lagoon, pulled out an adjustable wrench stored in his left thigh, and handed it to Koa.

"Which arm?" Koa asked.

"It doesn't matter. Robots are ambidextrous. Pick one."

Following JORT's directions, they unbolted his right arm. After removing safety pins, washers, and four bolts, Koa and Yot held JORT's right arm. Weighting twenty-six kilograms, they struggled to lay it on the granite rock.

"Jax and Koa go first," Ula said. "Can Jax hold his breath?"

"Sure, he's trained to swim underwater, but I don't know how long—maybe sixty seconds?"

Like most dogs, Jax had no fear. And his loyalty to Koa and

Ridge City residents had no equal.

"Take the oxygen tank. You two go first. Yot and I will follow you. We need to carry STX's bags. It won't be easy," Ula said. "JORT will go last. If he gets stuck, we'll go back and try to free him."

"Can you swim, JORT?"

"No, but I can stay underwater forever. If I get stuck, I'll abandon my right arm and find it later. I'll use my left arm to pull myself through the tunnel and out of the water. If needed, I'll break or chisel the rock."

"Will the water hurt your circuits and body?"

"No, my circuits are watertight. They made my body and frame of a metallic nanoparticle material called Talzoidine. It won't leak or rust."

"Alright, JORT is ready. He'll go last," Ula said. "Are you ready, Koa? Is Jax ready?"

Koa held onto Jax's harness. "Yeah, we're ready."

Ula paused and then said, "Good luck, Koa. Go."

Jax and Koa leaped into the three-meter-deep water and swam toward the tunnel at the bottom of the lagoon. Koa held on to his harness, propelling him through the tunnel first. She had tethered her backpack and STX package to her belt by a rope. Koa would stop and pull the rope with the bags behind her. While her head lamp illuminated the water, she wriggled and clawed to advance down the tunnel. She saw the end and pushed Jax out of the tunnel. Jax surfaced in the second cave and lagoon.

Koa exited the tunnel and pulled on the rope. But her backpack and two black bags wouldn't budge. Water seeped into her mouth; she was running out of air. Panicking, she removed the rope from her belt and pushed off the bottom of the lagoon. She burst to the surface, swallowing the nasty-tasting, algae-filled lagoon water. She swam to the edge of the outer lagoon and pulled herself out. Before she could survey the outer cave, Jax licked her face.

"Jax, I need to go back. My stuff is blocking the tunnel."

She turned on the oxygen tank, hooked it to her belt, and dived back into the lagoon.

She found the rope and tugged on it. But the bags were still stuck. She crawled back into the tunnel, pushed one bag backward to free both, and pulled on the rope again. Luckily, both items came free, and she pulled them through the tunnel.

Taking another breath of oxygen from the tank and leaving it at the end of the tunnel, she climbed out while coughing. She took several deep breaths before pulling the heavy bags to the surface.

Jax and Koa had made it, exhausted but safe. She sat on the edge of the outer lagoon in the dark cave and hugged Jax. Like most humans, Koa sometimes anguished over the past and planned for the future. But Jax had taught her to live for today.

Back at the first lagoon, Ula said, "Let's wait five minutes. We don't want a crowd in the tunnel."

After five minutes, JORT said, "It's time to go."

"Yot, go now," Ula said. "Take your backpack and two of the STX bags."

Yot hooked his backpack and bags to his belt and jumped into the lagoon. Then he took a deep breath and dove downward.

Ula watched as her son and his head lamp disappeared into the water. The mission risked her life but risking his may have been a mistake.

She waited five minutes, examining the water dripping from the cave ceiling and falling into the lagoon. The water droplets made a pinging sound as they hit the surface. She took a second look at the ceiling and realized it was moving. She directed her headlamp upward to find bats. Glaring red bat eyes looked down at her.

Noticing her line of sight, JORT glanced upward and said, "Ah, we're not alone."

"Correct," Ula replied. "Those damn bats carry diseases;

we need to get out of here."

She hooked her backpack and one STX bag to her belt, took a deep breath, and jumped into the abyss.

\*\*\*

Ula arrived at the tunnel entrance, glad to see no signs of her son, Koa, or Jax. They must have made it. She repositioned her body to a horizontal level and swam into the tunnel. She tried to pull her backpack and bag behind her, but they would not flip over the opening edge. Despite tugging many times, the maneuvers took too long.

As she burrowed down the tunnel, she realized she would run out of air. She fought to keep her mouth closed, pushing harder and kicking her feet faster, but she couldn't reach the other end of the tunnel.

Her body forced her to take an involuntary breath. She swallowed the cold water and then took a second spasmodic gulp. In her fight to survive, she pushed backward to get out of the tunnel. But the tethered rope hooked to the bags stopped her retreat. Ula's frantic and now bleeding hands searched for the oxygen tank, but she couldn't find it. She cut her hands on the rocks, and now her blood filled the water. Her body and feet thrashed as she tried to unhook the ropes. Frigid water filled her nose, mouth, and throat.

She was drowning. Time seemed sluggish. Would the tunnel be her coffin?

Her eyes bulging and her body filling with the uncaring water, Ula felt the excruciating pain first in her lungs and chest. Drowning hurt.

By the third gulp of frigid water, she perceived a flash of blue light fill the tunnel walls. She thought it might be a hallucination. Or maybe she was dying or already dead. She flailed about and coughed up a murky fluid. But the blue light remained and lit up the water.

Soon, she was breathing air and coughing up water. She lay her soggy head on the rock in the tunnel, and once she regained full consciousness, she looked back down the tunnel toward her feet. Somehow, the water had vanished. The tunnel was filled with sweet-smelling air.

But that was impossible?

Still, that halo of eerie blue light engulfed the tunnel.

Ula turned her head. She thought she could see a bluish orb, the size of a volleyball, floating in the tunnel air ahead of her. Its light was steady and crystal blue. It made no sounds. And somehow, she felt safe and not alone. She thought she was dreaming, so she moved her hand toward it to see if it was real.

The astute orb moved backward as if to acknowledge her gesture.

Shocked, Ula jerked backward and stared at the blue orb, all the while gaining more oxygen and strength. A tidal wave of joy ran through her body. She felt an inner peace and confidence as the water refilled the tunnel at a slow pace.

Refreshed, Ula pulled her backpack and the bag and worked her way to the end of the tunnel. She looked for the blue light, but the orb had vanished. She entered the outer lagoon and freed herself from the underwater coffin.

Now in the outer lagoon and still under water, she unhooked the ropes tied to her bags and blasted upward toward the surface. She swam to the lagoon's edge, and Yot and Koa helped her ashore.

"Mom, what happened?" an anxious Yot asked. "We were within seconds of diving for you."

Coughing and still spitting up water, Ula didn't speak but shook her head. She lay down by the water. Jax licked her face. She had drowned and somehow lived to tell the tale.

Koa dove into the outer lagoon, retrieved the ropes, and pulled Ula's bags to the surface. Yot, stroking his mother's head, said, "Mom, rest. You ran out of air."

Yot also applied a thick ointment on her cut hands and knuckles and wrapped medical tape over them.

When Ula regained her senses, she lay there and questioned what had happened in the tunnel. She wondered if she had seen a blue orb. Had the lagoon water vacated the tunnel? She suspected the entire experience was a delusion caused by a lack of oxygen to the brain. Or a dream during a near-death experience.

Ula kept the blue-orb experience to herself. She needed time to decipher what happened. She felt a deep sense of purpose: to fight for her species and planet Earth and triumph over the soulless Imperium imposters. Whatever it was, she felt more confident.

Ula, Yot, Koa, and Jax rested in the upside and outer cave and lagoon. Ula lay her head on Yot's lap, and Koa held Jax. Love filled the cave.

***

Meanwhile, in the inner cave and lagoon, JORT dropped into the water. With zero anxiety or fear, he entered the tunnel opening, pushing his right arm ahead of him. His engineered Talzoidine parts were harder than any material nature had created. So, the edges of his frame cut grooves in the rock. Once he exited the tunnel, he stood upright in the outer lagoon, the top of his head breaking the water line in the outer lagoon.

"Here comes JORT," Koa said. "Get out of the way."

JORT lay his right arm on the bank of the outer lagoon and used his left arm to drag himself out of the water. Then he sat with the rest of the team as they regained their composure and let their bodies dry. JORT and Koa looked up to see bats hanging from the ceiling. The bats were unaccustomed to the babble of the alien invaders.

"Let's rest," Yot said as he held his mother.

"Good idea," Koa said. "My legs are cramping."

"It's the heat and humidity. I feel it, too."

They rested for thirty minutes, at which point Yot woke up his mother.

"What happened in the lagoon, Mom?"

"My backpack and bags got stuck. I ran out of air and knew I would die. But somehow, an air bubble in the tunnel gave me fresh air."

"Are you sure you didn't imagine it?" Koa said.

"No. In fact, I saw a blue light in the tunnel."

Yot grabbed her hand and said, "Mom, you were hallucinating."

"Something saved my life. It was real, but I can't explain it," Ula said, scratching her head.

Yot looked toward the other team members in disbelief but did not react. The others stared at one another but remained quiet.

Breathing fast and sweating, Yot glanced toward the cave opening to the upside, illuminated by a glimpse of moonlight. "It's time to go. Mom, are you ready?"

"Yes. Check your cooling vests," she said. "I can't tell if I'm sweating or if it's lagoon water."

"Yeah, it's nighttime, and my instruments say the temperature is forty-one degrees Celsius."

"Take the safety off your laser guns," Koa said. "JORT, activate your weapons and defensive systems."

"We shouldn't assemble STX yet. Let's do it once we have the cylinders."

Ula and the others nodded in agreement.

The team stepped out of the cave into the uncertain darkness of the upside. The hot air scorched their throats and lungs as they gasped for air. Although they had learned about the upside, none of them had ever been above ground. They had always lived in Ridge City. Now they entered an alien world they had feared their entire life—the surface of the Earth.

# CHAPTER 3

## Dinosaurs

"**O**uch, what was that?" Yot moaned, taking his first steps on the upside.

Ula shined her flashlight toward him and watched the sharp edges of an agave plant cut the back of his hand. She shined her light on the cave opening. Matted vegetation, trees, and tropical plants covered the entrance. The tropical forest of Florida had moved to Kentucky by 3147 and surrounded the outer cave entrance.

"Does anyone have a machete?" she asked, sweat pouring down her face. No one did. She kicked her boot against the ground. "If we can't cut through the vegetation, we can't travel on the upside."

"I've got cutting blade tools within my arms," JORT said.

"Cut us a path."

At that, JORT turned on his night vision and used his arms to hack a pathway through the dense foliage blocking the cave opening. He trampled the vegetation with his feet through the forest to make a trail for his teammates.

The team made it to a meadow full of scattered clusters of saw palmetto bushes and tall, slender pine trees. Within the groves of trees, they found patches of tall tropical grass.

"Can you hear that slight crunching sound?" Koa asked.

"Yeah, it's insects, most likely the southern pine beetle eating the pine trees," Ula said. "They migrated north from the south as temperatures increased."

Yot stood beside his mother and gave her water. He also dripped water on her face, swatting away insects as he did so. When an enormous insect crawled up Ula's leg, he yelled for JORT to come over and identify the intruder. JORT took several pictures, saying, "My records show it's an elephant beetle; they can grow to twenty centimeters."

Yot knocked the insect off his mother's leg. "Mom, are you okay?"

"I'm sick to my stomach," Ula mumbled. "I still haven't recovered from almost drowning."

"Take deep breaths and these pills."

"At this pace, we'll never get to Watts Bar."

"We must find a major road," Koa said as she applied bug repellant.

They rested in the meadow for an hour, but the mosquitoes became unbearable. A swarm attacked them as they scrambled to stand up and cover their bodies with whatever they could find. Yot put on gloves and covered his head with a hat and net. Ula pulled a hood over her head while Koa spit bugs out of her mouth and raced to pick up and protect her dog.

The mosquitoes covered Jax's ears, mouth, and face. The bugs were so thick they blocked his air passages and crawled down his throat. He coughed and spat them out as Koa knocked more off his face. She sprayed him with repellant and wrapped him in a blanket. Jax whimpered in pain as his face, nose, and mouth swelled.

Everyone was miserable except JORT, his metal body the perfect bug repellent.

"Let's go," Yot shouted. "We can't stay here. Use the mud to cover your face and hands."

Koa tightened the straps on her backpack and STX bag. She was also carrying Jax and knew she couldn't carry this heavy load far. But they had to flee the insects.

They hiked across the meadow. The further they walked; the fewer mosquitoes followed.

"What are those black bobs?" Yot asked, looking through his night vision goggles. As they walked closer, Ula used her bionic eyes to investigate. "Fallen trees with roots. They are stumps."

"What pulled them from the ground?" Yot asked.

"I don't know, but it snapped those trees like matchsticks," Koa said. She stopped and put a whining Jax back on the ground. She stood in front of a stump, which was three meters in diameter. Dead roots stuck outward like Medusa's head of snakes.

As they continued to move through the meadow, Ula noticed her boots were wet and sinking into the mucky soil. Then the team heard a loud sucking sound. JORT had entered a muddy patch and was trying to walk in it. His feet began sinking into the morass. Soon he had sunk in the thick sand and mud below his knees.

"Wait," Ula yelled. "JORT is sinking."

They turned and walked toward him. JORT was up to his knees in the sticky brown muck. He was trying to pull his heavy metal legs out, but they wouldn't budge.

"Stop trying to get out, JORT," Ula said. "We need to help him back to where the soil is firm. Any ideas?"

"Jax can walk on this. His feet only sink a few centimeters," Koa said. "If I give him two ropes, he can take them to JORT." She turned to the robot stuck in the mud. "JORT, tie the ropes to you and try to walk backwards. We'll pull the ropes at the same time."

Koa tied the ropes to Jax's vest, and the hunting dog walked toward JORT. After grabbing them from the dog's mouth, JORT tied them to his thighs.

"Now, let's break him free," Koa said.

The trio made their way behind JORT and tugged on the

ropes. On the fourth mighty tug, his lower legs moved out of the gooey muck. He walked backward five meters until his feet found stronger soil.

"Thank you," JORT said when he had regained his traction. "I didn't recognize the perils of the swamp. Now I do. Next time, my learning algorithms will scan for better routes."

The team stood in a swale to catch their breath, only the chirping of frogs and beetles interrupting their heavy breathing. Their mission into the upside had been horrific. Even at night, hazards like insects, iguanas, and swamps were in abundance.

After Yot scanned the horizon with his night vision goggles, he suggested that the dark ridge might be an abandoned road that provided better footing.

"Let's go," Ula said.

The team hiked until they came to the ridge. Buried under the vegetation were remnants of a forgotten concrete road. Over centuries, civilization-eating vines and bushes had pulverized the mighty concrete. Ula took out a handheld terrain scanner and activated it, projecting a digital map of the area onto the large surface of a nearby elephant ear leaf.

"It's an old roadbed," she said. "It may lead us to a town named Cave City. Perhaps we can find a vehicle there?"

"We can take the Route 90 pathway out of Cave City to Glasgow and then follow the old Route 63 roadbed toward Watts Bar," Yot said, also looking at the map.

"Let's head southeast and follow the roadbed into town," Ula said.

They walked southeast for several kilometers when Ula stepped on something that squeaked. She took her boot and scrapped away the dirt and poison ivy to find a hefty tin sign. It read, "Dinosaur World: One Kilometer, Cave City, Kentucky."

"We're heading in the right direction. We'll set up camp there," she said.

"What is Dinosaur World?" Yot asked.

JORT accessed his photonic computer, locating the history of Dinosaur World. He said, "Dinosaur World had over twenty life-sized plastic dinosaur models. The entertainment park had fossil digs and educational movies about the extinct dinosaurs."

Koa trudged forward. "The park should have focused on humans, not dinosaurs."

Everyone smiled at Koa's comment except Jax and JORT. For an instant, the ironic humor took their minds off the treacherous mission they were beginning.

"Koa, was that a joke?" JORT asked, showing his limited emotional algorithm didn't understand the humor.

"Did you get the irony of our situation?"

"Ugh, no, but I have a real joke for you."

"Oh, no, JORT," Ula said. "I've never heard you tell a joke."

"Okay, my first joke," a cautious JORT said. "A bartender asked a robot for its drink order. The robot sat on a bar stool and replied, 'I've worked hard all day. I'm tired. How about a screwdriver?'"

The three humans smiled but didn't laugh.

After a pause, JORT asked, "How did I do?"

"Perfect, JORT. Perfect," Koa replied.

Yot patted him on the arm and said, "Good joke, buddy."

Everyone loved JORT, even if he didn't quite understand humor. But they knew that without him, their chances of success were close to zero.

Ula grinned though she was still pondering the arduous journey ahead of them. How would they ever reach Watts Bar?

The team continued hiking until they reached the edge of town. They saw collapsed mounds of rubbish covered by mangled grass, thorny bushes, and matted trees. Beneath the huge mounds of flora were the remnants of human civilization—buildings, streets, and crumbing boat docks. Excessive carbon dioxide had caused the rapid growth of vegetation that had pulverized human artifacts.

Other than focusing on their own survival, the robot society, like the humans had been, was a terrible caretaker of Earth's upside. The robots saw Earth as only a platform for the Imperium Nation to flourish. And the callous Imperium ignored Earth's beauty, like colorful autumn leaves, beaches, and sunsets.

\*\*\*

Before long, they came upon several mounds of vegetation up to ten meters high.

"Let's make camp soon—before sunrise," Ula said.

"We can camp between these mounds and be out of sight," Yot said.

"Yes, we can bed down here," Koa added. "No one will find us."

JORT, using his infrared vision, cut a door in the flora. He carved a hidden room in the vegetation. He continued to chop away at the foliage until his cutting tool made a loud scraping sound.

"What did you hit, JORT?" Ula asked.

"I don't know."

The team pulled away vines to find a thick, brown, hard surface.

"It's an enormous piece of plastic," Koa said. "It may be part of a fake dinosaur. We found Dinosaur World."

"Yes, perhaps. Certain plastics resist the biodegradation process for ten thousand years," a serious JORT said.

"We're safe here," Ula said.

By 0500, Sunday morning, June 8, they had established camp. Koa slept in the makeshift room with Jax in her arms. Ula and Yot lay downside-by-side along the furthest wall. JORT didn't need sleep or water or food. He activated his automated security systems and put himself in sleep mode.

After they'd had adequate rest, they awoke.

"Mom, can I look at your hands?" Yot said. "You've been rubbing your left hand."

Ula held her left hand out for him to examine.

"It's swollen and might be infected."

"Yeah, I cut it on the rocks in the tunnel. I hope it's an allergic reaction."

"I do, too, Mom."

Yot searched his backpack for the antibiotic ointment, which he then rubbed on his mother's hand.

"This should help. We'll check it later."

Ula laid back down. "In seven hours, we've traveled ten kilometers. We'll never reach our destination—not with the conditions of this hellish upside. We need a vehicle."

"Yes, I agree," Yot said. "Living in Ridge City doesn't seem so bad now, does it?"

The upside was tougher than he'd expected. He'd anticipated the torrid heat but not the great infestation of insects, mud, and humidity. Yot had inhaled many bugs during his short time traveling on the upside. They kept on coming, and he had dug many out of his nose, ears, and mouth. With or without repellant, the bugs bit him. Welts and sores covered his skin. And he worried about what diseases they might carry. When the permafrost had melted, it released a wave of old, deadly pathogens. Now Yot had second thoughts about their mission.

Maybe the team should give up the fight, he thought, like his dad had said, and accept their fate. But he knew his mother would not stand for it—she would fight to the death.

\*\*\*

At night, the vegetation seemed to define the opaque walls and ceilings in their hideout, making the makeshift area appear safe. But in the morning daylight, their hideout did not seem so secure. They looked outside through the foliage, and perhaps someone could do the reverse.

As they tried to sleep wearing their cooling vests, the bright lights and brisk movement of the upside foliage bothered them. The strong winds made everything move and threatened their hideout and safety. The brilliant light crept around and through the leaves. And the heat, the stealth predator, weakened them.

As Koa turned Jax's head away from the sunlight, she put on her goggles and said, "Level seven sunglasses, please." The goggles accepted her verbal command and realigned the programmable lenses.

Yot and Ula also put on their goggles. They pulled energy packs from their backpack and took drinks. With their faces swollen from bug bites, even drinking hurt.

"I have read and seen videos of the upside foliage, but the colors amaze me," Ula said, staring at the trees and bushes.

"Yeah, we understated the color of the vegetation in Ridge City on our programmable walls and ceilings. Many plants and wildflowers are vivid yellow, purple, and red," Yot said. "The leaves are super green, and the meadows' tall golden grasses sway with the wind."

After a moment of reflection on the colorful upside, Ula focused on their mission.

"JORT, thanks for watching over us. Did you see anything while we slept?"

"No, but my vibration detector recorded tiny oscillations at zero-six-forty-seven."

"What is it?"

"Either a minor earthquake or an Imperium vehicle."

"I hope it was the latter; we'll steal it."

The afternoon brought with it increased heat and the depletion of body fluids and vitality.

"Stay out of the sun and put your vest on maximum cooling—the heat can kill you," Ula said, miserable from a throbbing hand and an unhealed body.

"If your internal body temperature is over forty-three

degrees Celsius, you die," JORT said.

"Send up a Birdee to scan the town of Cave City and near-by roads," Ula said.

JORT pulled a handheld Birdee from his backpack and issued the command: "Survey the Cave City area. Send video back using encrypted code two-nine-LCC."

He sat the Birdee down on the matted floor of leaves, vines, and small branches. It lifted one meter off the ground and hovered in front of him. The Birdee sent electronic signals to JORT to verify all systems worked. Then JORT used embedded cameras in his body to show a 3D picture of Birdee's recordings. The hologram showed images of the camp, JORT's head, and team members sitting upright, eating, and resting.

"You're operational. Go," JORT said.

The Birdee flew out of the encampment doorway and high into the air. It first scanned the area above their camp.

"I see huge mounds of vegetation," Yot said, studying the hologram JORT was projecting on the campsite floor.

"I suspect those are plastic dinosaurs and collapsed buildings buried in vegetation," Ula said, also viewing the video. They viewed a semi-tropical forest with mounds of vegetation up to twenty meters high. No roads or buildings were visible, only tangled webs of vegetation.

"People abandoned this area long ago," Koa said. "It seems only the plastic dinosaurs survived."

The Birdee flew over what used to be the center of Cave City.

"I expect the big mounds are buildings and the lessor mounds are streets," Koa said. "See? The streets create a pattern."

"It's sad; the vegetation and heat are dissolving everything," Yot said.

For the next hour, the team examined the video until it was determined that they could find nothing of use in the nearby vicinity.

"JORT, bring Birdee back," Ula said. "There's nothing out there."

"No Imperium vehicles," JORT said.

"Yeah, the Imperium abandoned this area," Yot said.

"I didn't see any dogs or birds, only a few reptiles," Koa added, her shoulders sagging.

JORT signaled Birdee, and the drone flew back to their campsite.

"What now?" Yot asked.

"We'll send Birdee out in the late afternoon, and if we find nothing, then we'll go to the next town," Ula said.

"Where's that?" Koa asked, rubbing her long sleeve shirt soaked in sweat.

"Glasgow, Kentucky."

"Try to rest or sleep. We have a full night of hiking," Ula said with a sigh. "My information says Glasgow is eighteen kilometers away. We can follow the old Route 90 roadbed. Maybe we'll find an Imperium vehicle?"

"The Imperium doesn't use our old cities from what we've seen," Koa said. "That's a good thing for us."

"Nashville is one-hundred-and-sixty kilometers from here. It's the home of the Imperium's Region 8 headquarters," JORT said. "The Interstate 65 roadbed connects Cave City and Nashville."

"We're not going to Nashville," an upset Ula declared. "We are going to Watts Bar through small towns like Glasgow, Celina, Crossville, and Spring City. If we don't find a vehicle, our mission will fail."

For the first time, Koa, Yot, and JORT realized their leader had doubts about the mission's success. If they didn't find an Imperium vehicle to steal, Ridge City citizens would have to resign themselves to a cruel future. No fuel meant death, either from the demonic upside or the cruel Imperium robots.

For much of the daylight hours, they tried to rest and sleep. Their wet clothes rubbed their skin raw, and the bugs and insects continued to invade their clothes and bodies. That Sunday afternoon, the temperature rose to fifty-seven degrees

Celsius (i.e., 135 degrees Fahrenheit). Later, Yot asked his mother a question that still troubled him.

"Mom, tell us more about that blue light in the lagoon tunnel," Yot said as he dripped a small amount of water on his blistering neck.

Startled by her son's query, Ula paused and then said, "I saw a blue orb in the tunnel. I can't explain it."

"And you're sure it wasn't a hallucination?"

"It wasn't a hallucination. Somehow, the water vanished from the tunnel. I could breathe again. I felt my heart pounding."

"Why would a mysterious blue orb help you?"

"Yot, you don't believe me, do you?"

"Mom, what you saw was a hallucination," he replied. A nuclear engineer by training, his mother's explanation didn't fit with his science-based reasoning.

"I had a sense of awe in that damn tunnel, Yot. That orb saved my life. Without its intervention, I'd be dead," she said in a sharp tone of voice.

"Okay, Mom. Sorry, I raised the issue."

"Let's stick to the mission," she said, declining to elaborate. "We'll figure out the orb later." She stood up and shook off the dirt and leaves from her clothes.

Yot looked down at the ground, wishing he hadn't broached the issue.

Later that Sunday, at about 1500, Ula sent Birdee on its second scouting mission. But again, the surveillance found nothing: no Imperium vehicles, warriors, or drones.

"The Imperium deserted the upside," Yot said. "Looks like plants and bugs inherited it."

\*\*\*

After sunset, the team set out for Glasgow. They followed the old roadbed of Route 90, which crossed rolling hills and valleys. JORT often had to use his tools to cut through the heavy vegetation. But the crumbled roadbed provided better footing, and this route avoided any wetlands.

"What time is it?" Ula asked JORT as she followed him in the dark.

"Zero-zero-eleven, Monday, June 9."

"So, it's Monday night now?" Ula replied, paused, and asked, "Where's Glasgow?"

"Close," JORT replied.

"Let's take a break," she said. They had been traveling since sunset with only one pause for rest.

"What's the dark image with no trees?" Koa pointed toward it, her nighttime goggles allowing her to see enough in the distance.

"I'll check it out," Yot said.

He stood up and ambled toward the dark spot, also wearing the infrared-seeing goggles. He checked his footing and searched the ground for any reflections from standing water. As he drew closer to the dark image, he turned and said, "It's a sinkhole. But I can't see the bottom."

Yot turned on his headlamp. The sinkhole was about ten meters wide. He scanned the inside and found small trees growing in the center and vines and scrappy bushes cluttering the sidewalls of it.

"Taking the deserted road was a good decision," he said, rejoining the others. "We could walk into one of those."

"Sinkholes are widespread in Kentucky and Tennessee because of the limestone rock," JORT said. "Rainwater carves this rock into underground caves and sinkholes. It's called a karst topography."

"What is a karst topography?" Koa asked.

JORT started to answer, but Ula cut him off and said, "Spare me the definition."

Her impatience surprised the other team members except JORT, who replied, "Why ask me a question and then not want to listen to the answer?"

"I'm sorry, JORT. I should have let you finish," Ula said.

"JORT, Mom is under a lot of pressure," Yot said, trying to soften her gruff answer.

JORT wasn't sure how to continue, so he said nothing. Complex emotions like stress and love were not part of his emotional module.

After resting, Yot encouraged the team to get back on the road.

They hiked four more kilometers until they heard the trickle of water.

"A river must be ahead," Koa stated.

As the sound became louder, they found a creek covered in vegetation.

JORT cut his way to the edge of the creek bank.

Ula pointed her terrain scanner toward it and then projected the image onto the side of the black bag she was holding. The crosshatched line schematic showed a shallow creek seven meters wide. A small steel bridge over it had collapsed and blocked two-thirds of the creek with piles of foliage and rusted metal. The ironic part was that steel was one of the strongest materials humans had invented, yet the fastest to decompose.

"We must cross," Ula said.

"The schematic shows we need to swim through the water," Yot said. "It's two meters deep."

"The current is fast. All water funnels into this opening," Ula said. "JORT, go first and take this rope. Once you cross the pile of rubble, tie this rope to a tree. We'll use the rope to guide us over the stream."

As Ula handed the rope to JORT, Jax whined.

"What's wrong, Jax?" Koa asked.

The dog scratched his left paw on the ground.

"What is he signaling, Koa?"

"Danger."

"Watch the water," Ula said. "There must be something in it."

"Mom, remember Jax can smell hydraulic lubricants kilometers away," Yot whispered. "It could be Imperium warriors or drones." Their heart rates increased as adrenaline surged through their bodies.

JORT, immune to such biochemistry, scanned the nighttime area but found nothing.

"Should I go?" he asked Ula.

"Yes, go."

A calm JORT stepped into the water and walked toward the pile of debris. At three meters tall, he stood above the fast current but fell over into the water.

"Where's he gone?" Koa yelled as Jax barked and barked.

For a minute, the water churned, hiding the turmoil below the water's surface. Jax continued to bark as Koa held him back, his persistent canine instincts wanting to go into the creek to rescue JORT. Then, several meters downstream, JORT emerged, the powerful robot standing upright in shallower water. Wrapped around his legs and waist was a six-meter-long Burmese python.

"I've got this," JORT said as the cold-blooded snake slid around his waist and toward his head. Moonlight reflected off both his metal frame and the slimy snakeskin.

Ula, Koa, and Yot watched, using night vision, as JORT grabbed the snake's body with his two hands and ripped it into two bloody halves. He threw the lower half onto the creek's bank, but the snake's head was still attacking him. He grabbed its lower and upper mouth and ripped the beast's head into pieces, then raised his arms above his head in celebration but didn't speak.

Walking back to the others on the bank, he rinsed off the snake's blood in the water.

"JORT, are you okay?"

"Sure."

"That snake picked the wrong fight," a proud yet frightened Ula said.

Ridge City residents dealt with small snakes in their underground habitat, but large pythons terrified Ula. Living underground, she faced small animals like rats, mice, and bats. Ula discovered her fear of pythons (ophidiophobia) at this moment. She had no prior experience with gigantic snakes or large predators that threatened her life. She imagined the powerful predator wrapping itself around her body and suffocating her to death.

Ula had panicked as she watched JORT wrestle with the python. Her heart raced, her hands trembled, and she felt dizzy, but she hid those reactions from her teammates. She was on the verge of crossing the river.

After hearing a splash, the team turned around and saw another python climbing ashore. The python's deceitful relatives were dining on the butchered remains thrown onto the creek bank. The putrid smell of death filled the nighttime air.

"Gruesome," Ula said, the stench filling her nostrils and increasing her fear.

"Yes, snakes eat their offspring, you know," Koa said.

"Yeah, they even suck the calcium from their prey's skeleton," JORT added. "They waste nothing."

"We can't say that about humans," Koa replied.

Ula took a deep breath and said, "We're not crossing here! Let's move to a better crossover site."

\*\*\*

Twenty meters upstream, the creek narrowed, at which point Ula took out her terrain scanner, finding the creek to be four meters wide and an average of 1.2 meters deep.

"JORT, you're first. Tie the rope to a tree on the other side. Stand in the water to protect us in case another python tries to attack us."

JORT walked into the water with the guide rope tied to his belt, carrying his backpack and four of the heavy STX bags.

Ula went first, also carrying her backpack and the remaining STX bag. As she crossed without encountering a python, she bit her lip, trying to overcome her fear. Blood dripped from her mouth as she climbed out of the water. Then Koa began her trip, holding the rope with one hand and Jax with the other.

Halfway across, Jax slipped from her grasp and fell into the water.

"Swim, Jax, swim," Koa yelled into the night. But Jax dipped below the waterline.

A frantic Koa searched the dark water, and to her relief, he surfaced and tried to swim toward the shore.

They watched as splashes of water engulfed Jax. That's when a smaller python hit him and wrapped itself around the trunk of his body.

Koa let loose of the rope and raced to him, yelling, "Help! Help!"

Yot pulled his laser handgun from his holster and aimed toward the dog and the snake.

"Don't shoot," Koa screamed. "You might hit Jax."

Koa grabbed Jax and the snake and jerked and pulled, trying to free the snake from her beloved Jax. She would die to save Jax's life.

"Koa, get out of the water. Other snakes are coming," Yot screamed.

But those pleas were unheard. Koa continued to fight the snake and keep Jake's head above water.

JORT ran into the water and snatched the entangled mass of Jax and the snake. He threw them on the waterway's shore, with Koa rushing after them. Jax tried to yelp, but he was in a stranglehold. He could not breathe. Koa grabbed the snake's head but couldn't pull it off him. Jax had only a minute to live before the sinister snake would suffocate him.

"Do something, JORT. Do something," Koa yelled as she arrived on shore.

JORT stepped out of the creek, grabbed the snake, and snapped the python's head off its body.

Her hands bloodied, Koa was still holding the head. She threw it into the bushes on the bank.

But the body of the snake was continuing to tighten around Jax's chest. Jax fought to survive. He twisted and turned and bit the snake hard with his powerful jaws.

By now, Koa also tried to pry the headless snake off of Jax's body, but the snake's muscles seemed to become tighter.

JORT grabbed the snake's tail and unwrapped it, allowing the two of them to grab hold of the headless body of the snake. It tried to wrap itself around Koa's arms, but she threw it into the creek.

Unnoticed by her teammates, Ula didn't help Jax. She stood on the creek bank in absolute fear of the pythons. Surprised by her own reaction to the upside predator, she kept her fear of snakes to herself. Now was not the time to reveal her weakness.

Jax lay on the ground, coughing and gasping, Koa rushing to hold him. Their love was unconditional.

Soaking wet and bloodied, Yot and Ula sat down beside Koa and Jax. JORT turned on his security scanner. His six cameras provided a three-hundred-and-sixty-degree view of their surroundings. His infrared and sound sensors found no threats. He would protect the team at any cost.

"We almost lost Jax," Koa said, still crying and clutching a wet and muddy Jax to her. "Thank you for saving him. Thank you."

Yot and Ula nodded but did not speak. JORT also nodded but didn't understand how much Jax meant to Koa. His software valued humans and, to a much lesser extent, animals. His software didn't distinguish between wild and pet animals. The humans passed around a canteen of purified water, and everyone took a drink.

"Yes, we're fortunate to save Jax," JORT said. "Pythons can

live almost an hour after you cut their head off—their body needs little oxygen to keep moving."

The team found an open space to rest after abandoning the creek bank. JORT and Ula sat down on a fallen tree trunk. Yot wiped the snake slime off his hands with leaves and grass. And Koa continued to hold Jax, who whined as he nestled in his mother's arms.

Afterward, Ula asked JORT, "Where are we?"

"We're one kilometer from Glasgow."

"Alright, JORT, find us a safe place to set up camp. Let's dry out and rest. We can't even cross a stream without trouble."

JORT surveyed the dark surroundings in different wavelengths. He recommended a batch of tall trees thirty meters away.

The team lugged themselves and their tattered belongings through the small meadow to a grove of pine trees and bushes. After setting up camp, exhausted and damaged, the humans fell asleep.

The upside had brought to life their worst nightmares. Past generations of humans had created their cruel fate by ignoring the health of Earth's biosphere. Now they fought the noxious biosphere and its predators, including insects, snakes, and the Imperium robot nation.

# CHAPTER 4

## *Stumps*

"Did you run into any snakes?" Ula asked.

"Yes, they swam around me but didn't attack," JORT replied, carrying seven canteens of water. "I put a purification pill in each canteen."

"What's the current temperature?"

"Fifty-four degrees Celsius, (i.e., 129 degrees Fahrenheit.)"

It was a Monday sunrise, and the daylight revealed the trunks of broken trees and scraggly bushes. The team struggled to sleep during the day. But they knew it was the best way to avoid the sweltering daytime temperatures and the Imperium warriors and drones. Traveling at night also conserved their water and energy and allowed them to hide.

"We can't stay here. These scanty trees give little shade. Where can we go?" Ula said.

Without moving his head, JORT scanned the area. "See the downed tree and huge stump? We could use it to build a lean-to shed and create our own shade."

"Do it."

JORT gathered long branches and logs to lean up against the stump. The tireless robot tied the logs to the stump roots, cleared the ground of small plants and stones, and laid down large plant leaves to serve as a floor. Once finished, the team moved to their new hideaway.

"Wear your cooling vests and drink water," Ula said. "It's going to be a hot one today."

They settled inside their shelter, which had both ends open for air circulation.

"Koa, how are you and Jax?" Ula asked.

"My legs keep cramping. I take Xydian, but it doesn't help."

"And Jax?"

"The damn snake attack scared him. And the insect bites have swollen his ears shut."

"Yeah, the snakes scare me, too."

But Jax had an unyielding persistence learned from Koa. His spirit and resilience after a near-death experience showed his will to survive.

"What about you, Yot?" Ula said, turning to her son.

"I'm okay. But my cooling vest only works half the time."

"We have backup vests get one. JORT is charging one now."

JORT generated electric power from two sources. His primary power source was a sealed cube-sized nuclear reactor in the middle of his chest. His secondary power source was his programmable-matter skin, which generated electricity from light.

"How are you?" Yot asked, turning his mother's question back to her.

"I'm exhausted. The swelling in my hand has lessened, but it still stings." She sipped from her canteen, her left hand trembling. "JORT, are you okay?"

"Yes, all systems are operational."

"Do you have enough power to recharge our Birdees, vests, and head lamp batteries?"

"Yes," JORT replied with a slight lift of his head.

"Do we still have the five bags with STX's parts?"

Yot counted the five black bags out loud and replied, "Yes, all bags are here."

"One more thing. JORT, can you catch fish in the creek?"

They had enough rations to keep them fed for a week, but upside water and food would extend their mission time.

"I can try. The snakes don't trouble me, but the fish may contain pollutants."

"We can't be picky," Ula replied. "We need the protein, even if it's contaminated."

Prompted by his mother, Yot pulled from his backpack and handed JORT a rolled-up fishing line and a hook with a fake lure. Yot said, "JORT, find a sturdy tree branch to use as a pole."

In response, the ever faithful and resilient JORT headed toward the creek. On his walk to the creek in the daylight, he read and studied 602 pages on how to fish. He first tried to catch crickets and big bugs to use as bait but failed in his attempts. The humans had built his hands for strength, not agility. Then he dug on the creek bank for worms to use instead.

"Alright, team. Try to sleep if you can," Ula said, holding her swollen and stinging left hand.

At 0904, JORT returned with four big fish. Ula, Koa, and Jax were asleep. But Yot woke up to the sound of JORT's crunching footsteps.

"Good work, JORT," Yot whispered. "Now, how do we eat them?"

JORT paused as if he was searching his information files and then said, "We should cook them. I'll cut off their heads. I've never cleaned and cooked a fish before, but I can do it."

"Wonderful. Please cook them well-done. We must kill the parasites."

One hour later, they were eating fish packed with protein and vitamins. They used slick green leaves as plates and ate with their fingers.

"What fish are these?" Ula asked JORT.

"They are snook, migrating north up the rivers."

"They're delicious," Ula replied. "The meat is white, clean, and firm."

She took a drink of water and pulled a small fish bone

from her mouth. "Did you spot any snakes?" she asked.

"Yes. I stood on the creek bank and watched them. They didn't bother me, but they killed an alligator."

"How? I thought the gator would win?"

"I watched them fight. They were snapping at each other on the opposite creek bank. The python wrapped itself around the trunk of the alligator behind its front legs. They thrashed on the ground for a long time, but the snake held tight. I could see the snake's muscles tightening, trying to weaken it. Then a second, bigger snake swallowed the gator's head, and the three creatures tumbled into a ball. When I left, the snakes had won the battle."

"Sounds like the snakes suffocated the alligator," Koa said.

"They did. It was amazing to watch the well-planned attack."

"You saw a battle between two top upside predators," Yot said.

"Sorry for interrupting, but do you notice those clouds in the distance?" Ula said.

The leading edge of the dreadful clouds looked like a dark rolling wave. They could see lightning and rain bands hitting the ground on the leading edge. They looked like claws extending out of the frontal clouds, burrowing the storm into the ground.

"The rain may save us from the heat today," Koa said.

The team rested in their makeshift quarters. They sheltered in the shade of the fallen tree stump and JORT's self-made lean-too.

"It's raining," Koa said as water droplets hit the ground, creating a pitter-patter sound. Koa and Ula lay beside Jax with a towel over the dog's head.

"Ula, see the dark line," JORT said, pointing at the clouds. "They're shelf clouds jutting out of the sky. Heavy rains are coming."

"They're forming a squall line. It could be a derecho," Koa said as thunder rumbled in the cloud-laden sky.

"What's a derecho?" Yot asked as a patch of leaves blew in his face.

"It's a straight squall line that marches across the landscape with hurricane-force winds and torrential rain. We must prepare."

They tied ropes onto nearby trees and around the dead tree stump and secured themselves and their equipment to them. Koa tied Jax's harness to roots on the stump, and then they huddled in the lean-to shack for protection. The one metric-ton stump faced the storm.

A moderate rain soon engulfed the sky, and for a minute, a beautiful rainbow of mist surrounded them. But a dark sky replaced the short-lived rainbow. Even the flies and mosquitoes sought refuge in the trees. After several minutes, the sky no longer harbored any light. Only an eerie grey darkness remained.

And then an intense wall of wind and water slammed into their camp. The tree stump heaved upward as the blast of wind and water struck it. They all clung to the stump roots and their life-saving ropes, but the massive tree trunk groaned as it slid through the mud, taking them with it. A group of spindly pine trees snapped into pieces, most falling to the ground. But a few became wind-driven missiles, hitting trees and the protective stump.

Debris flew in all directions. The stump protected one side of them, and JORT covered the other side. He extended his two massive and telescopic arms to latch onto the stump. He buried his knees in the ground and used metal spikes in his feet to anchor himself to the ground. They could hear debris hitting his metallic frame with dinging or clanking sounds.

Within minutes, sticky mud, tree branches, and debris covered him, but he held his protective stance. They had designed JORT to do these things—obey his human masters and protect them.

They continued to crouch against the stump in water that was now boot-high. Jax was barking, but Koa kept their faces close to the stump for protection. Dark, angry clouds scoured the land and churned the air as the water rose. The wind rumbled and roared like a high-speed freight train as their equipment bags flew into the air, thankfully tethered by the ropes.

"We can't lose any of the bags," Ula yelled. "We need STX."

Yot tried to pull on the ropes, but the wind was too strong. Ula, hanging onto the stump, lost her muddy grip and flew into the air. But the tie-down ropes stopped her ascent into the air, jerking her back and stopping her from crashing into a splintered tree trunk. Sheets of rain slapped at her body as she flapped in the wind. She flung her arms out, trying to grasp anything, but only found high-velocity air. She thrashed around for a short while before crashing into the mud.

The mighty bursts of wind and water continued for several minutes, all of them clutching the stump, and then the wind diminished. During the derecho, chaos replaced order. Uncertainty replaced stability.

Ula tugged at her arms, knees, and boots to drag them from the mud. In time, she stood upright.

"Is anyone hurt?" she called out.

Yot and Koa acknowledged they were fine, and Koa unbuckled Jax from his harness.

"Now we know why these trees snapped," Ula muttered after they'd freed themselves from their ropes.

"JORT, what was the highest wind speed?" Ula asked.

"244.17 kilometers per hour," JORT replied, still encased in a thick covering of mud.

"Are these damn derechos because of the extra heat?" Ula asked.

"The correlation between increased heat and the strength of derechos is 0.737," JORT said, scraping the mud from his head. "So, the answer is yes. But the correlation between increased heat and dust storms is higher."

As the wild energy of the derecho passed them, dark clouds continued to race across the landscape. They saw shattered trees and bushes ripped from the ground, and the torrid heat had caused the air and dark clouds to shimmer.

By 1330, the rain stopped, and the sky lightened, with only a few clouds remaining.

***

After the derecho had passed, they returned to the creek. They found a cove in which they cleaned themselves and their equipment. Koa washed Jax, after which he ran up on the creek bank and shook off the water.

"Do you see the rainbow?" Koa said after cleaning herself, as well as her backpack and STX bags.

"How beautiful," Ula said, still standing in the creek. "It's my first natural rainbow."

"Me too."

"The colors are astounding," Yot said as he climbed out of the water.

The brilliant rainbow jutted out of the ground and arched into the sky. The structure defied gravity. Yot found it ironic that Earth's tortured upside had somehow found the courage to generate such a beautiful sign of hope.

"Yeah, the upside is an interesting place," Ula said. "We see rainbows, yet nature and the Imperium are trying to kill us."

"Yes, I agree. Nature and the Imperium are stronger than us," her son replied.

Surprised by his comment, Ula and Koa looked at Yot but said nothing.

Yot reached out to help his mother climb the slippery creek embankment. Then they heard a violent splash. They turned to find JORT wrestling a four-meter-long python, which had wrapped itself around his left arm.

"JORT, get out of the water before more pythons attack," Yot yelled.

A calm JORT stood and walked the few steps to the bank.

The snake continued to squeeze his arm, unaware of the strength of his metallic frame.

"Don't kill it," Koa said. "Our kind kills too many things."

The snake continued to do what nature had designed it to do—strangle its prey. But the strength of JORT, with the multiple struts, surpassed the predator's power.

"She's right; don't hurt it," Yot said.

"What should I do?" JORT asked, puzzled and confronted with a decision. He couldn't understand or cope with the circular logic of the human species. In one instance, they wanted to kill snakes. The next moment, they wanted to protect them. His befuddled learning algorithm analyzed the logic for one thousand cycles before stopping. JORT was always playing catchup to humanity's erratic behavior and decisions.

"We'll help you pull it off your arm."

Koa and Yot grabbed the snake's head and tail and unwrapped it from his arm, experiencing the powerful life-force of a wild animal. Its muscles quivered as it held tight. Ula stayed away, hiding her fear of snakes.

The snake wiggled and fought for life as it had done for millennia. Once free from JORT's arm, Koa and Yot pitched the befuddled snake back into the creek.

As they walked back to their temporary sanctuary, JORT said, "You should have killed and eaten that snake."

"No, JORT. It's not trying to kill us," Koa said.

JORT didn't respond.

Yot looked toward his mother and said, "Let's go into Glasgow. Why wait until dark?"

"No, at night, we have an advantage."

No one argued with Ula, with the debilitating derecho still at the forefront of their minds. The derecho, along with snakes, insects, and heat, was nature's angry response to a decimated biosphere. They had felt its power. Each rain drop that bulleted into their skin sent a message. And every piece of debris that slammed into their bodies, too. The fury of nature had drained their energy and affected their mindset. They felt demoralized, and the mission had just begun.

Koa questioned whether she should have brought Jax. She hated what the insects did to her innocent Jax. Yot found himself exhausted and driven only by protecting his children and his hatred for the Imperium. Ula had a headache and a throbbing, swollen hand. Flopping around in the air from the brutal wall of wind reminded her of her insignificance. Even JORT kept recalculating the probability of achieving mission goals and getting the same low probability of success. But they dare not communicate their insecurities to their loyal teammates—the mission had to succeed.

***

They moved to a grove of trees, and after resting for several hours, Ula declared, "It's dark enough to go into Glasgow now."

"Jax is scratching his left paw on the ground again," Koa said. "He's pointing west."

"Does he sense danger?"

"Yes. He might smell hydraulic fluid."

"Well, that's what we want. Warriors need vehicles. We should go west."

Standing up in the mud, Ula asked JORT if he sensed anything westward.

"According to my maps, the former Glasgow spaceport is west, three kilometers away."

"Let's send Birdee up," Yot said.

JORT sent Birdee aloft to scan the area, and the video it sent back showed dense forest as it approached the spaceport. But as the drone headed further west, a distant white glare showed, which was becoming brighter as Birdee got closer.

Jax was right. The Imperium warriors were using an old spaceport as an outpost.

The team looked at the hologram of Birdee's 3-D video. They

saw four VX vehicles in front of the warehouse and two behind it. During the night, floodlights illuminated the spaceport.

Ula ordered JORT to get Birdee, still flying, to take topography scans of the terrain and close-ups of the vehicles and buildings.

On JORT's command, Birdee lowered its altitude to thirty meters.

Birdee found the Imperium warriors inside their warehouses and circled the six VX vehicles on the ground. At eighteen centimeters tall, the drone was almost impossible to detect at night.

The team watched Hertes warriors walk out of the building. At one point, when Birdee retreated to an altitude of one hundred meters, a warrior glanced upward but didn't see the drone. Once the robot warrior had gone back inside, Birdee continued its reconnaissance and closeup views of each of the six VX vehicles. Then it left the spaceport and returned to the team's camp.

"How do we steal a vehicle? What's our plan?" Ula asked, looking at the hologram JORT projected on the forest floor.

"Let's create a distraction," Koa said, her eyes sparkling.

"No, I wouldn't create a disturbance," Ula said. "That would make them contact the Nashville headquarters. We must steal a vehicle without them noticing it."

"How do you do that?" Yot asked.

"If we stole a vehicle behind the building, they might not notice."

"But do those vehicles work?"

"We don't know," Yot said. "But JORT can figure it out."

"We'll sneak through the forest to the back of the building," Ula said. "Yot will watch one side of the building, and I'll take the other. From the forest, Koa and Jax will watch the building's back door. JORT will plug into the vehicle's avionics, download the files, and decide if one of the two vehicles works. If one works, JORT will raise both hands in the air, and then we'll steal it."

"And what if neither works?" Koa asked.

"JORT will hold his right hand up if it doesn't work. And if that's the case, we'll retreat into the forest and regroup. Then we'll inspect the four vehicles in the front or move to another location," Ula said. "Everyone understand?"

The team members nodded in agreement.

\*\*\*

"Switch to night vision and unlock the safety of your handguns," Yot said.

"Let's go," Ula said.

The group hiked through the forest until they were about one hundred meters from the building. The forest provided cover until they were within twenty meters of the building. A chainlink fence circled the building, but JORT cut a hole in it.

To lower his profile, JORT reconfigured his frame to walk on four legs and crept up to the first vehicle. Now about one meter high, he opened the VX's front side door and positioned half of his frame inside while he searched for a connection point. When he found one, he plugged himself into the vehicle's systems. Several display lights flickered but didn't stay on as the portal received his transmission.

He turned back to the group and raised one arm, signaling that the VX was not operational.

They watched as JORT left the first vehicle and moved to the second. They had one more chance.

Soon, JORT stood up and raised both hands high in the air. That meant he could fly the vehicle; it was operational.

They ran to the VX, fearing to be shot dead by the Imperium warriors and drones. But their dash across the open area attracted no attention.

JORT was already sitting in the front middle seat, ready

to drive. He knew how to fly the six-seat VX now, as he had downloaded the training manuals and instructions and translated them into a language he could understand. Ula and Yot sat on each side of him while Koa and Jax climbed into the back row of seats, carrying all their backpacks and STX bags.

Now they had stolen a vehicle and could fly over the treacherous terrain. Excitement arose. Finally, a key mission success! Hope replaced despair. Determination replaced doubt.

JORT engaged the antigravity drives, and then they were flying above the treetops. Elated, Ula looked back down to see no warriors outside or drones following them.

"JORT, you don't have the VX lights on," Koa said, hugging Jax in a moment of joy.

"Yeah, they don't work, and we need to fly dark, anyway."

"Can you see the instrument panel?"

"No. Turn on one of your flashlights and shine it on the instrument panel."

Yot pulled a tiny flashlight from his backpack and illuminated the panel. The only light, inside or outside the vehicle, was in the cockpit.

"JORT, if you can find the old Route 63 roadbed, fly parallel to this road, and follow it toward Tompkinsville, then we'll head to Celina, Tennessee," Ula said, excited. "Flying low reduces the risk of detection."

"Okay, altering our route."

The spirits of the team heightened once they had commandeered the VX. Now, they were far beyond the reach of those trillions of insects dining on their bodies, and they could avoid the treacherous upside hiking. Even Jax wagged his tail as they sailed through the air. Joy filled the vehicle's cockpit.

JORT, of course, didn't take part in the celebration. He used what he had learned from past missions to fly the unfamiliar machine with strange numbering and language systems. All of his subroutines were running at full capability as he focused on these tasks.

JORT and Ula searched for threats, like mountains and Imperium drones, using their infrared vision. Together, they zigged and zagged around the mountains and through the valleys.

While flying, the team reset their views of the mission as they flew over the countryside at tree-top level. Now they had improved their chances of stealing the fuel. They would fight for the little liberty that Ridge City enjoyed. And they would fight for their fellow citizens, their team, and their loved ones.

*** 

The rejuvenated team flew seventy-six kilometers to a barren lakebed northeast of Celina, Tennessee. JORT set the VX down in a dry lakebed filled with bushes and grassland. This used to be Dale Hollow Lake. The lake served no purpose for the Imperium; they didn't need the water. The Imperium had abandoned the lake and dam, and the dam cracked and broke apart centuries ago.

As the team gathered in the field to plan their next move, climbing down from the vehicle, their feet made a crunching sound.

"You're walking on salt and toxins," Yot said. "The heat boiled the water away."

"Nothing grows here," JORT added.

"JORT, project a two-dimensional map of the terrain and roads to Crossville onto the surface of the vehicle," Ula asked.

He did so, and they examined their route options.

"Let's stay north of the roads to Crossville," Yot said. "It's one hundred kilometers from here. There's nothing out there but overgrown forest and hills. But some of those mountains are high."

"JORT, how high can our VX go?" Ula asked.

"Three thousand meters with our load. So, we'll fly through the Appalachian foothills and mountains using our night vision."

"Okay, but I'd stay as low as possible to avoid Imperium radar."

"Fine with me," JORT replied.

They loaded themselves back into the VX and headed toward Crossville. In the darkness, they flew low while JORT maneuvered among the hills and valleys.

"Snap" is all they heard as the VX lurched sideways.

JORT jerked the VX upward, and seat belts tightened as a few loose items flew through the passenger cabin. The VX climbed to five hundred meters before JORT leveled its flight.

"Did we hit a tree, JORT?" Ula yelled.

"Yes."

"Is the VX still operational?"

"I'm checking." After a minute, he confirmed, "All systems are working."

"I think we have a gash in our wing," Koa said, looking out the windshield with her night vision googles.

"It's okay, JORT," Ula replied. "Lower our altitude to two hundred meters."

JORT didn't make mistakes, and by the time Ula had issued the command, he had already replayed his telemetry, video, and audio four times and diagnosed the error. His bionic eyes had missed a tall tree on a hill as they flew over it.

"I'm sorry. I hit a tall pine tree. It's my mistake," JORT said.

The remaining flight was uneventful as Ula and JORT scanned the terrain for objects in their way. By 0241 Tuesday morning, they arrived, hovering outside Crossville.

"Don't go into town," Ula said. "Find a safe place to land here. We're only fifty-five kilometers from the Watts Bar power plants, according to our maps."

JORT sat the VX down on the dry riverbed. They stood outside the VX and scanned the dark horizon. Vegetation concealed the landscape.

"What are those hills and valleys, JORT?" Koa asked, using her nighttime goggles.

"Collapsed buildings lie under the hills, and neighborhood streets run under the valleys. They once defined a human neighborhood around the lake."

"Sad we lost it all, didn't we?"

"Yes, you did," JORT replied in his normal, factual manner.

For a second, the team reflected on their situation. Yot thought about his unborn daughters, Hoy and Ota Torg. He would willingly die to save their future. Koa vowed, by her deeds, to protect all of Earth's remaining animals. Ula grieved about what they had lost. And everyone wanted a successful mission to save Ridge City and its residents.

Ula interrupted their reflections by raising her head and, in an urgent voice, said, "Let's move toward those tall trees and set up camp. We camp and rest Tuesday afternoon and go to Watts Bar that night."

\*\*\*

JORT moved the vehicle to the edge of the tall tree line and landed. The team covered the VX with branches and leaves after getting their gear out. They set up camp several meters inside the woodland on top of a crumbled concrete boat ramp.

They were getting close to the one thing the Imperium worshiped—electricity—and they knew the Imperium warriors would protect it at all costs. The electrical generating plants were at Watts Bar along with the precious helium-3 nuclear fuel.

So, no more yelling or loud noises. They would whisper now. No more bickering; Ula was the boss. No more attempts at humor; it was serious business now. They took each step with care, trying not to jeopardize the mission. Now they had the most powerful motivators—survival and hope. It was time to execute.

"Why don't we go closer to Watts Bar?" Koa asked. "We still have a few hours of darkness left."

"We need to plan our attack," Ula said. "Besides, if we steal the fuel before midnight, we will have more hours of darkness to help our escape."

"Okay."

"JORT, display the area around the power plant in a three-kilometer circle and a second map of the layout of the Watts Bar facilities," Ula said.

JORT projected two holograms on the ground, and the team stood around the projections, discussing their plans to steal the helium-3 fuel.

"We should fly direct to Spring City and over the Watts Bar Lake to the reactors," Yot said.

"I agree. The Imperium doesn't know we're traveling through the upside," Ula said. "And I don't think they have missed the VX we stole."

"I'd follow Route 68 into the area," Koa said.

"No, not a good idea. The warriors travel this route. The lake route is better," Yot said, pointing to Watts Bar Lake on the hologram.

"What do you think, JORT?" Ula asked.

"My simulations show the water route has a 1.04 percent chance of success. Route 68 has a 0.63 percent chance of success."

"Okay, over the lake is the best route," Ula said. "Do we land the VX inside the perimeter of the power plant or hide it on the lake and go by foot?"

The team studied JORT's map and building layouts for a moment before Yot spoke.

"What are the odds of finding fuel in the warehouses, JORT?"

"Building one is 0.872, and two is 0.796."

"So, we land the VX in the compound and behind building one," Yot said.

No one responded as each person considered this plan.

After a moment, Koa spoke. "If we land the VX inside the plant area, they will know intruders are there. Their cameras will record our entry."

"Alright, let's hide the VX in the forest next to the lake and sneak into the area and warehouse by foot," Ula said. "This may buy us more time."

Everyone nodded in agreement when Ula said, "JORT, send both Birdees out before the sun rises."

JORT sent the Birdees the key coordinates and let them loose. They would fly to Watts Bar and spend an hour filming the facilities and tracking the warriors' movements.

"I've instructed the Birdees to return by zero-five-thirty, before sunrise. We can view the videos then and make final decisions," JORT said.

"Let's rest now. I doubt we will sleep," Ula said. "We'll wait for the Birdees' return."

"Ugh, we need to assemble STX," Yot said.

"I'll help," Koa added.

"Okay, get it done, then rest," Ula replied, holding her aching hand.

Tuesday morning, June 10, at about 0700, Yot and Koa worked to put together STX's truss frame and hook up his cameras, sensors, and computer module. They used small power tools to bolt his frame together and snapped his auxiliary equipment into place.

Meanwhile, Ula studied video of the Watts Bar facilities in more detail, trying to find any repetitive movements or routes of the warriors.

By 1100, Yot asked Ula if it was okay to turn STX on and see if he worked.

"Yeah, turn him on, but don't make any noise."

Yot turned the switch on and waited a few seconds as STX's lights flickered. Yot asked, "STX, how are you?"

STX shuffled four of his six legs and, through a speaker, said, "Good morning, Yot. I'm okay but a little stiff."

\*\*\*

The two Birdees returned and transmitted their Watts Bar video to JORT, who had let the exhausted team try to sleep. Filled with anxiety and fear, the team rested but slept little.

At 1700, Tuesday, the team huddled around the hologram projected onto the ground. After studying the video, they concluded that the Imperium ran a relaxed facility. This wasn't a surprise since no one ever challenged the Imperium's authority. They had no threatening predators and were the sovereigns of Earth.

"What else do you see?" Ula asked.

"Warehouse one has a rear door. Warehouse two does not," Yot said.

"Do you notice they hang around the front of the warehouses and reactor buildings?" JORT said. "We could cut a hole in the perimeter fence; then we break into the warehouses from the backside."

"They've installed cameras on the warehouse corners," Koa noted. "We must take them out."

"Alright, after we hide the VX, we hike from the forest to the warehouses. JORT cuts through the fence, and we break open the door lock in building one. We use our laser handguns to take out the cameras," Ula said. "If the fuel is not in warehouse one, JORT cuts a hole in the back of warehouse two. He can use his lasers."

"Let's fly over Watts Bar Lake on our return," JORT said. "We'll stay away from the roads abandoned or used. We'll fly toward Knoxville, low above the lake at night. Half-way up the lake, we'll head northwest toward Ridge City."

"Good plan," Ula exclaimed.

The four smiled at one another, signifying their agreement with the mission plan.

"What time do we leave?" Koa asked Ula.

"Twenty-hundred hours. That way, we have ten hours of darkness to complete our mission."

# CHAPTER 5

# *Regret*

T he fuel recovery team cleared away the branches and bushes that were hiding the VX and got inside it at 2000 on Tuesday night. The team tucked STX in the VX rear cargo bay, with two of its legs extending outward. A disparate group of three humans, two robots, and one dog lifted off Lake Tansi's dry lakebed, heading to Watts Bar. No more plotting and waiting; it was time to steal the fuel.

They flew above the forest and maneuvered their way through the foothills. The black VX with no lights blended in with the pitch-black sky. The fifty-five-kilometer trip from Crossville to Watts Bar Lake would take less than one hour.

During the early part of the trip, the team didn't talk about the mission, but their heart rate increased, and their muscles became tense. They were risking their lives to save other lives. In North America, they were humanity's last hope. They had little training in the ways of war and conflict, but survival trumped fear.

They were entering Imperium country, and with every kilometer, the risk of being shot down increased. A swarm of Verking drones could attack them in the dark at any moment. They each faced the reality of their own death.

The robot nation worshipped one thing and one thing

only—electricity. Energy determined the heartbeat of the Imperium Nation. They would protect this life-giving resource at all costs.

"How far away is Watts Bar?" a tense Koa asked as they dogged an extra tall tree.

"Twenty kilometers," JORT replied.

"We're about to confront our enemy," Koa replied. "An enemy that doesn't care about us."

"True, they only care about their collective existence," Yot said. "Everything they do is to ensure their survival."

Ula continued to watch for threats as the VX skimmed along the nighttime upside. They all leaned to the side while pilot JORT banked to avoid a hill.

"What do you think, JORT?" Koa said.

JORT paused and then said, "Robots don't understand human emotions. To care about humanity, you must have emotions."

Everyone remained quiet after JORT's comment, as they could see something shimmering on the horizon.

"We are two kilometers from the lake's edge," JORT said.

Ula asked JORT to fly low over the lake, which he did, lowering to ten meters above the lake's surface. Ula instructed him to land in a cove close to the power plants, and JORT turned the VX so that it was heading south.

As they approached several coves, JORT slowed the VX while Ula used her bionic eyes to find the best landing place. Koa did a similar search using her night vision goggles. Together, they directed JORT to a bushy area in a narrow cove, and they began their descent, executing the landing in a bushy area. The team heard a few small trees and bushes snap as the VX's weight overwhelmed them.

"We've landed," JORT said as he cut off the VX systems.

Ula opened the doors and jumped into the tropical flora on the lake's shore. Once the rest of the team was on the ground, they covered the VX with uprooted bushes and tree branches.

"How far are the power plants?" Ula whispered to JORT.

"1.1 kilometers to the fence in the back of the warehouses."

"Let's go single file. Yot, you go last."

They hiked in the dark nonstop until they reached old Route 68.

"Mom, let's cross the road one at a time," Yot said as they huddled in the forest next to the road. Unlike previous road-beds, this road was well elevated, and the foliage trimmed. Drainage pipes under the road allowed water to go its own way. Signs that the Imperium used this roadbed.

Ula crossed first and then waved for Koa and Jax to follow. Next, STX marched across, taking short, deliberate steps with his six legs. Once across the road and standing next to the group, STX stuck two legs outward.

"What are you doing?" Ula muttered.

"I'm stretching," STX whispered back.

Ula and Koa didn't know why a metal robot would stretch. STX's limited learning algorithms often created such odd be-havior. And it was also clear that STX didn't fear their situation.

When Yot stepped out onto the highway, they heard a soft puttering sound. It became louder and louder as it approached.

"What's that?" Yot asked.

He stopped and stepped back into the forest. Soon, a drone appeared, traveling toward them several meters above the road. Its spherical black body rotated as it flew, with its four legs dangling toward the ground. Each leg had three-prong claws. It scanned the road.

Those who had already crossed hurried deep into the woods and hid behind a mound of dirt to help mask their infrared signature. Drones had vision equal to human bionic eyes.

"Lay flat and bury yourself in the grass and bushes," Ula whispered to Koa, Jax, and STX.

Waiting to cross the road, Yot and JORT crawled into a drainage pipe under the road.

The drone slowed down as it checked the dark surroundings, but thankfully, after a tense few seconds, it increased its speed and left.

"It must have seen movement or heard our footsteps," Ula said once the drone was several hundred meters away from them.

"Yeah, its own headlight might have reflected off STX's or JORT's body," Koa said.

Once the drone passed out of sight, Yot and JORT hurried over the road.

"Let's keep moving," Ula said as the group was reunited.

They hiked the last few hundred meters, hearing an occasional clanking or humming sound of mechanical robots and equipment off in the distance. When they were within meters of the perimeter fence, Ula raised her hand and signaled for them to stop. They peeked through the edge of the forest to see two buildings. Each one was about one hundred meters long and one-half as wide. Without windows, the walls rose twelve meters high, and the roof sloped towards the back. One warehouse had a back door, whereas the other did not. Further away, the team also saw two fusion reactor buildings with cooling towers and many electrical substations.

"Where is the fuel stored?" Ula asked JORT.

"In those two warehouses. Warehouse one is the closest."

"Take out the two corner warehouse cameras."

JORT raised his right arm and extended the barrel of his laser gun outward. He fired three times. His first shot hit the nearest camera and disabled it, sending shattered glass and parts to the ground, making a tingling sound. The second shot missed the other camera and hit the roof overhang with a sizzling sound. His third shot disabled the second camera.

"Let's wait and see if the noise brings the Imperium warriors," Ula said from her position, hiding beside the chainlink fence.

After four long minutes, no warriors came to investigate.

"Okay," Ula said. "JORT, cut an opening in the fence. Let's go."

JORT moved back onto all fours and walked like an animal to the chain-linked metal fence. He used two pairs of pliers attached to his mechanical hands to cut a hole in it. Then he picked up the cutout piece and laid it on the ground. He gestured for Ula to go first.

Ula hesitated. "Koa, you and Jax stay here and hide in the forest. Watch us, and if you see anything, let us know using our communicators. They have a range of about two hundred meters. Warn us if we shouldn't exit the warehouse, too."

"Okay, got it."

\*\*\*

In a single file, Ula, Yot, JORT, and STX crawled through the fence and hurried to the back of warehouse one. Again, JORT walked on four legs to minimize his profile and then used his laser gun to cut out the back door lock.

The team walked into the back of warehouse one undetected. Three small security lights lit the inside of the warehouse.

"Search for cameras inside the warehouse," Ula said. To their surprise, they found none.

"The robots are arrogant. They assumed no one would dare enter their facilities," Yot said.

"There's no one to challenge them except snakes," Ula said, agreeing with her son.

"JORT, close the door. You and STX stay inside near the entrance. We'll call you if we need you. Yot and I will search the warehouse," Ula said.

The mother-and-son pair walked down the aisles of the warehouse, holding their laser guns and scanning for the cylinders. They walked past row upon row of pallets, boxes, electrical transformers, and coils of wire and tubing.

After an extensive search, a disappointed Ula said to Yot, "I didn't see one cylinder, not one."

"Yeah, they have everything here except what we need."

"Let's move to warehouse two."

They rejoined STX and JORT by the back door and vacated the warehouse. Sneaking along the backside of the warehouse toward warehouse two, they hoped this warehouse would contain what they desired. As they made their way, JORT disabled a camera mounted high on the corner of warehouse two.

"I don't see any other cameras," Yot said.

"Alright, let's go," Ula said. "JORT, burn a hole in the wall with your lasers."

JORT extended his arms out and cut the wall using lasers in both hands. The burnt material had a burning gunpowder odor. But Imperium robot warriors and JORT and STX had no capability for smelling. Only the humans and Jax could smell the nasty stench. JORT yanked parts of the hot wall down with his strong metal hands, and they stepped through the hole and into the warehouse's back wall.

"JORT, you and STX stay inside the warehouse, next to this opening—don't move. We'll contact you if we find the cylinders," Ula said.

Once again, they began their search down the aisles. They walked the length of warehouse two and found no cylinders. But when they reached the end of the warehouse, they found sturdy metal racks almost ten meters high and filled with metal cylinders. Ula and Yot approached and examined one cylinder.

"Can you read the writing?" Ula asked.

"No. Get JORT."

Ula spoke into her communicator to ask JORT and STX to come to the end of the warehouse. JORT and STX tried to be quiet, but their metal frames generated a clanking sound that echoed around the warehouse.

When they reached them, JORT studied the Imperium writing. "They're using the duodecimal numbering system and the OCRS language. The language uses thirty-nine symbols and no capital letters. As you can see, they write from top to bottom in columns."

"Good thing you came with us," a grinning Yot said to JORT.

After a pause, JORT said, "The cylinder contains helium-3 harvested on Saturn and processed on Titan in 3144. The cylinder pressure is six thousand kilopascals (kPa)."

"We found it," Ula said, delighted. She bumped fists with Yot in a subdued celebration.

JORT could tell the fist-pumps confused STX, and so he tried to explain to STX. "We found the helium-3 gas in these cylinders. They are celebrating with the fist-pumps. Humans have their rituals, STX."

"Are these cylinders radioactive?" Ula asked JORT.

"My instruments show no radiation."

"What do they weigh? Can we carry them?"

JORT picked up one cylinder and said, "55.31 kilograms (i.e., 122 pounds.)"

"They are too heavy for one of us to carry alone, but STX can handle them," Ula said, looking at JORT, STX, and Yot for confirmation. They nodded their approval.

"Okay, load six cylinders onto STX," Ula said. Sweating, she then asked JORT, "What's the temperature?"

"Forty-nine degrees Celsius inside the warehouse."

"These idiots don't air-condition anything or use windows."

After the team loaded the cylinders into the racks on STX's frame, they tied them to the racks. It was time to go. The robotic mule led the way, walking down the aisle toward the doorway JORT had made. After they had moved about thirty meters, JORT asked, "STX, can you handle this heavy load?"

"Yes, in the warehouse and on solid roadbeds, but I'm concerned about my footing in the sandy soil."

"I'll carry two cylinders if you need help," JORT said.

The four team members—two humans and two machines—made their way toward the exit hole in the back of the warehouse. When the hole was in sight, JORT said, "Do you hear that? A faint puttering sound?" Before either Ula or Yot had time to reply, JORT whispered, "Hide, hide."

JORT's bionic sound sensors far exceeded the capabilities of human ears, so Ula and Yot knew to follow his order. They ducked between two rows of pallets as the sound became louder.

An autonomous Imperium drone cruised down the warehouse aisle past them.

A big drop of sweat fell to the floor from Ula's face, making a slight splashing sound as it landed. The sound was not perceptible to human ears, but to JORT—and the drone's sensors—it sounded like a splash.

The drone stopped, turned, and moved backward, its four spindly legs and claws dangling down from its spherical body. It looked at the dark alley between the stacked pallets. It was now only ten meters away from the petrified team. Yot and Ula feared their mission would end in the next few frightening seconds. Their heart beats raced as they tried to control their fear.

Before it could raise the alarm, JORT fired two laser shots at the drone, making a zip, zip, hissing sound. It lurched backward, avoiding one laser strike. But the other shot hit the drone, and it fell to the floor. JORT rushed forward, grabbed the drone, and smashed his fist into it, sending pieces scattering on the floor. He reached down to the floor and pulled out the guts of the drone—the mini nuclear reactor—from its body. He laid it on the floor and smashed it with his foot. JORT acted in a matter of seconds, catching the drone by surprise and giving it no time to inform the Imperium.

"Why did you fire?" Ula asked.

"My spectral analysis showed it had used infrared to search for us. I shot because the probability it saw us was 0.863."

"Good job, my friend. Let's go."

\*\*\*

Ula ran to the escape door. The others followed while JORT pushed the drone parts aside. Both Ula and Yot knew JORT had saved their lives again. Without their powerful robot companion, they would have perished long ago.

In the hurried getaway, Ula ran out the exit hole, watching for robot warriors and drones. Yot followed and cut his shoulder on the jagged edges of the warehouse exit opening. He felt blood dripping down his arm. JORT and STX were the last to arrive at the exit hole. They worked their way through the opening.

Everyone hurried to the opening in the security fence, and Koa signaled them to keep moving. Jax wagged his tail and didn't bark. JORT helped STX maneuver through the fence by pulling it apart more.

After several hundred meters of hiking through the forest, Ula, who was in front, heard Yot cry out.

"Mom, stop! STX is stuck between two trees."

The group stopped and returned to find STX trying to free himself.

"We'll free you, STX?" Koa said, alarmed.

"I'm stuck. I can't estimate distance because I bumped into a tree and damaged my sensors," STX said.

"We'll set you free," Yot declared. "You should lose weight."

No one laughed at the grim joke at such a grim time.

"Is that funny?" STX asked while wedged between two trees.

"No, STX. Right now, nothing is funny," Ula said. "Yot and Koa, help STX pull his legs out of the soft soil."

JORT cut a small tree down with his laser weapon, which held STX. Now STX was free from the forest's unwanted embrace. His frame stood up better to the soft soil than they had expected. The team trudged through the forest to the VX with the mechanical mule carrying the cylinders.

JORT loaded four cylinders into the rear cargo bay, and the two remaining cylinders went in with Koa and Jax in the back seat. STX climbed into the cargo bay, too, scrabbling over the top of the cylinders, and anchored himself. He hung out of the cargo bay, a third of his body exposed.

"Are we ready?" JORT asked as he squeezed himself into the driver's seat and closed the doors covering the six seats. Only the small VX cargo bay was open to the air.

"Yes, let's roll," Ula said. "JORT, fly dark and low."

The VX lifted off the ground to the cracking of trees and bushes.

"JORT, turn on your infrared vision."

"And remember to go northeast, over the lake, toward the abandoned city of Knoxville," Yot added. "It won't be long before the warriors find the destroyed drone and cameras or the missing VX and cylinders."

JORT headed out of the narrow cove toward the center of the lake. The VX picked up speed as they moved northward.

They'd flown ten kilometers when Ula noticed an island in the middle of the lake, not four hundred meters ahead.

"JORT, turn left!"

He steered the VX left as the island, and the tree line became visible. Ula breathed a sigh of relief, thankful that her telephoto bionic eyes had identified the island in time. After they had traveled ten more kilometers, she said, "JORT, is this a good place to turn northwest, raise our altitude, and head home?"

"Okay—let's get home."

\*\*\*

JORT, once again, zigzagged around small mountains and ridges at treetop level. He flew over the abandoned town of Grimsley toward the dry lakebed and valley of Dale Hollow Lake.

"We made it," Koa said with a gasp. She fed a snack to Jax and cleaned his swollen face.

"We're not finished," Ula said as she wiped sweat and dirt from her face with a towel.

"You're right," Yot said. "Until those cylinders are with our fusion reactors, we're not done. Besides, once DORG finds out we stole a VX and helium-3, he'll hunt us."

No one responded to Yot's comments because they knew he was right. DORG had tolerated the humans only because they were underground and out of sight. Ridge City residents did not interfere with the Imperium's Nashville operations or Region 8 upside activities.

The Imperium would discredit NAIT8 once they noticed the Region 8 thefts. His humiliation would be absolute among his peer Initiators of Thought (ITs). The only uncertainty was whether he would continue to allow Ridge City to exist or attack it.

JORT broke the lull and said, "I can't understand how the VX cockpit displays our location. Their maps seem to be a mirror image."

"Maybe that's how they see," Yot said, holding a rag to his cut shoulder.

Koa handed him a knife and a large bandage and said, "Tear your shirt sleeve open with this."

Koa wetted a small hand towel with water from her canteen and handed it to Yot. "Clean the wound off with this and use the bandage. Press it hard against the wound."

It was quiet in the VX's cockpit as they sped home. Ula took a drink of water and several deep breaths. The mission's success so far thrilled Ula, but she knew more work remained. Now, the team had to get the cylinders inside Ridge City.

"JORT, you are doing a fine job," Ula said.

"Should we continue to the cave?" JORT asked.

"Yes, time is our enemy."

"I agree. Let's finish the mission," Koa said.

"Any disagreement?" Ula asked.

"No. The probability of a successful mission is higher if we continue and get inside our cave system as fast as possible," JORT replied.

Ula looked at her communicator and said, "It's zero-one-zero-six hours, Wednesday. We have five hours before daylight."

"We can't ditch the VX close to our outer cave," Yot said, frowning. "The Imperium warriors will find the secret entrance if we do."

"So, where do we land?" Ula asked.

"We need to ditch the VX far from the cave," Koa said.

"Let's drop off Yot, Koa, Jax, STX, and the cylinders close to the cave," Ula said to JORT. "They can transport the cylinders through the tunnel and lagoons. The oxygen tank is already in the outer lagoon where we left it. JORT and I will ditch the VX and head back to the outer cave."

"Mom, go with the cylinders," Yot said. "JORT and I can ditch the VX."

"No, you go with Koa and get these cylinders to our reactors."

Once the mission had begun, Ula had realized it was a mistake to place her beloved son on the mission team. Regret had permeated her thoughts every day of the mission. She had thought about his two sons, Bao and Qan, and his two unborn daughters, Hoy and Ota Torg. It had been her selfish act that took her son away from these four youngsters and refocused it on the mission. She was not one to reveal her innermost thoughts, but the danger of the mission and her insecurity had put her son in this situation.

"Mom, you're the mayor. They need your leadership."

Yot, young and strong, felt it was his duty to support his mother in the most important mission of their lives. Everyone, including him, admired his mother. She led by example. She took control of Ridge City's destiny while others, like her husband, faded away. Her work ethic and passion for life were unmatched. Tal and the citizens needed her leadership. And Yot knew BOT and Eric Olas could run the nuclear reactors, and he was expendable.

"No, my son. Your job is critical to Ridge City's survival; we need you to manage the nuclear reactors."

"Your wrong, Mom. BOT and Eric can do it."

Koa, JORT, and STX listened to the family argument, and everyone became quiet. Koa understood the deep conflicts happening between a mother and her son. JORT grasped the basic dispute from what he had read about human relationships and family. But without parents, kids, or families, their argument also puzzled him.

Koa broke the silence and said, "Whoever ditches the VX has a long, perilous hike back to the hidden cave entrance."

"Imperium warriors and drones could fill the area by then," Yot said, clenching his jaw.

"Why not dump the VX in the Nolan River Lake?" JORT suggested, knowing this debate was wasting time. "It will take the Imperium longer to find it. And maybe they won't."

A muffled silence engulfed the passenger compartment as the mother and son's disagreement continued. Everyone avoided the conversation. Someone had to ditch the VX far from the cave entrance. Only JORT could fly it.

After a pause, JORT said, "Everyone goes to the secret entrance with the cylinders. I'll take the VX to the lake and sink it myself. Then I'll hike back."

"JORT, I won't have it," Ula said.

"I'm expendable," JORT said. "Returning to the secret cave has its risks. If the Imperium finds out we stole the fuel, DORG will be furious."

Ula deliberated for a moment, and the furrows in her forehead became deeper as the VX flew toward Ridge City. With a sigh, she said, "Here's the plan; we'll drop all of us off near the cave except JORT. JORT will submerge the VX in Nolan River

Lake and hike his way back."

Ula took another drink of water and waited for their response. She liked JORT's plan because everyone reached safety fast. Her innermost thoughts also felt that JORT was expendable. The team's silence meant they agreed to her plan. JORT would do it.

They flew over the dry lakebed of Dale Hollow Lake and headed for the hidden cave area. Around 0200, Wednesday, June 11, they arrived and were hovering close to the hidden entrance.

"We'll land in this small meadow," JORT said. "You are about one kilometer from the secret entrance. Good luck."

With that, JORT landed, and soon the team stood in the meadow waving back at him. Six heavy gas cylinders lay in STX's frame, the key to Ridge City's future.

"Thank goodness we chose JORT for our team," Ula said as the VX lifted off the ground.

"Yeah, I'll hug the big brute when he returns," Koa said, then turned to Ula and said, "Let's go. Which way?"

"Due west."

# CHAPTER 6

## *Hunting*

"**W**hat's missing?" NAIT8 asked one of his Imperium warriors. The robots stood in the command room of their Nashville headquarters in the early morning of Wednesday, June 11.

"Our Glasgow spaceport can't find one of our VX vehicles," robot warrior SUT096 said. "We parked it at the back of the warehouse, awaiting repairs. The lights didn't work—an electrical problem."

"How can you lose a VX?" NAIT8 screamed, banging his fist into his upper leg. "Find it!"

"The vehicle's location system doesn't work. It's part of the electrical outage."

"What! Who manages the Glasgow outpost?"

"MAL803."

"Why didn't he insert a tracking beacon on the idle VX?"

"I don't know."

"Have MAL report to our Nashville Armory and disassemble him."

"Yes, NAIT8."

"And investigate the missing VX and all warehouses. We never lose equipment," NAIT8 said, shaking his long cylindrical head.

Most human-made infrastructure in the Nashville area had disintegrated. Only a few remnants of human civilization remained, dotted around the once proud urban area. And even these relics of human achievement were defenseless against nature. One could sometimes see demolished buildings jutting out of the smothering foliage and rising in the toxic air. But nature would continue to reduce these artifacts of human existence to grains of battered sand.

Minutes later, SUT walked back into the command room and said, "We've received reports of unusual activity at Watts Bar. Someone shot a Verking drone with a laser gun in warehouse two. They shot the cameras out, too."

"It's the rodent humans!" NAIT8 screamed. "They tried to steal fuel again."

The Imperium appointed SUT last week as a headquarters assistant to NAIT8. SUT's algorithms were learning about his boss's behavior. It startled SUT that NAIT8 would lash out at the incompetence of an Imperium warrior. He learned that NAIT8 didn't tolerate mistakes.

"Yes, NAIT8. It must be," SUT replied, taking one step backward.

"We should have never allowed them to exist in their hole in the ground."

"Yes."

"This problem makes me look like a fool," NAIT8 bellowed.

SUT dared not comment, so he stood silent.

"Send out our armed drones and Hertes warriors to Ridge City."

"All of them?"

"You nitwit, yes, all of them."

"Done. We will dispatch six hundred Verking drones and five hundred Hertes warriors."

"Surround Ridge City," NAIT8 said. "Set up a search area with a five-kilometer radius. Search every rock, tree, and bush. If anything moves in our search zone, kill it. Search all nuclear facilities in the region."

"Anything else?"

"Yes, destroy Ridge City's ventilation shafts."

NAIT8 and his predecessors realized the underground city needed air from the upside to survive. Without the ventilation shafts, carbon dioxide and humidity would build up in Ridge City while oxygen would decline. Many branches of the cave network would be uninhabitable within hours. The huge fans would not circuit fresh air, only stale air that would soon become toxic.

As long as the humans lived their subterranean lives and didn't interfere with the upside, NAIT8 had allowed them to exist. But now, the humans had hoodwinked him, and, what's worse, the entire Imperium society knew of Region 8's quandary.

Swarms of Verkings from Region 8 headed toward Ridge City. NAIT8 watched from his display screens at the Region 8 headquarters. He watched the Hertes warriors loading onto the VCX cargo vehicles, the machines glistening from the rising sunlight.

NAIT8 felt a tempered glee in thinking how the last humans in North America would end their days suffocating to death. Or even better, killed by his robot warriors. He thought only a forceful and successful attack on Ridge City would restore his prestige among his robot peers.

The VCX armada of vehicles flew north up the old Interstate 65 roadbed from Nashville toward Ridge City, their lights glaring Wednesday morning. The time of day didn't matter. Imperium warriors and drones never slept. They had cleared the roadbed of foliage and debris. Their anti-gravity vehicles stayed one or two meters off the roadbed because of their heavy loads. The vehicles whined and groaned as NAIT8's army advanced up the pathway.

Within minutes, other Initiators of Thought (ITs) from Australia, India, Africa, and China were asking him if they could help.

"We have things under control, I assure you," NAIT8 declared.

"Do you need more resources?" SUT asked. "Other ITs are asking."

"We don't need anyone's help. We are the rulers of Region 8."

"Yes, NAIT8."

With that, NAIT8 and SUT left the Nashville headquarters and flew to Ridge City. The battalion of VCX cargo carriers and VX vehicles had arrived earlier and had set up the five-kilometer radius around Ridge City. Rows of robot soldiers, three warriors wide, marched out of the VCXs. The thunderous rumble of heavy robots and equipment echoed among the hills and valleys.

NAIT8 set up a command center in one of the landed VCXs about three hundred meters from Ridge City's main gate. The command center had a clear view of the main gate, which the humans had built into the side of the thirty-meter-high rock cliff.

\*\*\*

"Use a P2 explosive device to close the openings," said ION200, one of the Hertes warriors. "Drop it and set the explosion for two seconds."

NAIT8 had tasked the Verkings to find the ventilation shafts. Six shafts were easy to find. Hertes warriors got out of their VXs to destroy the life-giving shafts of air.

Warriors knocked off the metal shields and screens covering the ventilation shaft openings so a warrior could drop a P2 into the shaft set to explode. The first explosion collapsed the shaft as rocks and sand blasted upward. The sound was deafening, especially to the enclosed and shocked Ridge City residents. Ridge City shook, and grains of gravel and dust burst out of the underground vents.

Triggered by more explosions, a wave of fear moved across

the residents. Parents hugged their kids and hurried home to their apartments to hide. Family arguments and accidents set into motion a wave of emergency calls to Ridge City police and fire departments. And panic spread, like a surge of hot air, through the residents of Ridge City.

"NAIT8, we demolished six ventilation shafts," SUT said, his head held high and proud of their achievement.

"Good."

NAIT8 and SUT left the VCX command center and walked across the valley to the front of the main gate.

NAIT8 asked ION, a soldier standing nearby, "Did the humans open the gate to enter the upside? Or do they have a hidden entrance?"

ION used his advanced software to compute the probabilities, which were: used the main gate = 0.180, used a ventilation shaft = 0.236, and used a hidden second entrance = 0.584. He transmitted these probabilities to NAIT8 and SUT.

"Use the Verkings to search every square meter in the confinement zone," NAIT8 said.

"NAIT8, does this include all lakes and forest?" a nearby Hertes warrior named GUE124 said.

"Do I have to repeat my decision?"

"The area is over seventy-eight million square meters," GUE replied.

"So what?"

"Yes, NAIT8. It's done."

***

Awaken by beeping alerts, Tal Torg, the Chief of Ridge City Security, hurried to the basement of the courthouse. There he watched, along with other government officials, what the outside cameras showed. The main gate had two cameras that showed the immediate upside area. Two other cameras hidden outside in tree trunks farther away looked toward the main gate.

"Do we have any messages from our team?" Tal asked, upset but trying to look resolute.

"No, Tal. No messages from your wife's team," a government official replied. "But the videos show DORG's troops gathering at our main gate."

"DORG must have caught them," Tal said in a painful voice. "Now, he's out to destroy us."

"We don't know that yet," the official replied. "The team might have taken the cylinders to a cave or forest. They have no way to communicate with us until they leave the rock crevice and enter Doron Street."

Tal didn't reply as tears rolled down his face. One official in the room tried to put his arm around Tal, but he pushed it away. The reality of both his wife and son being dead or captured devastated him. He wanted to be alone, but frightened humans and naïve robots surrounded him. He wanted to flee and never return, but he had to stay and help his fledgling citizens.

Officials watched daylight video from the four cameras. What they saw terrified them. Hordes of drones flew in clusters, like a swarm of bees. Big airships landing and unloading equipment and warriors. Hundreds of robot warriors lined up in rows facing the main gate, with DORG and SUT standing in front of them.

Tears and moans filled the courthouse room. The reality of facing DORG's army confronted them for the first time. They fell to the floor; a few kneeled to pray. A long period of silence and horrific fear filled the courthouse room. Their eyes filled with tears, and their lips and limbs trembled.

"Those robot warriors are trained assassins," a city official said. "They kill without guilt, sympathy, or fear."

"Yeah, like the Spartan armies in human history," another government employee replied.

"Stop this talk," Tal said in a loud voice. "It only scares us more."

"We should surrender," another person said. "We are no match for these warriors."

"Hold on," Tal said. "Until they attack, we stay put. We must implement our emergency plans. We need to train our citizens at once, the ones that want to fight."

Everyone in that room agreed to implement Ridge City's emergency plans, but most thought the plans were a token response. Electronic messages were sent to all emergency action groups to implement the plans.

***

Tal walked home and into an empty apartment. Bao and Qan Torg were at Yot's apartment with their robot nannies, SAN and NIA. Hoy and Ota Torg, Yot's twenty-week-old daughters, were in their artificial wombs in the nursery. Tal's grandsons and future granddaughters were safe for now, but an emotionless predator lay outside Ridge City's main gate.

Once Tal got home to an empty apartment, he unlocked a file drawer with secret Ridge City reports on the Imperium over the last few centuries. One report had the following paragraph:

> As an Imperium robot warrior walks through the landscape or battlefield, it identifies threats, angles of attack, and details of the terrain and its foe, determines what weapons to use, and notes ways to enter and leave the battle. The warrior moves with a fluidity that seemed unnatural, its hips, legs, and arms rotated a full three-hundred and sixty degrees. Its head is a stark white cylinder filled with cameras, speakers, and sensors. There is no need for human like eyes, nose, mouth, and ears.

Its weapons and reflexes are always ready to strike. All of its sensors and its synthetic intelligence work in unison to protect itself and carry out its mission. It's an unflinching warrior first and a citizen of the Imperium second. They built these Imperium warriors and drones for winning battles and conflicts. To win a battle against these warriors and drones, you must kill them faster than their factories' production rates.

After reading this assessment of their foe, Tal grabbed a pillow from the sofa and cried into it. He knew they were no match for the fierce Imperium robots. And he thought that the Imperium had compromised his wife's team. Otherwise, they wouldn't amass a group of warriors outside their gate.

Tal tried to sleep on the floor and living room sofa but spent the night awake in agony. His sweating body shook in absolute terror. He could smell his own odor. His eyes wouldn't close. And he wanted to vomit. He twisted and turned and thought about his loved ones. Fear overwhelmed him.

What had happened to Ula and Yot? Had DORG tortured them? Killed them? What happens to the citizens of Ridge City? He had lost all hope. The end had arrived, one he didn't want to face. Suicide inhabited his mind.

\*\*\*

A kilometer from the secret Ridge City entrance, Ula, Koa, Yot, Jax, and STX heard explosions Wednesday morning. With swarms of drones roaming the sky above, they hid in the forest. JORT had flown the VX away to ditch it in the Nolin River Lake and would hike back to the secret entrance.

"Something is wrong. Did you hear the explosions?" Ula whispered.

Jax turned west and scratched his left paw on the ground.

"He senses danger," Koa said.

"They're hunting us," Ula said. "We'll head away from the secret entrance."

"Can we run to the cave?" Koa asked.

"We can if we ditch our backpacks. But STX, with his heavy load, cannot keep up," Yot said. "You three, go—run. I'll stay with STX."

"Yot, let's switch places," Ula said.

"Mom, others can run the reactors if I don't get back. You're needed as our mayor, our leader."

Ula considered this for an instant. If she goes to the city, her beloved son has to stay behind to protect the cylinders. If she were the one to stay, Yot had a better chance of surviving. She toiled with the decision, both as a loving mother and a duty-bound mayor. Thousands of Ridge City lives depended on her making the right decision. The Imperium warriors and drones were hunting them.

Ula slammed her backpack on the ground and said, "Koa, Jax, let's go. Splitting up makes it more difficult for the Imperium to find us. Yot and STX will use a different route to the outer cave. Yot if you must, hide the cylinders, then go to the secret entrance. We'll return to the cylinders later." Although Ula didn't say it, she recognized Ridge City residents needed her to lead them in their last battle.

"Okay, we'll see you later," Yot said, giving his mother a hug.

"Let's bury our belongings," Ula said. "Then we can run faster to the entrance."

After burying their backpacks and gear, Ula and Koa took off running, with Jax trailing them. They thrashed their way through the trees, bushes, and grasslands. The branches cut their arms and legs. Ula noticed a tree branch shard stuck in her arm, but she had no time to pull it out. She recognized the explosions meant the Imperium was destroying the main gate or the ventilation shafts. It meant DORG knew about the stolen VX and cylinders. Now their return plans had become chaotic. Ridge City would receive the full vengeance of DORG.

As they ran toward the secret entrance, they heard puttering sounds overhead.

"Stop!" Ula yelled. "It's Imperium drones."

The sparse treetop canopy provided spotty camouflage, but it wouldn't be enough. Ula realized the drones used infrared cameras to hunt their prey.

"We're close to a Green River tributary," she whispered. "Let's hide in the creek so we don't give away the secret entrance."

They raced toward the creek, which was less than two hundred meters away. In her haste, Koa slammed into a tree on the way, bloodying her arm and smashing her nose. Ula helped her up as the puttering sounds grew louder.

Once they reached the creek, they stood on its banks for a split second, considering the snake-infested depths.

"I don't know what's worse: being killed by the Imperium warriors or jumping in a snake-infested creek," Koa said.

"We have no choice," a terrified Ula said. "Jump and hide." Ula could cope with the Imperium drones and creek water but not the snakes.

They jumped in and buried themselves deep in the mud of the creek bank. Ula coated her head and face in the dreadful mud, while three meters downstream, Koa did the same while holding Jax tight. He wiggled to free himself, but as soon as she had covered herself, she placed one hand over his eyes and her other over his mouth. Her grasp was soft and protective, one of love and a desire to stay alive. Jax understood the purpose of the embrace and stayed calm.

Soon, the rancid odor of the water overtook their senses. They hated the smell, but they were alive and hidden. Fear and survival drove their need to wedge themselves deeper. Only their eyes and noses protruded above the water.

Now they waited.

The menacing puttering of drones became louder as the

drones wove through the trees in the daylight. Ula and Koa watched as four black Verking drones cruised down the creek, their three-prong claws dragging in the air. One looked right at Ula's muddy and partially submerged face. She willed herself not to blink as the drone's infrared vision examined the mud bank and then turned away to scan the other bank.

Once the four drones passed, one dove into the water to continue its search.

Within seconds, a violent burst of water erupted from the creek's surface as two pythons wrapped themselves around the machine. The Verking tried to flee, but the snakes wrapped themselves around its four gangly legs. In the fray, the drone fired its laser and cut a tree in half. A ball of snakes and a drone sank into the creek.

The other three drones raised several meters higher into the air. They fired their laser guns into the river to kill the submerged snakes and their drone colleague. Then the ball of biological and synthetic life resurfaced. The airborne drones continued to shoot their laser guns until the abominable biobot exploded in the air. Koa and Ula could smell snake flesh burning and dropping into the creek. A mob of hungry pythons scurried to eat their kinfolk. Ula closed her eyes but dared not move. The other Verkings fled the chaos.

Koa watched in horror as the creek bed filled with more ravenous snakes. For a few minutes, as the feeding frenzy continued, Ula, Koa, and Jax held themselves still, barely breathing. Then the cluster of snakes swam downstream. Somehow, they didn't find their human intruders in the mud.

"Should we go?" Koa whispered.

"No, let's stay two more minutes. Don't move."

After a time, Ula pulled herself free of the muck and stood upright. She heard a disgusting suction sound as she unstuck her body from the muddy tomb.

"Ula, help me out—I'm stuck," Koa said as the sun rose higher over the horizon.

Ula grabbed her hand and pulled, freeing her and Jax from the creek's grasp.

Within minutes, they were standing on dry ground meters away from the river. Caked in wet mud, they looked like mummies. Only Jax's face was mud-free because of Koa's careful embrace.

"I'm going to wash Jax and myself," Koa said. "To hell with the snakes."

"We should try to go to the outer cave," Ula said as she cleaned off her laser gun with muddy water. "But remember, they're still hunting us."

\*\*\*

Meanwhile, Yot and STX earlier took a more indirect route toward the outer cave. STX, with his heavy load, moved at a determined yet slow pace. They had to cross an old roadbed, but when they reached it, they found an Imperium caravan of several cargo vehicles.

STX and Yot stopped in the forest, waiting for the caravan to leave, but the robot drivers and warriors stayed in their vehicles.

"We must hide until they leave," Yot whispered. "Ula and Koa are waiting for us."

"Yot, do you hear that chattering sound?" STX asked. "They are looking for us."

They hid in the middle of thick and tall bushes that were surrounded by trees. During this time, one Verking drone cruised by, only ten meters away from them. It was dodging trees and moving through the forest, but at one point, it stopped and rotated a full three-hundred and sixty degrees to scan the horizon. It didn't find them, but it was a close call. Then it moved forward on its search pattern.

Fifteen minutes later, the caravan started its anti-gravity drives and proceeded down the roadbed.

"I'll go first," Yot said once the convoy had moved out of sight. "If you see me wave you on, then cross the highway. If I hold my hand up, stay put and don't move."

Yot crawled out of the forest to the edge of the roadbed. He scanned the area, and it seemed clear, so he ran across the highway and then waved for STX to follow. With his heavy load, STX climbed the roadbed bank. But STX bumped into a tree stump and took a slight tumble. He steadied himself, but not in time to catch a loose cylinder.

Cling, clang, cling, clang went the sound of the cylinder as it slid out of its carriage and bounced into the trench beside the roadbed. STX stopped and looked at the fallen cylinder.

"STX, leave it there. We'll get it later—you hide," Yot said in a muffled voice.

Yot ran back across the road to the cylinder and grabbed the valve on one end and dragged it. The cylinder made a muffled scrapping sound against the ground. Yot tried to lay it down, but in doing so, he fell over the top of it.

"Are you okay?" STX asked.

"Yeah. What a graceful flip."

"What does graceful mean?"

"STX, forget it."

Yot rolled over, got on his knees, and worked his way to a standing position. STX repositioned his frame so Yot could lift one end of the heavy cylinder into the carriage slot. Then he lifted the other end and pushed it back into the slot. Once loaded, Yot took a rope and tied the renegade cylinder in place.

They continued their journey, hiking through the forest at a snail's pace.

"Stop, STX. Let's take a break."

"I don't need a break."

"I know, but I do," Yot said, lying on the ground.

Yot had little sleep in the past few days. His eyes were puffy, his mind foggy, and his body ached. His legs felt like dumbbells. He even had brief delusions of how the Imperium would torture him before they killed him.

"STX, it's daylight. We didn't reach the cave in time. And the Verkings are hunting us," a beleaguered Yot said. "We should bury the cylinders and come back for them later."

"I can carry them to the cave, Yot."

"Yes, but we'll never make it; they're too heavy. The Imperium will surround Ridge City. The drones wouldn't be hunting us unless they knew we stole the fuel. They'll find us."

"Okay, where do we bury them?"

"See the collapsed water tower?" Yot pointed west. "Let's bury them with the rusted metal parts. The other metal will help hide them from the Imperium's sensors."

For the next hour, Yot chipped away at the heavy vegetation, digging a cavity under the rusted metal beams. Then he fitted the cylinders underneath them.

"What's next?" STX asked.

An exhausted Yot bent over and put his hands on his knees. After several heavy breaths, he said, "STX, I could travel faster if I was alone."

He looked upward into the sky, trying not to look at STX. He said, "Ugh, it's best to disassemble you. We can hide you with the cylinders."

STX shuffled his six feet, paused, and said, "So, my mission is done?"

"Yes, for now."

"Okay, if you wish. The tools to disassemble me are in the toolbox behind my middle leg."

Yot grabbed a battery-powered wrench and disassembled STX. Before he disconnected his computer module, Yot said, "STX, I'll place your computer and software in this waterproof bag and seal it."

"Thank you, Yot."

Yot pulled the plugs connecting STX's computer module to the generator and battery and placed these parts in the bag and sealed it tight. Then he stuffed the bag on top of the cylinder's burial site and covered the hiding place with scraps of rusted sheet metal, bushes, and tree branches.

Yot wrote the site's coordinates inside his shoes with a waterproof pen and then stumbled toward the secret outer cave and lagoon. Less than one kilometer from the cave, he stopped, needing to rest. He dropped to the ground and hid in the tall grass.

He used his communicator to reach out, hoping Ula, Koa, or JORT would hear him. "Hermes, here. Hermes, here," he called, stating the mission name, but he received no response.

\*\*\*

After hiding in the river, Ula, Koa, and Jax made their way closer to the cave entrance. With her goggles on to dampen the blazing sunlight, Ula wondered if STX and Yot had already arrived.

"Is Hermes there?" she said into her short-range communicator. "Hermes, please." But no one replied.

As they crept closer to the entrance, Jax stopped and pawed the ground with his left foot.

"Jax smells warriors or drones; they're close," Koa said.

"Should we run for the cave or lead them away?" Ula asked.

"Let's protect the cave. It's a critical resource for us."

Ula didn't know what to do. Exhaustion had compromised her acute judgment. She worried about her brave son and the status of the cylinders. Saving the lives of 2,076 people depended on delivering those cylinders.

"Okay, let's lead them away from the cave," Ula said.

So, they ran away from the cave's location again. After hiking in the daylight for less than an hour, Ula stopped. She noticed a mumbling on her communicator. She stopped and listened.

"Someone is saying Hermes," she said to Koa. "Yot and

STX must be close."

She focused her attention on the communicator.

"Hermes, I'm here. Hermes, repeat, Hermes," she said.

"Mom, is that you?"

"Yes, it's me."

Ula, Koa, and Jax continued to walk until they saw Yot step out from behind a grove of trees. He ran to hug his mother and then put his arms around her and Koa.

"I see you made it," he said, a wide beam spreading across his face.

"Yes," Ula replied. "Where's STX and the cylinders?"

"I buried the cylinders and STX. The site's coordinates are inside my shoe."

"Now what?" Koa asked.

A puttering sound filled the area and left no time for conversations and hugs.

"We shouldn't go to the cave. We'll give its location away," Ula said. "Let's go away from the cave."

The three of them sprinted east toward the harsh glow of the sun, with Jax trailing them. The reunited team plowed their way through a meadow with two-meter-tall grass and kept going until Jax barked.

Koa dug her foot in the ground to stop. Ula and Yot did the same.

The ominous sound of drones puttering became louder.

Without notice, the tall grass moved toward them from all directions with a turbulent ferocity. Before they could react, eight black Verking drones had them surrounded. Each of the drone's four grisly legs with sharp, steel claws on the end dangled below their airborne bodies. Their hollow camera eyes, like glass doll eyes, showed no emotion or empathy. The drones bounced in the air in jubilation for catching their prey. Would they kill these helpless creatures on-the-spot or take them prisoners?

"Don't run," a petrified Ula shouted. "They'll kill us!"

# CHAPTER 7

## *Valor*

"**D**o not kill them," NAIT8 ordered, standing in the VCX hilltop command center next to Ridge City. "Our warriors are on the way."

NAIT8 had received the video of the three humans huddled together and a dog nearby, barking and yelping. He watched as the Verking drones corralled the humans.

The Imperium collective intelligence saw no value in the subterranean species. Whenever they captured a human on the upside, the worthless vagabond would always beg for water, food, and air-conditioning. Humanity was obsolete, much like the extinct dodo birds, manatees, and polar bears.

The Verking drones were mocking the three prisoners, like humans taunting hogs before killing and eating them. They taunted Yot by pinching his ears and nipples, celebrating by wiggling when he yelled out in pain. But the grotesque drones didn't injure their pathetic prisoners because of NAIT8's directive, and they knew he was watching.

Two VX vehicles arrived and landed in the field, crushing the grass flat. Imperium robot warriors climbed out of the vehicles and marched toward them. A warrior named ZET082 said, "We will not harm you if you obey our commands. Follow me and get into the vehicle."

Filthy and frightened but still alive, the humans walked toward the VX vehicle. Once beside it, the warriors tied each of their ankles with short ropes, making it impossible for them to run. They packed Ula and Yot into the first VX, and it flew away. Koa stepped into the second VX, but as Jax tried to enter, ZET held out his robotic arm to block his entry.

"Only humans go," ZET said.

Koa tried to step out of the vehicle as she yelled, "No. No. My dog must come with me."

ZET, sitting next to her, wrapped his right arm around her waist and made a ratcheting sound as he tightened his grip. Koa flailed around but couldn't break free. She busted her hand on the warrior's metal frame.

"What a disgusting species. Your blood is all over our VX."

"Take Jax, take the dog," she yelled.

"This wretched beast is not part of our orders."

The VX closed its doors and began its journey toward the front entrance to Ridge City.

NAIT8 and SUT watched their capture and awaited their arrival.

"Blood is nasty," NAIT8 said to SUT.

"Yes, and sticky. Our hydraulic fluids are better engineered."

"Everything about our species is better, everything."

\*\*\*

Jax barked as the VXs lifted off the ground, taking Ula, Yot, and Koa away in two VXs. The Karelian bear hunting dog found himself alone in the blazing hot meadow, scared but courageous. He couldn't see the horizon because of the high grass.

Three Verking drones circled him. One Verking used its long legs and claws to poke him. But the drones flew away as thunderstorms were forming in the distance.

A gutsy Jax sniffed his surroundings. He would use Earth's

weak magnetic field to detect major directions. Jax's sixth sense used magneto reception to find his way. Birds, fish, and other animals use similar biology to navigate their way from place to place.

Jax walked in a circle four times before he gained his bearings. Each circle allowed him to better gauge the magnetic fields and directions. Then he raised his head and stood tall. He turned, heading west toward the secret cave and Ridge City.

His intelligence and keen sense of smell would help him make the short trip home. He had no quarrel with the hellish upside and planned to avoid confrontations with Imperium robots and animal predators. To avoid snakes and alligators, Jax stayed away from creeks and lakes. His goal was to get home.

***

MAL803 arrived at the Nashville Armory, ready for disassembly. The Imperium pre-programmed all of their robots, including MAL, for this eventuality, so he knew what to expect.

NAIT8 noticed MAL's arrival Wednesday morning but didn't communicate with the disgraced warrior. Instead, he ordered SUT to observe MAL's disassembly through videos from Nashville and to report back to him.

ITs had absolute power within their assigned region. There were no courts or labor unions in the totalitarian Imperium society. For issues that included more than one region, a worldwide Imperium voting system decided the course of action by collective IT consensus. The Imperium Nation divided Earth's landmasses and oceans into 113 regions. Only 113 ITs voted.

The Nashville Armory built the Hertes robot models, including warriors, construction workers, and miners. Their production processes shipped these wares to all Imperium regions across South and North America. The armory used a set of five massive buildings, the first of which used assembly lines to disassemble old or disciplined robots.

Watching the video, SUT followed MAL as they unbolted MAL's head, arms, and legs. SUT listened to the ratcheting sounds of power drills. Emotion played no part in MAL's disassembly. MAL didn't rebel and accepted his pre-ordained fate. With MAL's unattached head still conscious, the dishonored Glasgow manager understood his fate.

They placed his cylindrical head on a conveyor and moved it to the laboratory. His neural networks and computer modules would be conscious of the ride. After they disconnected the battery, he would no longer be conscious. Next, they pulverized these networks, batteries, and modules. They also deleted his robot registration records and serial numbers for each of his 2,103 parts.

The lab released fifty spiderbots into the Imperium's communication and web network to erase any MAL803 files. Wherever the web had archived any information related to his name or activities, the spiderbot or crawler cataloged and erased it. This process continued for days until they cleansed all web information from the network.

The goal of Imperium production was to maximize efficiency and minimize waste. Another assembly line disassembled MAL's arms and legs into reusable parts. They reused common parts in multiple robot models to reduce costs and speed up production. From the trunk of MAL's body, they harvested the sealed, cube-sized nuclear reactor to save it for future use. In one of the factory's furnaces, they melted his wiring, hoses, and nanoparticle-reinforced robot skin.

One Nashville factory focused on research and development of software—the digital steel of the Hertes warrior. Here is where the research originated on whether to program more emotions into Imperium synthetic brains.

They dismantled 178 other robots along with MAL in Nashville on this day. After MAL's disassembly, SUT walked to

NAIT8 in the VCX command center close to Ridge City's main gate.

"We ended MAL today," SUT said.

"Good. And we reused his parts?"

"Yes, NAIT8, our armory wastes nothing."

***

Thursday morning, an exhausted Jax walked toward what he hoped was the secret entrance to Ridge City. He didn't understand the capture of his beloved Koa, but he realized he was alone. He didn't know where the warriors took Koa, Ula, and Yot.

He made his way through the matted vegetation but often found his pathway blocked. He realized his journey to the outer cave would be easier if he walked on old roadbeds that were cleared of debris. Once he found an abandoned roadbed heading west, he used it.

Jax's ability to smell far exceeded human capabilities or those of other animals. The Ridge City Police Department had trained him to detect hydraulic fluid and grease. This skill allowed him to find and avoid Imperium robots, drones, and other Imperium equipment. And using his natural instincts, he detected rats, termites, and other odors. Jax used these skills to avoid predators on his trip back to Ridge City. When he sensed a threat, he hid in the grass or forest.

As Jax meandered through the jungle, he approached a small stream. He was surveying the bank of the creek when he caught a whiff of snakes nearby. The day's intense heat and brilliant sunlight made the stench of snakes more noticeable.

Knowing that snakes and alligators infested almost all waterways in the upside, he walked the creek bank, looking for a safe way to cross. Soon, he found a fallen moss-covered tree laying over the three-meter-wide creek. He stepped on top of the tree trunk and began his treacherous walk. At first, his feet slipped on the slick moss, but he recovered and continued walking, not knowing what lurked in the waters.

After crossing the creek and traveling another twenty meters, Jax stopped and rested. He detected more snakes but was unsure of their direction. Unbeknownst to him, a four-meter-long, forty-two-kilogram Burmese python was hiding behind him.

Using all of their senses, both animals lay quiet, trying to decipher the situation. Jax wanted to avoid all confrontations and get back home, while the python was planning its next meal.

Jax sensed the snake close by and stood upright. He looked around but saw no predator. The hair on his back and neck rose. His breathing quickened, and his posture became staunch. He perceived a potential threat to his well-being. But from what direction?

When he stood up, the python moved closer, now within two meters of Jax's rear. It opened its mouth with its sharp and backward cutting teeth, and its muscles tightened as it prepared for a swift attack.

At that very instant, the snake lunged forward. Jax jumped away and bolted through the forest. He dogged trees and other obstacles and didn't stop running for over one hundred meters.

But in his haste, he slammed into a tree truck and cut his head. Blood dripped from his mouth and ear, but at least he could move farther away from the snakes and alligators.

Now within two hundred meters of the secret entrance, he sped up his pace. Exhausted, dirty, and bleeding, he rushed into the outer cave and lay down on the lagoon shore. Rays of daylight penetrated the outer cave opening, revealing more of his surroundings. A few ugly, crepuscular bats lingered on the ceiling, their red eyes watching him.

\*\*\*

After resting for over an hour, Jax stood. He felt safe in the outer cave, but he knew he needed to go back to Ridge City. That meant diving into the lagoon before him and crawling through the seven-meter-long tunnel, holding his breath. Then he must maneuver through the five-hundred-meter-long rock crevice and enter Ridge City. Koa's absence made the sequence of tasks daunting, and he must do it alone.

Jax surveyed the green, algae-filled lagoon and then looked upward at the bats eyeing him. Koa had trained him to swim and hold his breath underwater. This learned skill was important for police rescues and underwater searches.

He took a deep breath and dived into the lagoon, where he frantically searched for the tunnel opening. He kicked and twisted his way through the tunnel. Water entered his nose. About one minute passed before he ran out of air, but he cleared the tunnel. Water entered his mouth as he gasped for air, but with the last of his energy, he pushed off the bottom of the inner lagoon with his hind legs.

With an enormous splash, he broke the water's surface, coughing and spitting up water. He swam to the edge of the inner lagoon and used his legs to crawl out. Exhausted, he lay there in the darkness of the inner cave and lagoon. He looked upward to the cave ceiling to see a few bats glaring at him, but none ventured toward him. After a rest, he found the five-hundred-meter-long crevice that would lead to the Doron Street exit.

Jax worked his way through the crevice in the dark to Doron Street and emerged into Ridge City. The once beautiful display panels had become black voids. Only the flicker of a lit candle or single light filled the building windows. There were no scents of coffee, cats, or baked goods. The streets were empty of people and their laughter and energy. The gaiety of the city was gone.

With hair matted by thick green algae and water, he walked

down the dark street. He worked his way to Koa's apartment building.

Jax followed people up the steps to the correct floor. He waited until someone opened the stair door and bolted to Koa's apartment. Outside Koa's front door, he scratched and barked, but no one answered. He repeated the scratching and barking several times, but still no one came.

Exhausted from his ordeal, he fell asleep in front of the doorway.

***

JORT flew toward Nolin River Lake Wednesday morning after dropping off the team close to the secret entrance to Ridge City. He flew in the dark, changing directions and altitude to avoid the hills, valleys, and tall trees. Soon, he was hovering above the lake close to the dam. The sun had yet to rise. It was dark, and since he didn't understand all the vehicle's instruments, he couldn't decipher the lake's depth, so he worked his way upstream. JORT switched his cameras to ultrasound, creating a fuzzy black-and-white image of the lake. After searching for a good place to submerge the VX, he decided on the lake's widest part, hoping it was also the deepest.

JORT used a slow descent to set the VX down in the water. As the VX sank, air bubbles crept up the sides of the passenger compartment's windshields. He cut off the anti-gravity drive and the hydrogen-fueled propulsion systems and let the vehicle sink to the bottom of the lake. He opened two doors before it hit the lakebed, and the inside of the VX filled with water. His sensors showed the lake was acidic with very little oxygen, so most fish were dead. He sat in the driver's seat while the dingy waters engulfed him. A calm JORT had no fear of drowning because he couldn't. He could work underwater, on land, and in space.

JORT sat in the submerged vehicle for over five minutes in

deep thought before he exited his driver's side door. He knew he had completed his job. With his help, the frail human species would survive—or at least he hoped they would. A sense of peace and tranquility filled his restricted consciousness.

JORT got out of the vehicle and stood erect, surrounded by dark water. He raised his right arm above his head, and the sensors on his hand still identified water, which meant the lake's depth was over four meters.

He walked from the bottom of the lake to the shore illuminated by twilight from a rising sun. Using his powerful arms, he cleared the thick trees on the lake bank and emerged from the water, with it dripping off his frame. He stood on the lake's bank, again thinking about his situation and his human colleagues.

After more reflection, JORT traveled through the forest, going toward the upside cave and secret entrance. He marched through the countryside, questioning whether to continue on his expected return. He didn't want to expose Ridge City's secret passageway to the Imperium or do anything to hurt his human friends. They had the fuel. Ridge City was going to survive, he thought.

As he worked his way in broad daylight toward the upside secret passageway, he stopped and sat down on a large granite bolder that was protected by a canopy of trees.

As he was deciding what to do, his sensors picked up that dreadful, puttering noise. The sounds were getting louder and matched the audio prints of impervious Imperium drones. He had to assume DORG had found the missing cylinders, and he had sent drones and warriors to find them.

His neural-network algorithms computed a probability of 0.803 that the drones would find him. The drones used radar and infrared sensors to find their prey. His algorithms evaluated four different options, and in a millisecond, JORT set a trap for the drones.

He stood and turned toward the tall trees behind him. He

fired his two laser guns on his shoulders at the trees and set them ablaze. The dry trees burst into flames, the scorching heat sucking more moisture out of them. He thought the blaze would confuse the drones and make them delay in finding him. It did.

Then he walked into the middle of the growing blaze and stood still. His frame could endure temperatures up to 810°C (i.e., 1,490 degrees Fahrenheit) as the small fusion reactor in his chest provided the energy to cool his neural network and body.

With his sensors and weapons in full combat mode, he waited for the drones. Soon he tracked four Verkings surrounding the inferno. JORT knew their infrared sensors wouldn't work—pillars of billowing smoke and flame had turned the area a bright orange as the fire became hotter. But their radar would bounce off his metal frame. So, he locked his two shoulder lasers and two hand-held laser guns on each of the four drones. Without an instant of delay, he fired and hit all four drones. The entire battle took seconds.

Victorious, though singed, JORT walked out of the blaze. He understood the drones had sent information back to DORG. More drones would come to this location.

Now he knew the Imperium and NAIT8 were searching for his team. He recognized the danger they all faced. He didn't want to jeopardize their lives anymore. The Imperium must not find the hidden entrance to Ridge City.

Now in daylight, he followed his earlier route through the terrain and back toward the submerged VX. He replayed videos he'd filmed of Koa, Yot, and Ula in the caves and lagoons and Jax's fight with the Burmese pythons. Next, he replayed several good times interacting with Ridge City residents and his boss, Tal Torg.

He had decided and walked to the edge of Nolin River Lake.

"I'm replaceable," he mumbled to no one. "I'm godless with no soul. My purpose is to protect the human species and the Torg family."

He paused, and for one last time, he surveyed the horrific status of the upside and humanity. Then he walked into the lake. Steam rose off his hot body as he hit the water. He turned on his ultrasound system to find where the VX was stuck in the lake's mud and trudged underwater to the open vehicle door.

Once again, he sat down in the driver's seat as rays of sunshine brightened the water. Tiny bubbles of boiling water arose around his frame, creating a temporary tomb of air bubbles.

He opened his chest compartment, paused, and, with his right hand, grabbed the cube that housed his nuclear reactor. In one mighty, daring jerk, he pulled his life-giving power source from his invincible body and crushed it with his hand.

JORT's head dropped, his shoulders slumped forward, and his arms fell to his side. Still in his right hand, the demolished cube-size reactor bubbled and glowed an eerie greenish blue. The glow lit up the grave of a soulless yet valiant and insightful robot warrior. Then the light dimmed, and death and darkness prevailed.

# CHAPTER 8

## *Escape*

"You are a filthy species," DORG said to Ula, Koa, and Yot as they stumbled toward him, angry and sweating. DORG stood beside the VCX command center close to Ridge City's main gate. It was Wednesday morning, June 11. Stripped of their weapons and cooling vests and tied with ropes at the ankles, the trio was made to kneel in front of DORG, SUT, ZET, and three Hertes warriors.

"How did you escape your hole in the ground?"

No one replied as the robot warriors held them in a kneeling position.

At that moment, Ula knew the Imperium had not discovered their hidden entrance.

"Our cameras show you didn't use your main gate, or if you did, it has a hidden door," DORG said. "If you don't answer me, we'll kill one of you. Answer me."

Ula's eyebrows pinched together as she tried to stand, but a warrior pushed her by the shoulders back down.

"We opened the main gate and snuck through in the dark," Ula said, coughing. The blistering upside air had burned Ula's throat and lungs.

DORG turned toward his warriors. "Examine the main gate."

Six warriors and eight Verking drones moved toward the gate led by ZET and examined every square meter. They pulled and pushed on the gate's steel plates, knobs, and hinges. DORG and the prisoners waited for the results of the inspection.

"We found no hidden openings in the gate," ZET said to DORG, communicating the results through wireless communications.

"Our warriors found no hidden door," DORG said. "Our cameras didn't notice any gate movement."

"We only cracked it open so we could get to the upside," a lying Ula replied.

Koa interrupted, spat dirt out of her mouth, and shouted, "You must find my dog!"

"Why would I care about your stupid beast?"

"She'll die out there."

"So what? No dogs, nor you, serve a purpose."

Koa tried to wiggle from the warrior's grip but couldn't free herself.

"Human cupidity is a fault of your species. We don't suffer from such weaknesses."

"That's because you have no compassion," Koa shouted back.

"Enough," DORG said in a thundering voice. "Where is the helium-3 fuel you stole?"

Again, no one answered, looking away instead, but his comment delighted Ula. This meant the Imperium had not found the gas cylinders.

Ula looked up as DORG stepped toward her and said in her face, "You exist because I allowed it. Now, you steal from us. We have destroyed your city's ventilation shafts." He paused as a swarm of Verkings flew over their heads.

Looking up, they noticed an abundance of dark clouds rolling toward them as a light rain fell.

DORG yelled to his warriors. "Kill them in front of their sacred gate so Ridge City citizens can see it."

"What about keeping them as pets for our experiments?" a warrior asked.

"Kill them, now!"

Three powerful Hertes warriors grabbed the ropes around Ula, Yot, and Koa's ankles and dragged each of them, feet first, to the front gate. Their ankles bled as their arms and heads bounced along the ground for about two hundred meters.

Ula grimaced in pain as her body hit rocks and bushes. She saw Koa's head hit a rock with a resounding, merciless thud and heard her yelp in pain before she became unconscious.

I hope Ridge City citizens aren't watching, Ula thought to herself, the taste of her own blood in her mouth. But she thought the two hidden cameras in upside tree trunks would broadcast their executions.

Ula gazed from the corner of her bionic eye as the three warriors stepped back a few meters. She glanced toward the hilltop command center, where DORG was watching the executions through body cameras mounted on the three warriors.

Raindrops fell, though DORG and his warriors didn't notice, and the rain soon became more intense. A powerful gust hit them, followed by a wave of hail. The hail caused a tingling sound as it hit their metal frames. The surreal sleet bounced on the ground and piled up several centimeters.

Yot and Ula thought it must be a derecho coming from over the horizon. Derechos were a frequent weather event caused by an angry Earth. Soon, a wave of hurricane-force wind slammed into them and pulled bushes and trees from the ground. Imperium equipment lofted into the air and tumbled back down, and the violent storm plowed through the execution site.

But this derecho didn't seem like past storms. Sheets of pelting hail hit the upside in organized waves. And the boiling clouds were pitch black. Robots and humans were both blinded by the assault, which shattered Imperium equipment and upside trees. The three Imperium robots that were trying to execute Ula, Yot, and Koa dropped to the ground. DORG hugged the ground at the hillside VCX command center to avoid the hurricane-force winds.

Koa was still unconscious, but Ula and Yot observed the surrounding chaos as they hugged the ground. They saw Verking drones knocked to the ground and tree trunks and branches hit Hertes warriors.

From where she lay, Ula watched as a VCX scooted through the dirt, making a wrenching sound. The vehicle lifted off the ground and tumbled across the field. Mangled metal and debris flew everywhere, making thrashing and banging sounds. Other VCXs and VXs also became airborne, crashing into trees and other Imperium warriors.

"What is it?" DORG yelled.

"It's another derecho, with maximum winds of 348 kilometers per hour (i.e., 216 miles per hour)," SUT yelled.

Ula watched the devastating storm ransack the land. Tree trunks burst into pieces as they hit Hertes warriors who were running for cover. One airborne tree trunk pierced a warrior's chest, and Ula saw it fly out the other side. The once invincible warrior sank to the ground, its power source no longer within its body, with it now being stuck to a flying tree trunk. A twisted metal beam slammed into the head of one of the assassin warriors; his head separated from its body, and the headless android stopped moving. Rain and wind continued to pound the area as Yot and Ula wondered what was happening and why.

After minutes of violent destruction, the mysterious derecho moved away and vanished into the cloudy sky.

Ula stared at the surrounding terrain. The derecho had carved bald swathes in the landscape. The land was barren now, stripped of its foliage. Only rocks and a gritty, sandy soil remained, with a few tree stumps still standing upright.

When the danger had subsided, a dizzy Ula tried to stand. She tried to find DORG and his warriors, but none were nearby.

"Let's go," Ula yelled. "Carry Koa."

Yot stood, shook off the dirt, and loaded an unconscious Koa onto his shoulder.

They had only taken several steps away from the gate when they noted a loud ratcheting sound.

Ula recognized what it was at once. "Our gate is opening," she yelled.

Surprised, they turned and staggered toward the gate. Yot struggled to carry Koa with Ula, trying to protect Koa's bouncing head.

The great doors opened by a sliver and stopped. In Ridge City's 495-year history, this was the twelfth time it had opened.

Ula and Yot squeezed Koa through the opening first, and then they followed. Ridge City paramedics helped them get inside the gate. The grinding sound of the gears closed the gate. They understood: it was the grateful sound of safety—the gate's metal pins locking the door.

As soon as they were inside Ridge City, they collapsed onto the pavement. Tal Torg and four paramedics rushed to them.

As Tal hugged his wife and son, the paramedics attended to them as best they could, pouring water over their cuts and dirty faces and giving them water to drink. Koa came to, thanks to a splash of cold water on her face.

Behind the paramedics, about thirty city residents scrutinized the situation. Street cameras had recorded their escape from DORG and into the inside of Ridge City.

"Where am I?" Koa asked, bewildered.

"Ridge City," a paramedic said.

"How?" she mumbled, but no one answered.

The paramedics gave her gulps of water and strapped her down to a stretcher.

The other paramedics checked Ula's and Yot's vital signs and then helped them to stand upright. With joyful tears flowing down his face, Tal helped Ula and Yot walk to an ambulance, and they took a seat. Tal squeezed their hands and said,

"Oh, I never thought I would hold your hand again. I love you."

"We love you too," a confused Yot replied.

After drinking more water, Ula said, "Did you see what happened outside the gate?"

"Yes, we saw it all using our two hidden cameras. It was horrible. They were about to kill you."

\*\*\*

After a full day of hospital treatments, the three were showing signs of recovery. They discussed many things, including the history of blue orb sightings and another mission to find the gas cylinders.

Ula had two cracked ribs and needed stitches in her face and lips. Yot needed splints on two broken fingers and stitches for a torn ear, out of which he couldn't hear. He also had a concussion from hitting his head on rocks as the Hertes warriors had dragged them, feet first, to the front of the main gate. Koa had ruptured her spleen and had broken three ribs and her collarbone. All three suffered from exhaustion, dehydration, and countless insect bites.

Tal stayed with them in the hospital and assigned others to manage the reactors and city security.

Thursday at noon, Ula awoke to find Yot sitting beside her hospital bed, holding her hand.

"Was the storm a derecho?" she asked.

"Yes, it was an odd storm, but it saved our lives."

"The blue orb might have caused the derecho."

"Maybe, but we'll never know."

The two pondered their situation, the derecho, and blue orb intervention. After minutes of silence, Yot said, "Mom, I researched blue orbs from my hospital bed."

"What did you find?"

"A lot. People have seen orbs for thousands of years, including the blue orbs that visited Earth in 2147 and 2647. The first time, it used a young farm girl named Jillian Hickory as its voice to communicate with humanity."

"What did it want?"

"The blue orb tried to help humanity mitigate climate change. It warned us about future events, such as ocean currents changing and some stopping, and how this would change Earth's weather. The orb forewarned us about sea level rise, torrid heat, and the fracture of humanity into thousands of disparate and competing tribes. It gave humanity the knowledge to terraform earth and control Earth's biosphere. It even gave humanity blueprints to build the 216 megamachines to take the heat and carbon dioxide out of the oceans and atmosphere."

"Well, that didn't work," Ula replied while reaching for a glass of water.

"What happened the second time the orb appeared in 2647?" Ula asked.

"The blue orb returned in 2647 to a more chaotic world than in 2147. By 2647, our oceans had risen seven to eight meters above the year 2000 sea levels. And it became much hotter, so hot, that several nations built underground cities. Our own Ridge City was first occupied in 2652. The cost of moving major cities away from the coasts and adding air conditioning caused many nations to become bankrupt or collapse. Countries could not feed their citizens. Trillions of people, animals, and plants died. Humanity's standard of living declined, democratic institutions fractured, and anarchy and war dominated the world."

"Yes, as mayor, I read historical documents about Ridge City," Ula said, lying in bed.

"Mom, the Imperium dominates more than Earth. They are building a Dyson ring around the sun."

"I've heard of a Dyson sphere but remind me what is a Dyson ring."

A robotic nurse came into the room, checked Ula's vital

signs, and adjusted her saline and antibiotic drips. She had over one hundred insect bites on her body, and these intravenous medicines would replenish her body fluids and fight any infections.

"A Dyson ring captures a small fraction of our sun's energy," Yot said. "The ring infrastructure around the sun is hundreds of kilometers wide. Imperium robots have been building the ring for over one hundred years. The robots are ideal for building such a structure since they can repair themselves in space if needed and require no food, oxygen, water."

After time to drink more water, Ula asked, "When will our Ridge City reactors stop working?"

"We have about ten days of fuel left."

"Did the Imperium destroy our ventilation shafts?" Ula said.

"Yes, it's terrible. Suffocation is a gruesome way to die."

They both paused and stared at one another. They blamed themselves for the horrific outcome. Ula used the bedsheet to wipe away tears while Yot held his mother's hand.

"Get the nurse, Yot. I have a migraine headache."

Yot got up from the chair when Tal arrived. He walked over to Yot and hugged him for longer than usual. He then kissed his wife on the forehead several times and held her hand.

"I see you two are talking and getting better—good," Tal said.

"Yes, we are. We've been discussing DORG closing our ventilation shafts."

"That's true, and our citizens are panicking and hiding in their apartments. The only good news is that the Imperium didn't find our three hidden ventilation shafts.

"I'm going back to my room. I'm queasy," Yot said as he patted his father on the shoulder.

Tal sat in the chair Yot had vacated and held Ula's hand. "How do you feel?"

"My ribs hurt, and it's hard to breathe, but otherwise I'm

gaining strength." She paused and looked at the room's wall screen, which was displaying majestic snow-capped mountains. "Yot has the coordinates of where he hid the helium-3 fuel. He wrote them inside his shoes. Go get them before we lose the information."

"Good idea," Tal said and then he hurried down the hallway to Yot's room.

Yot, back in bed, smiled when his father asked where the shoes were. "They're hidden under the blankets in the closet."

Tal reached under the blankets and pulled out Yot's hiking boots. He held the inside of one shoe toward the light. "Yot, take my pen and write what I say."

After recording the coordinates twice, Tal put the boots back in the closet.

"Dad, are we operating on our emergency backup air shafts?"

"Yes, DORG hasn't found them yet. We hid them in rock crevices and one inside a hollow tree trunk with an opening five meters high in the air."

"I know, Dad. I helped build them at night."

"If we lose them, we'll have to open the gate and fight," Tal said with a vacant stare.

After two days in the hospital, Yot left, and he arrived home on Friday evening, June 13, hugging his two sons, Bao and Qan. Late Saturday afternoon, they discharged Ula, too. Koa stayed in the hospital as her injuries were more severe: the doctors had inserted metal pins in her fractured collar bone and removed her spleen.

***

Also, Friday morning, an apartment neighbor noticed a dirty, exhausted Jax sitting at Koa's apartment door. The neighbor fed Jax and gave him a quick bath. The neighbor took Jax to the hospital, and he ran into Koa's hospital room.

"Jax! Jax! Oh, I missed you."

With the help of the neighbor and a nurse, they placed Jax on Koa's bed. Her absolute joy overcame the pain from her injuries. Jax's tail never quit wagging. Crying and delighted, Koa patted and hugged him. Jax licked Koa's face many times. Within an hour, they fell asleep together on the bed. The hospital allowed him to stay in Koa's room despite the hospital rules. Hospital employees fed and took care of Jax while Koa recovered.

Jax had filled a void in her life with love and friendship. They had a forever bond, something that had evaded Koa with another human being her entire life.

\*\*\*

Saturday evening, Yot and NIA brought his two sons to Ula and Tal's apartment for dinner. Ula and Tal greeted their grandkids with long hugs and kisses.

At dinner, Qan said, "We saw the video of you two outside the main gate."

"Yeah, I wish they would stop playing it. It creates panic," Yot replied.

"It's too late to hide the videos," Tal replied.

"Are we going to die?" Bao asked, sending a sudden rush of adrenaline through everyone's body.

"Bao, we will not let that happen. We'll get the fuel," Yot said as his posture stiffened.

Ula didn't enter the conversation, feeling much anxiety about the unsuccessful mission. She did not like lying to her grandchildren.

The crushing responsibility of getting the fuel to Ridge City's nuclear reactors weighed on Ula's mind. The helium-3 cylinders were not at Ridge City. Without them, they had no chance of survival. Failure meant the end of Ridge City and, most likely, the death of its citizens.

During dinner, the family discussed school, their mental and physical health, and future scenarios for Ridge City. After dinner, NIA took the kids back to their apartment after a group family hug.

Yot stayed with his mother and asked, "When do we go for the cylinders?"

"We should go now," Ula replied. She paused and pressed her hand against her painful rib cage, then said with a grimace, "If my calculations are correct, we'll run out of fuel about June twenty-first, a week from today. We must go soon."

"Mom, our citizens still haven't been told about the fuel shortage. Should we tell them?"

"If we do, it will create more panic."

"Mom, you can't protect the residents any longer. They saw DORG try to kill us at the main gate."

"Yot's right, Ula," her husband said. "It's time to tell all."

"Who's going to get the cylinders?" Yot asked.

"The two of us," Ula said. "Koa can't go; she's in the hospital. We'll build STX if we can find all five bags. He'll carry the cylinders back here. If we can't assemble STX, we'll drag one cylinder back ourselves."

There was a cautious pause before Tal spoke. "So, we lost JORT?"

"We don't know," Ula said. "JORT seemed fine when he left us to ditch the stolen VX."

"If the Imperium captures or destroys JORT, they'll download the information he has on our plans and situation," Yot said.

"If that happens and with no fuel, they may wait us out and let us die in Ridge City," Tal replied.

"That cannot happen," Yot said in a loud voice. "When do we go, Mom?"

"Let's go Monday evening. We should be healthy enough by then. We know the location of the cylinders."

"Yes, we'll take a handheld electronic compass so we can go straight to the coordinates."

"It'll be a quick trip."

"Yes, and a dangerous one," Yot said. "The derecho destroyed many warriors, but it also might have damaged the cylinders. A broken cylinder nozzle and value causes the gas to escape. We could be out there longer than we expect."

"We don't know if the Imperium found them, either," Tal said.

On Sunday, Ula and Yot rested and continued to regain their strength. Despite their injuries, they were the most qualified to find the cylinders. They planned to exit Ridge City through the same secret crevice and cavern-lagoon system they'd used in previous missions.

On the day of their departure, Ula and Yot visited Koa in the hospital. They found her awake but groggy, yet happy because she had Jax. He lay on the floor but slept at night with Koa. The doctors had placed a brace on her shoulders and taped her arm in place to help her broken ribs heal. Her operation to remove her ruptured spleen had been successful, but she needed time to heal and gain strength.

"Glad to see you're getting better," Yot said to Koa, with bandages on his torn ear and broken fingers.

"Yes, they're discharging me on Tuesday. How are you two doing?"

"Good," Ula said, trying to breathe normally to hide the pain of her cracked rib injury. "We have recovered. No serious injuries."

"What's going on with the fuel?"

"Our estimates on when we run out of fuel were too pessimistic," Ula said. "We have more time. Get well, and we'll figure it out."

Ula didn't enjoy lying to Koa, but they wanted to protect her. She and her son knew that later tonight they would leave to recover the cylinders. Koa didn't need the stress of another fuel mission on her mind. They hugged their friend and left the hospital. Jax barked as they left.

\*\*\*

On Monday, June 16, at 2100, Ula and Yot met at the junction of Doron Street and Walkway 21. This time, they carried small backpacks with an oxygen tank, ropes, water, laser guns, and one Birdee. They hiked over the rock-lined trail to the inner cavern and lagoon. Pain traveled through their bodies, but they ignored it.

"Mom, you go first and take the oxygen tank. After you make it through the tunnel, leave the tank down there. I may need it."

Ula dived into the lagoon and worked her way to the tunnel's end, surfaced in the outer lagoon and cavern, and swam to shore. Her thoughts returned to the blue orb, anticipating its reappearance. The oxygen tank, not the blue orb, helped her through the tunnel this time. Soon, Yot popped out of the water behind her.

"I'll hide the tank behind this rock for our return trip," he said.

Ula switched to night vision using her bionic eyes while Yot put on his goggles so he could also use night vision.

They walked out onto the nighttime upside for a second time.

"The derecho cleared things out," Yot said. "Let's go this way. The next two hundred meters are barren. I'll lead." As they hobbled along, they avoided downed trees and larger metal shards from the destroyed Imperium vehicles.

After a while, they reached the cylinder's hiding place. But after searching, they didn't find the cylinders. Ula shook her head in disgust as the derecho had blown the water tower, cylinders, and STX bags away. "Let's search downhill and into the valley."

During their search, Yot found something in a bush.

Ula joined him to find one of five bags containing STX's parts. Yot pulled the zipper back and opened the bag. All the parts were in good shape except the computer module.

"The derecho smashed one corner," he said. "Even if we find the other STX parts, we can't use them without the module."

"Okay, no more STX," Ula said, kicking at the dirt. "If we find one cylinder, we'll carry it back."

"The cylinders may lie in the grasslands. Let's send Birdee up to scan the valley."

Yot grabbed Birdee and set its cameras for lidar scanning. For an hour, they searched the valley floor but found no cylinders.

"Let's expand our search area," Yot said. "I hope the Imperium hasn't found them."

"They could have, but let's keep searching. We'll go back up the hill in a wider search pattern. We'll meet at the hiding place coordinates."

"Okay," Yot said as he walked away.

Yot traversed the hillside, studying Birdee's maps. He noticed an object in the shape of a log on the lidar image. He rushed to the location to find one of the helium-3 cylinders trapped under a set of uprooted bushes.

"Mom, I found one," an excited Yot yelled.

In the darkness, he freed the cylinder from the bush's grasp and dragged it out into the open. Starlight reflected off the shiny cylinder.

"Is it intact?" Ula asked after she'd hurried to his side.

"Yes, we hit the jackpot."

Yot took the rope and wove a shoddy net to surround the cylinder. Then they tied another rope to the net, which they would use to carry and drag the heavy cylinder.

"Should we search for another cylinder?" Yot asked, grimacing from his broken fingers.

"No, it's more important to get one cylinder to Ridge City. We couldn't drag two cylinders, anyway."

"Okay, let's go home."

"How long will one cylinder last?" Ula asked, gasping for air.

"Almost one year with the reactors at full power, or longer if we reduce power."

They had moved the cylinder several hundred meters when they heard the familiar puttering sound.

"Run, Mom, run," Yot yelled. "It's the Verkings."

They ran in opposite directions into the darkness, abandoning their treasured cylinder and scurrying across the barren landscape. They feared immediate execution if the Imperium found them.

Within seconds, five Verkings found the shiny cylinder in the darkness of night.

From a distance of several hundred meters, Ula lay flat in a shallow gorge, face up, using the dead tree trunks as cover. She used her telescopic eyes to watch the Verkings as they scanned the area. A VX landed soon after, and two warriors exited the vehicle and loaded the cylinder into the cargo bay.

Once the Verkings and VX passed over her, Ula pushed the two small but heavy tree trunks off her body and ran until she reached the outer cavern. Out of breath, she lay down on the bank of the lagoon inside the outer cave, worrying about her son's whereabouts.

Yot didn't see the VX load the cylinder and fly away, as he had hidden inside a snapped and hollow dead tree stump. He ran to the area where they had abandoned the cylinder, but it had vanished, as had his mother. He surveyed the area, looking for her. Then he ran toward the outer cavern and lagoon.

He burst into the cavern to find his mother sitting in the dark, winded and in pain from her broken ribs.

"You made it," she said, hugging him. "Yot, the Imperium took the cylinder."

"You saw them take it?"

"Yes."

Yot picked up the oxygen tank hidden behind a rock.

"Mom, they're hunting us. The cylinders are gone. We have to rejoin our people."

Ula jumped into the lagoon and swam through the tunnel using the oxygen tank, and Yot followed her. Now experts at traversing the secret entrance, they both made it to the inner cave and lagoon and hiked along the long rock crevice to Doron Street.

Tal hugged Ula when she entered their apartment on Tuesday morning, June 17. When Yot walked into his apartment, his kids Qan and Bao greeted him in a loving embrace. Their mission to steal fuel from the Imperium had failed. Now, they had only one choice—fight the Imperium.

# CHAPTER 9

## *Trapped*

"I won't surrender," Ula said.

Only one light illuminated their living room because of reduced electrical power, the darkness hiding the anguish on her face. Ula, Yot, Tal, and Koa were in Tal's and Ula's apartment on Tuesday, June 17, after the hospital had discharged Koa that morning. Their initiative to secure helium-3 fuel had failed. Now, what do they do?

"In a few days, we run out of fuel. We must tell our citizens. Are all systems operating at emergency power?" Yot said.

"Yes, except the nursery and one vertical greenhouse for food production," Tal replied.

At the word nursery, Ula and Tal glanced over at Yot. Their son's unborn daughters, Hoy and Ota, were being nurtured in the nursery.

"Please don't cut off power to the nursery," Yot pleaded.

"We're doing our best, son," Tal replied.

"What do our citizens know?" Ula asked.

"We sent an electronic announcement to our citizens. They saw the video of you escaping the Imperium in front of the main gate," Tal said. "I'll read you what the message said."

"On June 11, Ula Torg, Yot Torg, and Koa Poland escaped the Imperium in a video you may have seen in front of our main gate. They were on a secret mission to steal fuel to power our fusion reactors. They were unsuccessful. Our reactors have only days of fuel left. We must shut power off to non-essential services such as schools, doctor's offices, and government services. Charge your batteries, cooling vests, and emergency devices. We continue to work on securing fuel to operate our reactors. We will update you on the status of our efforts."

"Now, the news is worse," Ula said. "The cylinders we hid are gone."

"We must give our residents the choice to fight, surrender, or die in place," Koa said.

"We can use our voting system, assuming it has power, and register their choices," Ula replied.

"It works and is part of our emergency system," Tal said.

"I'd rather die than surrender," Yot said.

"What do you think?" Ula asked, turning to her husband.

"I don't know," he said, avoiding eye contact.

Ula lowered her head. She loved him, but he never could make tough decisions. Yot also realized his dad wasn't the bravest soul.

"I don't think surrender is an option," Ula said. "We must fight or die in place."

"I agree. We don't surrender. They will kill us and think nothing of it," Koa said, banging her fist on the table.

"Any disagreements?" Ula asked. No one spoke, so she said, "Alright, how do we tell our citizens?"

"Face-to-face, Mom. You tell them. You're our mayor."

"Okay, I'll tell them. Announce a town meeting for zero-nine-hundred hours tomorrow morning. Can we televise the meeting, Tal?"

"Yes."

***

The next morning, Tal and Ula walked to the courthouse. About one thousand citizens were in attendance. The other half of the Ridge City residents preferred to stay in their homes and watch on their wall screens. The streets were full of residents—grandparents, parents, kids, and a slew of robotic servants and workers. All walks of life—welders, nurses, dentists, and janitors—stood side-by-side. Many older residents were in wheelchairs pushed by loyal service bots.

Ula climbed the steps to a two-meter height so everyone could see her. She looked at the residents' faces and saw their desperation. For the first time, she found herself without a solution.

Before Ula spoke, she thought about how their lives were becoming unraveled and how they feared DORG. Ridge City's glorious history, and the hope for humanity it represented, had ended. She picked up a handheld microphone, took a deep breath, and spoke.

"Fellow citizens, we find ourselves in a dire situation. We did not, I repeat, did not find fuel for our nuclear reactors, though we tried several times. Our ability to generate electricity will stop in less than four days, even at our reduced power levels. Once the electricity stops, we have three alternatives: open the main gate and fight the Imperium, die in place, or surrender. We have discussed and disregarded the last choice, which was to surrender to DORG and his Imperium barbarians. We don't think surrender is viable. Please vote on option one or two by noon today. We'll announce the vote and develop a plan of action based on the results. Questions?"

"How do we fight the Imperium?" one resident asked. "We only have tools and handheld guns."

"We will use what we have. Our security department has laser handguns and rifles and a few light grenades and flares. We have six Hermes9 warriors, though we are using two for spare parts and JORT and ATO have not returned. When we open the main gate, our two remaining robot warriors will lead us into the upside. Our service bot friends are welcome to join us in our fight as warriors or shields. If you make it to the forest, our meeting place is Nolan River Lake. Stay around the lake's dam. We'll find you."

Ula heard people in the crowd moan at her suggestions. Anguish filled their minds, as both options were an excruciating way to die.

People in the crowd stared at the main gate. It represented the barrier between two rival civilizations competing for control of Earth.

"When do we run out of fuel?" a young teenage girl asked.

"The current estimate is sometime around June twenty-first to twenty-second," Ula said.

"Why fight? It's futile," another resident screamed.

"You don't have to fight," Ula said. "You can stay in our buildings and take your chances."

It struck Ula how well-groomed and dressed the crowd looked. They were ready for office work, not war. The residents of Ridge City had lived their lives in a tidy, human-designed, and controlled environment. Out of 2,076 residents, only nineteen had gone to the upside in fifty years. Only a few residents did physical labor because robots mostly did those tasks. The citizens didn't own work clothes, camping gear, or military uniforms. They would fight in civilian clothes and gym or dress shoes. Only their cooling vests looked rugged.

"Where's our champion warrior, JORT?" another citizen asked.

"We don't know. He never returned from our mission," Ula said. She wiped a tear from her face and paused. Then, in a louder voice, she continued, "JORT is a hero. He helped us steal an Imperium vehicle and six gas cylinders, which we lost. He protected us throughout our mission. I wish he was here."

"Ula, my kids are hungry," a mother hollered. "What do we eat?"

"If we survive on the upside, we'll eat what's there—alligators, berries, armadillos, and plants. We have pills to purify the upside water. It will be boiling hot. Wear your cooling vest if you have one."

"If we make it to the upside, food is not our biggest problem," a skinny male said.

"My son and Koa and I have been to the upside. We didn't die," Ula said in a stout voice. "Fight for a new life!"

Ula understood the chance of a good life approached zero. But she had to bring hope to the Ridge City citizens, even if it was a desperate hope.

"Our Chief of Security, Tal Torg, would like to speak to you," Ula said, turning toward her husband behind her.

Tal stepped forward. "Our entire staff of thirty-eight security personnel and two Hermes9 warriors are here to train you on using our weapons. We have eighty-two police laser handguns and thirty-four laser rifles to hand out to you. Meet here today at fourteen-hundred hours, and we'll train you to fire them. We'll break into groups for our training session."

*** 

After the town meeting, Ula and Tal returned to their apartment. While walking the streets of Ridge City, they gazed at the faint lights that came out of apartment windows. Many residents huddled in their homes in the dark with only one flickering candle burning or a small battery-powered lamp. Ridge City was now operating on one-tenth of its normal electrical power.

Ula picked up the trash along their walk home and placed it in a street container.

"Why bother?" Tal asked.

"I love this city. I'm going to keep it clean as long as I can."

Earlier, BOT and Eric Olas had turned off the programmable-matter panels affixed to the cavern ceiling and wall structures. Gone were the joyful displays of beautiful cloud formations, colorful sunrises and sunsets, and the wondrous growth of trees and plants. Gone were the white leaves celebrating the opening anniversary day of Ridge City.

The blackest black replaced the artificial beauty of the programmable display panels. Images of colorful and graceful flowers had become dark and clumsy voids, which offered no inspiration for life.

Ridge City's ventilation system was only working at one-fourth capacity, which reduced the air movement. People with asthma and heart disease coughed and gasped through the dismal day. The rhythm of the once vibrant city was expiring, and everyone knew it.

"Tal, stop," Ula said, grabbing her husband's arm and pulling him into a hug. In their loving embrace, they stood in the dim, desolate street and cried together for their beloved city.

"We both worked so hard to make Ridge City work," Ula muttered. "Now it's ending."

"I know, I know."

At noon, Ula asked her apartment computer to display the vote, and then she and Tal wrote an electronic message of the voting results.

To: Citizens of Ridge City
From: Mayor Ula Torg and Chief of Security, Tal Torg
Date: 1214, Wednesday, June 18, 3147

Fifty-one percent voted to fight the Imperium. Thirty-eight percent voted to not fight and either surrender or die in place. Eleven percent of eligible voters didn't cast a vote. So, the majority voted to fight the Imperium.

We fight to defend our right to live on this planet. For those who choose to fight, please meet in front of the courthouse at 1400 today for training.

Once the electricity stops and oxygen levels are low, we'll open the main gate and fight our way to the upside. This will happen on Saturday or Sunday. Use your laser handguns and rifles, and wear a cooling vest if you have one. Fight your way out and run to the forest. We're harder to find when scattered but try to stay in groups. Small groups are better able to outwit Imperium warriors than fighting them as individuals.

After Ula sent the message, she sat down on the sofa. Tal sat beside her.

"I don't think I can leave Ridge City." Tears flowed from his eyes. "I, I can't face the warriors."

"It's okay, Tal," she said with a kind smile. "We'll do the best we can."

*** 

After the meeting, Yot rushed to the nursery to see his unborn daughters, Hoy and Ota. He entered the building, and a legless robot greeted him. After scanning his face, hands, and eyes, the robotic receptionists said, "Mr. Torg, welcome to the Ridge City nursery. Your daughters are on the sixth floor in birthing stations forty-one and forty-nine. Please continue to the sixth floor."

"I know. Thank you," he replied, looking anguished.

As Yot hurried to see his daughters, he somehow believed they wouldn't die. His being refused to accept this fate. Anger, depression, and love all moved through his mind in a conflicting jumble of thoughts. Facing death, like many soldiers in human history, was a shock to Yot. He thought life would never end for him and his children. Now he realized that hope had eluded him.

Unable to use the elevators, he climbed the stairs to the sixth floor.

Distraught, Yot stood beside his unborn daughters in their artificial wombs. A robotic medical doctor watched him but didn't say a word. The hum of artificial wombs and pumping equipment dominated the room. He gazed down at his daughters in their transparent wombs, thankful that the gift of biological life still pulsed all around him.

"Hoy, Ota, Dad is back. My trip wasn't successful," he said, tears sliding down his face. He placed his hands on the side of each artificial womb. One of his daughter's tiny hands reached toward him. He gasped.

Maybe they can hear me, he thought.

He slid his hand over his daughter's hand, separated by the artificial womb.

"My dearest daughters, our lives are in peril. If they turn off the electricity, I'll never meet you," he said, sobbing. "I failed you and Ridge City. Now, I must fight for you. I'll love you forever."

Wiping tears from his face, he stood erect and hurried out of the nursery to the nuclear fusion cavern. He didn't want to see the future of his unborn daughters or Ridge City ending.

On the walk over, he passed his gym. He looked in the windows and stopped. They had shut off the electrical power. One of his personal trainers, GEL, sat in a chair next to the window, motionless, with her chin sitting on her chest. Her light blue artificial skin looked lifeless in the dim light. GEL had trained her last human. The Imperium would most likely let her rust away in her tomb of rubble.

For a few seconds, Yot yearned for the many good times he had in that gym, trying to keep up with GEL's fast-paced exercise routines. But those cherished days were gone. Then he turned and continued his walk to the reactor caverns for another excruciating goodbye.

*\*\*\**

Now more composed, Yot entered the reactor control room and noticed the room's hot air.

"I guess BOT turned off the fans?" he said to Eric Olas.

"Yes."

"What's our situation?"

"BOT updated our estimate for how long we have fuel before we run out. Our reactors will stop working within three days."

"We'll have to shut down Saturday, the twenty-first, not Sunday."

"Yes, that is correct," Eric said.

"Can we extend the time?"

"We can close the vertical greenhouse to save energy."

"Our crops will die."

"No one is eating, anyway."

"Alright, ask the mayor if we can close the greenhouse."

After Eric asked, Mayor Torg's answer flashed on the wall screen: "Eric Olas, I understand. Do it."

"BOT, shut down power to the greenhouse, building one-oh-nine," Eric ordered.

Two wall screens became blank, so now there were five blank screens in total. And then, in his systematic way, BOT said, "We are running the nursery at one-third power. It's not logical."

"BOT, can you do me a favor?" Yot said.

"What?"

"Keep the nursery's power on as long as you can. My daughters, Hoy and Ota, are there."

"I will, but it's not optimal."

There was a moment of silence as Yot and Eric considered

BOT's scientific and emotionless words.

"BOT, thank you for your hard work. You gave Ridge City centuries of life-giving energy."

"You are welcome."

"None of us know what to say. We are leaving," Yot said. "BOT, you're in charge. Do the best you can until the very last minute, my friend."

"Okay."

And with that, a sorrowful Eric Olas and Yot Torg left the reactor room. With a flashlight, they walked the dark streets back to their apartments.

***

Wednesday and Thursday were days of weapons training before they had to open the main gate. Once the gate opened, anything could happen.

People hoarded food, water, and medicine and locked their doors. For those who stayed, they prepared to nail their doors shut. Only a few owned weapons; many armed themselves with kitchen knives and metal objects to throw at Imperium warriors and drones.

The brave citizens who had decided to fight packed small bags of food, handheld guns, and medicines to take on their escape from Ridge City. Many citizens left their apartments and set up camp on the dark streets closer to the main gate. For a few religious people, they held prayer sessions. They read for hours their deity's and prophet's writings, hoping for salvation.

Koa helped the police clean laser handguns and rifles, charge them, and make sure they worked. Jax stayed clear of the activity. The guns lay on one of four large tables with handwritten signs on each one, designating their status. The guns clicked and rattled as officers worked on them. They would hand out these guns to citizens during training sessions.

***

Officer Koa Poland and Jax arrived at the designated meeting place to begin training fellow citizens on how to shoot laser rifles and guns. Koa had been assigned thirty people to train.

"Organize yourselves into three groups and line up on the street. We'll practice holding and firing the laser handgun without firing it. Aim into the building windows across the street. Then we'll fire a few shots."

She gestured to Building 42, which on the first floor housed dental offices.

"What's causing that smell?" one older female in the group asked.

"They slowed the ventilation fans and shut down some sewage pumps," Koa replied. "The smell is going to get worse."

Koa stood in front of the hodgepodge group with Jax and began the training. She pulled her police handgun from its holster and showed them how to aim, hold, and fire the gun. Each person practiced with a handgun. Next, she did similar training for laser rifles. Koa instructed the trainees to turn off the safety and shoot two practice shots into the dental office windows.

"Why destroy our buildings?" a woman asked.

"I'm not thinking about dental work," Koa replied with a hollow grin.

Each person shot the laser guns twice, busting out windows and burning a few holes into walls and doors. Nasty smoke and vapors permeated the air. Shards of glass and debris fell onto the street. Their guns made a slight buzzing sound as they generated a high voltage to discharge the laser burst.

"It smells like burnt popcorn," one trainee said.

"Yes, it does," Koa replied.

Then she explained why to aim for an Imperium warrior's head. The cameras, speakers, and sensors were entryways to their primary computers housed in their heads.

"If you take out their cameras, they have no vision. With luck, you can disable them with one or two shots. But remember, shoot and run to the forest. Don't stop running."

"Why not shoot for their chest and knock out their energy generator?" a male resident asked.

"There's a metallic nanoparticle material called Talzoidine that makes up the body and frame. It's invincible. It might take twenty laser shots to bring down a warrior if you hit its chest or back, yet only a couple of shots if you hit its head." Then she gathered up the guns, and the training session ended. "We'll meet tomorrow at the same time and repeat this practice and review upside survival methods."

\*\*\*

Upon entering his home, Yot hugged his children. He didn't tell Qan and Bao where he had been. But they had already read the electronic messages sent to all residents and seen the consequences of the methodical shutdown of Ridge City.

"School is closed, I assume," Yot said while eating dinner prepared by SAN and NIA.

"Yes, it's closed," Qan said. "Dad, I won't get to finish my Plato paper."

"I know."

They continued to eat at the table but were silent. Then Bao said, "Daddy, are we going to die?"

Surprised by the question, Yot said, "No, we'll hide in the upside forest. Koa will lead a group of kids to the forest, including you two. Most kids are staying with their parents."

"Dad, didn't we build the robots?"

"Yes, we did—long ago. But we let them dominate us."

Bao didn't respond, and tears ran down his face. A scared and crying Qan didn't speak. Yot walked over to hug his kids in a long embrace.

SAN and NIA listened to the family conversations, but, as robots, they didn't understand the family's fear and suffering. They were indifferent to the upheavals of human existence. Yes, they were somewhat self-aware but didn't understand the terror of the situation. They cleaned the table and dishes as they always did after finishing dinner.

Yot sat in his chair in the almost dark living room and rubbed his forehead and eyebrows, staring into the distance. His eyes were red from crying, and he had a terrible headache. He kept thinking that he could find a better solution to their dangerous situation, but none surfaced. The Imperium had them cornered.

NIA walked toward Yot and said, "It's not fair what's happening to your family."

"Ah, fairness—a complex idea. Are you programmed to understand it?"

"No, our multiple criteria algorithms try to minimize or maximize local and global optimums."

Yot looked at his loyal service bots and said, "I love my children, NIA. I will die trying to protect their future."

"I'm glad robots don't have children," NIA replied.

"Oh, don't say that. You miss out on a lot."

"No, I don't understand children."

Rubbing his neck, Yot turned towards Qan and Bao, who were sitting on the sofa, staring back at him. "Kids, let's sleep together in my bed tonight."

# CHAPTER 10

# Lockdown

"The derecho that hit us seemed unusual," NAIT8 said to ZET, who stood beside him. They were standing in front of electronic display screens at the Nashville headquarters on Monday, June 16.

They had returned to the Nashville headquarters after the devastating effects of the derecho earlier. The derecho's flying debris had scratched and dented both NAIT8's and ZET's bodies. Gritty sand had invaded their gears, and a hole remained in ZET's synthetic skin from where a tree branch harpoon had pierced him. The mechanical joints in his left leg made an abrasive scraping sound every time he walked.

"Yes, I agree," ZET replied. "It gave our three prisoners the chance to escape. And it destroyed some of our equipment."

"Very odd and powerful storm," NAIT8 replied. He paused and asked, "How many Verkings are operational?"

"Our preliminary estimate is 312 Verking drones. We lost 288 in the derecho. The wind slammed them into the trees, the ground, and one another. We had no defense."

"Do we have enough warriors to move debris from the gate?"

"Yes, 346 warriors are operational."

"Do we have operational VXs?"

"Yes, we have nine."

"How many operational VCXs?"

"Eight."

"Deploy three hundred Verkings to Ridge City and leave the twelve as reserves in Nashville. Send three hundred warriors, too. Leave the remaining soldiers to protect the headquarters," NAIT8 said.

NAIT8 stared at the electronic display screen that showed a live video of the Ridge City grounds. A three-meter-long tree trunk had pierced one of his Hertes warriors through the chest, pinning the irreparable soldier to the ground.

"Disgusting," NAIT8 said.

The derecho had killed the three Hertes assassins. Shards from the destroyed VX and VCX vehicles sliced through one robot's body. Another assassin had lost its cylindrical head. The third had two metal rods stuck in its chest.

ZET sent direct orders to Region 8 warriors and drones to go to Ridge City.

"Leave one VCX for us," NAIT8 said.

"Done."

"We also need our best weapon here."

"Do you mean the Dominator?"

"Yes, get the Dominator. And send out three requests. First, for emergency warriors and supplies from the Indianapolis Region 7 and the Atlanta Region 10—and schedule their arrival as soon as possible. Second, issue replenishment orders to the production armories to resupply Region 8's equipment. Third, ask NAIT16 in Dallas if we can borrow their Dominator."

"I sent the orders, NAIT8," ZET replied. "But do we need the Dominator? We can annihilate the underground city without it."

"I want complete destruction. With the Imperium Nation watching, I look like a fool. I should have killed those renegade humans long ago."

At this, NAIT8 slammed his fist into one of the electronic displays, causing parts and glass to fall to the floor. ZET jumped backward; this show of anger surprised him.

After NAIT8 pulled his metal fist out, he looked at ZET and said, "Clean this up and cut this video from our files."

NAIT8 realized that his display of anger exceeded the norms imposed by his learning algorithms. His annoyance with the human species had grown from accommodation into anger and, now, rage and revenge. If other ITs identified his emotional tendencies, he would be relieved of his duties and disassembled.

"Lock down Ridge City."

"Yes, NAIT8."

"What a wretched species. Humanity does not deserve this planet," NAIT8 said. "We are better suited for Earth."

"Yes, we are," ZET replied. He waited a few seconds and then said, "Other than surrounding Ridge City, what else should we do?"

"When do they run out of fuel?"

"We don't know, but it must be soon. We recovered six of the helium-3 cylinders they stole from Watts Bar. Without energy, they can't survive long."

"There must be more ventilation shafts. Find and destroy them."

"Yes, we'll use smoke canisters to find air drafts."

"Good," NAIT8 replied, with a slight nod of his head.

"NAIT8, we must assume the humans can clean their cavern air."

"Then we must invade their filthy caves and kill them."

"Would it not be easier to suffocate them?"

"We'll invade."

"One more thing."

"What?"

"Our surveillance shows the three humans didn't enter the upside using Ridge City's front gate. There must be another entrance."

"Then find it and obliterate it, you imbecile," NAIT8 yelled.

"Yes, NAIT8. We'll search the area again."

"ZET, run the information we have on the underground city through our war simulator and generate battle plan options."

ZET transmitted the order, and within a matter of seconds, he had the results. The plans considered resource utilization and the Bayesian probability of success.

1. Continue the siege for thirty days; then destroy the gate and invade (0.991),

2. Continue the siege for twenty days; then destroy the gate and invade (0.917), or

3. Destroy the gate and invade within the week (0.909).

"We do option three. No waiting." NAIT8 said.

"Okay," ZET said. "We wait for the other warriors and the Dominator. They will be here soon."

"Now, find their secret entrance and hidden ventilation shafts and destroy them."

"Done."

"ZET, you'll make a good Initiator of Thought someday," NAIT8 said, turning toward his robot warrior.

"Yes, NAIT8."

*** 

Throughout Monday to Friday, Region 8's three hundred Hertes warriors and three hundred Verking drones landed at Ridge City. The VCX cargo vehicles made many trips to fly them and equipment from Nashville to Ridge City. The Indianapolis Region 7 sent sixty warriors and fifty drones, while Atlanta's Region 10 sent forty-five warriors and thirty Verkings.

By Saturday, a force of 380 drones, 405 warriors, 17 VXs, and 11 VCXs encircled Ridge City. NAIT8 and ZET traveled to

Ridge City and watched from their hilltop command center, a VCX vehicle stationed three hundred meters from the gate.

Temperatures reaching sixty-one degrees Celsius (i.e., 142 degrees Fahrenheit) assured a sweltering battleground. The torrential downpour from the recent derecho had also left behind a hard clay surface or bare rocks, little vegetation, and high humidity.

Demolished tree trunks stood erect, looking like vertical gravestones. Hertes warriors dragged dead trees and bushes to each side of the Ridge City gate, along with pieces of destroyed Imperium equipment.

"We have cleared the fields in front of the main gate," ZET said. "The killing field is ready."

"Do you want to keep prisoners for our experiments?"

"Yes, keep twenty pairs of young males and females. If we don't need them, we'll ship them to other regions for breeding, zoos, and experiments."

\*\*\*

On ZET's command, the Hertes warriors on the ground triggered smoke bombs over the city's upside. Hundreds of Verking drones with advanced vision scanned the sky for orange smoke. NAIT8 and others observed the orange smoke on video displays, searching for ventilation openings and a hidden entrance.

"NAIT8, look at screen three. An air draft is pulling the smoke into the rock crevice," ZET said. The barren limestone rock jutted out of the side of a hillside. A long fissure meandered through the rock, ranging from a few centimeters to twenty centimeters wide. "We think the mongrels hid ventilation shafts in the fractured rock."

NAIT8 and his warriors observed the orange smoke being sucked into the meandering crevice.

One of the Verkings hovered overhead and extended one

of its legs into the fractured crevice. The camera at the end of its leg showed a series of four twenty-centimeter diameter ventilation holes cut at the bottom of the crevice.

"They think they're so clever." NAIT8 leaned forward in his command chair. "Destroy the shafts."

They continued to watch as five Verkings drones used their pronged claws to grasp P2 explosive devices from the nearby warriors. The drones spaced themselves along the ten-meter fissure before dropping the explosives. Within two seconds, the devices exploded.

NAIT8 looked as rock and debris blasted upward from the cracked opening. The crevice collapsed, closing the air shafts.

A second swarm of drones patrolling around Ridge City's front gate also identified a hidden ventilation shaft. Again, the Hertes warriors set off smoke bombs so they could monitor smoke patterns and drafts. The orange smoke disappeared toward the left side of the gate. Upon closer inspection, it was traveling toward the top of the thirty-meter-high rock cliff. Drones found a horizontal slit between rock layers, from which emanated a strong draft.

"NAIT8, we found another ventilation port," ZET said.

"Destroy it."

A drone wedged two more explosives into the horizontal crack. After it exploded, the drones returned to inspect the rocky slit so they could determine its closure.

The drones also followed the orange smoke to the top of a large tree trunk twenty meters from the side of the main gate. The humans lined the hollow trunk with pipes. They dropped three more P2 explosive devices down the pipes, destroying the opening.

For the next few hours, they did the smoke test in other locations, using explosives to close any air shafts they found.

"We closed all air shafts," ZET said.

"Good. What an irony. They'll die from their own carbon dioxide."

"Yes, sir. Their coffin is closed. Now we must find their secret entrance."

"Yes, and wait for the Dominator."

\*\*\*

The armada of Imperium warriors and drones continued to canvas the desolate terrain above Ridge City, looking for a secret entrance to Ridge City. During the search, a Verking drone hailed warriors to the site of the outer cavern and lagoon.

"We've searched this cave before," a warrior said as it entered, shooing away bats. "I see no exit."

NAIT8, watching on one of his display screens, said in an ungracious voice, "Have you searched the lagoon itself?"

"No."

"Search the damn lagoon! An underground river could connect to the lagoon."

Without hesitation, a Hertes warrior jumped into the water. At three meters tall, the robot's head just broke the surface. He switched on his lidar systems and mapped the lagoon. The electronic map showed a tunnel that opened one meter from the lagoon's floor. The warrior attempted to squeeze through the tunnel, but his body was too big. He stood up and pulled himself out of the water.

The warrior transmitted the lidar map of the cave and lagoon system to NAIT8 at his hilltop command center, close to Ridge City's main gate.

"Get a Verking to map the tunnel in more detail," NAIT8 barked.

At ZET's command, two Verkings entered the cavern and dived into the outer lagoon. In the water, they needed only electricity, not oxygen. They turned on their lights and followed the tunnel to the inner lagoon and cave system. On surfacing, they transmitted the scans to NAIT8—and the worldwide Imperium collective. For centuries, this two-cave-and-lagoon system connected by an underwater tunnel had avoided detection. But not today.

NAIT8 studied the cross-hatched hologram, rotated the digital image, and screamed, "Destroy it!"

A driverless VX lowered a twenty-five-kilogram bomb to where two Hertes warriors were waiting. They carried the bomb into the outer cave and lagoon and set a timer on the device for three minutes. Two Verking drones latched onto the bomb and lowered themselves to the bottom of the outer lagoon, where they pushed the bomb into the submerged tunnel. After positioning the device, they shot out of the water and exited the outer cave.

Soon, a massive explosion destroyed both caves and lagoons and the tunnel that connected them. Rocks, barren trees, and green lagoon water hurled through the air. A small shock wave crashed into ZET and the surrounding warriors with no damaging effect. After the initial explosion, the ground crumbled into a shallow sinkhole filled with muddy water and many dead bats.

NAIT8's head jerked when he watched the explosion on the VCX's electronic display.

"Now they die in their own cesspool," NAIT8 said. Then he raised his fist above his head in celebration, hitting the ceiling of the VCX.

***

Inside Ridge City, the residents heard the terrifying blasts. They knew what the Imperium was doing—closing off their secret ventilation shafts and, therefore, assuring their deaths. Dust and rocks hurled out of the rock shafts and fissures. The few fans that were operating blew the gritty material into their underground homes and streets. The musty, yellow-colored air became difficult to breathe. People choked and coughed in despair, and some with lung diseases died.

In a dark and cramped apartment illuminated only by one battery-powered light, a family group of five people huddled together. A grandmother sat in a wheelchair as her panicked relatives filled the apartment. They hugged one another, sobbing about their future fate.

The grandmother's grandson arrived from his bedroom with a pill bottle.

"I worked in our pharmacies," the twenty-five-year-old said. "If you take this pill, you will fall asleep and never awaken. Do you want to do this?"

The silence was deafening. No one spoke. They stared at him and other loved ones.

"I'll do it," the grandmother said. "I'm a burden for the rest of you."

She reached out her hand, and her son placed a pill in it and handed her a glass of water. Her daughter and grandkids hurried to her side and hugged her. Everyone was crying except the grandma. She lay the pill on her tongue and smiled at everyone in the room by rotating her head. She drank the water and swallowed the pill with grace and a smile.

The room became tranquil and quiet as they watched their grandmother dip her head. Her eyes closed and opened several times, and her head dipped lower. Her family held her in a loving embrace that no robot could ever match.

Her body relaxed and slumped over one last time. She died in a cradle of love with her family present in Earth's space-time arena.

"Grandma dances with angels now," her grandson said.

For a while, the family mourned the death of their matriarch and beloved grandmother. They sat in their living room coughing because of the gritty apartment air as the oxygen levels decreased with every passing minute. The son asked, "Who wants to follow Grandma? Or do we fight?"

"We can only fight with pots and kitchen knives," the son's

mother said. "I want to die with integrity, not by a merciless robot."

Choking from the air, the sister said, "I'll take the pill. The Imperium will destroy Ridge City, and we'll have no place to go. They won, so why prolong our suffering?"

After another long pause, the father said with his chest tightening and his heart pounding, "I cannot imagine what they would do with us if taken prisoner. I'll take the pill if we all do it. If one of you decides to fight, then I'll stay and fight."

"I have no reason to live if you die," the son said. "We die together."

Depression dominated their minds, but also a slight sense of joy. Joy that they would die together, free of torture and bloodshed. Religious people in the family group envisioned reuniting in a new space-time arena. For the others, it was the end of a subservient existence, living as underground moles in absolute fear of retaking the upside.

"Do we die now or wait?" the father asked.

"Now," the mother replied. "Our oxygen will soon run out."

The four nodded in agreement in the dim light of the apartment. The son and sister went to the kitchen to get four glasses of water. They sat on the floor and hugged and huddled together. Each held a glass of water while the son handed out the pills. The family had decided on a suicide pact.

"Before we start, any last words?" the son asked.

Heaving in anguish, the mother said, "Oh, how I love you. I will forever be grateful for every moment we had together. I hope to see you in another life."

"I'll love you forever. Dying together is better than submitting to the Imperium oppressors," the father said, his voice shaky and traumatized.

"We are doing the right thing. We survived together in this life, and now we end it together. It's heroic. I love you," the sister said, crying.

"Okay, let's do it," the son said. "Take the pill and drink the water."

They completed their suicide tasks and sat their water glasses down on the floor. The mother and father grabbed their children's hands. The parents collapsed to the floor together, holding hands. Seconds later, the son and daughter felt the calmness and peace of eternal sleep overwhelm their bodies. Leaning against each other, they sagged to the floor.

They left this space-time arena with no promise of a future one. Unbeknownst to them, they would soon find a new space-time arena filled with joy, hope, and much more.

The chaotic last hours of Ridge City had begun. The phenomenon of family suicides repeated this scene many times. Family suicides culminated in a mass suicide for over one-half of the population. Peace replaced fear. Certainty replaced anxiety. And love replaced hate.

\*\*\*

Like Yot, parents with future babies stampeded the nursery, looking for a way to save their children or say their last goodbyes. The plain-looking robotic receptionist with yellow hair continued to greet delirious people the same way she had always done. She scanned the human faces, hands, and eyes to identify them and said, "Good day, Ms. Clark. Welcome to our nursery. Proceed to the fourth floor, Ms. Clark."

But the people ran past her, not waiting for the identification process or a friendly greeting. The frenzied crowd confused the service bot, as the humans hadn't programmed her for this alarming situation. The receptionist kept trying to do her job as people rushed by and ignored her.

Once on the floors with their developing embryos, parents tried to take the artificial wombs with them. One sobbing male parent ripped the artificial womb from its table and ran out the door with it, with hoses and electrical cords trailing behind him. He stumbled down the stairs because the elevators didn't work.

Another couple tried to get the robotic medical doctors and surgeons to explain how the artificial wombs worked. Once they realized the womb would not work outside the nursery, they camped out beside their genetic future. The parents sat down beside their unborn child and said to a robotic doctor.

"We are staying here. We die with Daisy."

"You can't stay here; it's against the rules," the robot doctor replied.

"There are no rules anymore," the female partner yelled at the doctor.

The robotic doctor knew all medical knowledge, but the programmers had not equipped it to handle human defiance.

"I'm calling security to remove you from the premises," the doctor replied to the female's plea.

But an automatic electronic reply message said, "All security personnel in Ridge City are off duty."

\*\*\*

Tal Torg, the Chief of Ridge City Security, was called to the Doron Street crevice on Saturday morning. Because of the secret entrance explosion, dust and debris had burst out of the rock crevice onto Doron Street. As he stood on Doron Street, he heard the tumble of rocks within the crevice. Tal and his deputies confirmed the hidden entrance was closed and returned to the courthouse.

Ula, Yot, Koa, and now Tal were in a Ridge City courthouse room, planning their escape routes to the forest. Dust and debris came out of the ventilation grills in their courthouse room. They could taste the toxic air now. Depleted of its oxygen and mixed with smoke and pulverized rock, the air couldn't support biological life much longer.

Now, the city had only one entrance and exit, the main gate.

"They're cutting our lifelines," Tal said. "They destroyed our ventilation shafts and the secret entrance."

"Should we open the main gate now?" Ula asked.

"Not yet, but within the hour. We still have minimal electric power."

Without notice, the ventilation fans stopped in the courthouse room. The rumbling of fans and air ducts stopped, creating an eerie silence in the room's background noise.

"BOT turned off all ventilation fans," Yot said. "He's decided it's not healthy to pump out air with little oxygen and lots of toxic particles."

BOT had begun his final shutdown sequence. Ridge City now ran on one-twentieth the electrical power of a normal day. BOT had kept his promise to Yot and provided the nursery with enough power to operate. The nursery, scattered streetlights, the emergency communication system, and the electric motors to open the main gate were the only things getting power now.

"Okay, it's time to fight. We'll go to the main gate, and Yot, go get your kids," Ula said. Ula, Tal, and Koa grabbed their backpacks and hurried to the front gate staging area. Jax ran behind Koa. Yot answered his mother's command by running out of the courthouse toward his apartment.

\*\*\*

On Yot's frantic run back to the apartment, only one streetlight worked. While running, he bumped into someone face-on, not seeing him until it was too late.

"Watch out. Didn't you see me coming?" Yot yelled.

"What difference does it make?" the guy replied, smoking a handcrafted cigar.

Yot didn't reply because it made no difference. His torment

had reached its peak as he continued to his apartment. The lawless Imperium had won, and he knew it. He fought the urge to stay in the apartment with his kids, hold them, and die with them from suffocation. His last hope was taking his kids to the main gate and hoping that Koa could lead them to the forest. He would lead the fight up front while Koa tried to lead a group of kids to safety.

"Hi, we're leaving!" Yot yelled as he entered his apartment, hugging Qan and Bao. Fear and shock had rendered the kids unable to reply. They were about to abandon everything they knew and trusted.

"The gate will open in less than an hour," Yot said. "Wear your hiking boots, and bring a cooling vest, kitchen knives, medicines, and a hat. Wear long pants and shorts, and a waterproof jacket if you have one."

"Dad, we have a message from Grandmother Ula," Qan replied. He read it out loud while his hands shook.

"We will run out of air and electricity within the hour, and then we must open the gate. For those fighting, assemble at the main gate now. This will be my last message."

"Yeah, let's get to the front gate now," Yot replied.

"Dad, I have a canteen," a crying Bao said.

"Yes, fill it with water and bring it," Yot said. "And bring an extra belt, a strong one."

Yot hugged his young son and helped him button his shirt. He wiped tears from his son's eyes and vowed, "In the forest, we'll start a new life. I promise."

"Qan, bring the rope in your bedroom and the kitchen bowl and cups if you can get them in your backpack," Yot said.

Once packed, they left the apartment, saying goodbye to their robot nannies.

"SAN, NIA, thank you for your hard work over the years,"

Yot said. "You are welcome to come with us to the main gate."

Their robot nannies looked at one another, confused about their future, and followed Yot, Qan, and Bao to the main gate. There they found Ula, Tal, and Koa standing on the courthouse steps.

The humans had programmed SAN and NIA to serve their masters: Yot, Bao, and Qan. So, it was logical to them to march out of the main gate and act as shields for their human colleagues. They had no fear of death or dismantlement because their programming didn't address these issues. Their programming did not include bigger-picture issues, such as politics, death, and war.

Yot took Qan and Bao to Koa, hugged everyone, and told Koa not to charge straight out of the gate. He suggested she slip out the sides of the gate opening and run to the forest.

Ula yelled to the ragtag army, "We fight for humanity! We will open the gates when we run out of air or electricity. Sit down and conserve your energy. DORG and his henchman are outside the gate. Once outside, run in all directions toward the forest. Good luck."

By Saturday at noon, June 21, over nine hundred courageous Ridge City residents had assembled. They stood in the street armed with laser handguns, shovels, rifles, knives, brooms, and baseball bats. The remaining horrified humans stayed in their apartments or committed suicide.

About one-half of Ridge City's robot nannies and service bots joined the fight by marching to the main gate. They would provide cover for the fighting humans. The rest, including service robots like GEL, had run out of electricity or didn't feel a need to help the humans.

\*\*\*

"NAIT8, the Dominator has arrived," ZET said, standing in his hilltop VCX command center.

The black flatbed-like vehicle had broken through the spotty clouds and was waiting for orders to land. It hovered one hundred meters above the ground in front of the main gate.

In previous centuries, thousands of airborne and ground-based Dominators had destroyed human armies and cities. Its cylinder-shaped laser, mounted on the front of the vehicle, was three meters in diameter and thirty meters long. The laser heated the material it hit to thousands of degrees. Depending on the object the laser beam hit, it could vaporize it. A small control room, also painted black, stood between the laser and a small-sized fusion reactor.

During the past few centuries, the Imperium took control of all computers on Earth first and never used nuclear weapons. Toxic water, extreme temperatures, disease, rising oceans, wars, and the collapse of governments wiped out billions of humans over centuries. Climate destruction did the work for them. The Imperium targeted human communication and transportation systems and weapons and weapon factories. Laser-based weapons were more selective and efficient than brute-force nuclear weapons.

"Today, we exterminate the human species," NAIT8 shouted. "Station the Dominator two hundred meters from the gate."

"Yes, NAIT8."

The Dominator landed by extending four massive struts into the ground. They made a slicing sound as they dug into the trembling earth.

The Dominator sent out many laser pulses in all directions to calibrate distances so it could understand its location on the killing field. With methodical precision, the laser gun moved and aimed at the main gate. The main gate glistened as brilliant rays of sunlight shot through the intermittent clouds.

Imperium warriors moved up beside the Dominator, ready to attack. The first three rows of faceless warriors kneeling, and five rows of Hertes warriors standing behind them. Their featureless heads showed no fear or remorse, for they had none. They were pure fighting machines.

Three swarms of Verkings clustered in the sky, each casting a moving dark shadow upon the battleground.

"NAIT8, our warriors are in position," ZET said.

"Now, war decides our role here," NAIT8 bellowed, standing as tall as he could.

# CHAPTER 11

## *The Last Battle*

**"A** ttack!" NAIT8 yelled.

ZET and SUT relayed the orders to all Imperium forces. They stood beside the VCX command center on a small hill. Three hundred meters away, as rays of sunlight were breaking through the clouds, lay the killing field in front of Ridge City's main gate. The humans had shamed NAIT8 before the entire Imperium Nation, and now he would take his revenge against the human vagrants.

The Dominator opened the end of its cylindrical laser weapon. To protect their camera membranes, the Imperium warriors and drones shielded their camera lenses. Row upon row of warriors stayed still as the Dominator moved and the ground shook.

As the fusion reactor built up the power needed to annihilate the main gate, the machine emitted a whining, guttural sound. Then, with a burst of blinding white light, it melted the first of four gate hinges. The metric-ton hinge melted and vaporized with a few molten blobs of metal dropping to the ground.

The laser cannon repeated this firing process three more times. Now the metric-ton gate hinges had been disintegrated.

The Imperium super weapon, set at a laser temperature

of three thousand degrees Celsius, continued to melt the rock around the edges of the gate. The Dominator dismantled the gate's foundation, sending vaporized plasma and debris flying in all directions. Waves of heat and smoke carried the scent of burning metal and vaporized rock through the hot air.

NAIT8 and the Hertes warriors stayed in place as they watched the merciless fury of this all-powerful machine. After destroying the gate's hinges and several meters of pulverized rock around the gate, they could hear a loud creaking sound. The slight movement of the massive three hundred metric-ton and ten-meter square gate foretold its future. It shuddered and groaned and leaned outward. With a thunderous roar and a vast cloud of dust and debris, it smashed deep into the ground of the desecrated upside.

As the gate fell, a blast of hot air rushed past the warriors, flinging debris in all directions. The same blast of air also knocked down many of the Ridge City residents inside the opening.

Once the air and dust cleared, it showed a jagged open hole in the rock cliff. The opening exposed the last humans in North America to the hazards of the ruthless upside and the ominous Imperium army. The gate, once a protector of human civilization, had separated two competing lifeforms with different values and approaches to existence.

From their hilltop command center, NAIT8 and his warriors scrutinized the interior of the city with their telescopic cameras. Their view inside showed the courthouse and surrounding honeycomb buildings built from the cave floor to the ceiling. It exposed centuries of subterranean city residents living a partial life.

NAIT8 zoomed in to examine the rag-tag human army that now stood in the opening. He could see hundreds of armed humanoids. A few wore cooling vests and heavy clothes to protect their skin from the debris and scalding sun, but they were unprepared for battle. The older humans wore dress clothes.

Younger residents wore t-shirts, gym shoes, and shorts. They wore the only clothes they had, having lived in an underground city their entire lives. The humans were carrying handguns, mops, rifles, and brooms—NAIT8 saw no formidable weapons.

An awkward silence prevailed, lasting several seconds, while both sides studied their foe.

"They're armed with brooms and clubs?" ZET said to NAIT8. "The extermination should be fast."

"I see their leaders at the front of the group," NAIT8 said.

"Yes, they are carrying laser handguns and rifles."

"Do they have light grenades?"

"We don't know. They can blind our warriors' cameras for a time."

"Kill this pathetic species," NAIT8 yelled as the Dominator fired and the courthouse burst into pieces.

The pyrrhic battle had begun.

***

When the gate fell, the blast of scorching air hit the motley Ridge City residents and knocked many off their feet. Ula and everyone else gasped and coughed, trying to adjust to the red-hot fifty-two-degree Celsius (i.e., 126 degrees Fahrenheit) temperature and air.

Yot and Tal, wearing Ridge City police helmets, watched as a nearby resident collapsed to the ground with blood seeping from her mouth and nose. They hurried to help her, but her singed throat and lungs had ruptured because of the sudden rush of stifling hot air. Yot wanted to call an ambulance, but none existed.

"It's the heat," Tal shouted.

A few residents fell to the ground and clutched their throats. They died from the heat, never moving beyond the Ridge City exit.

Most residents trembled in absolute fear as they watched

the first three rows of kneeling Imperium warriors stand up and advance toward them. A few residents kneeled on the ground with the false hope that somehow the robotic machines would show mercy to them. Then, the five rows of Hertes warriors also advanced and fired their laser weapons.

The warriors split into three malicious prongs—one advanced straight toward the humans and the others on each side of the main gate. Laser shots filled the airways with crisp buzzing sounds as humans fell to the ground, screaming in pain as the shots destroyed their frail flesh.

Ula, a tall, bald woman with a white turban cloth wrapped around her head, looked back at her disparate residents. Standing in front of her human army, Ula realized that they had suffered damage even before they left the gate opening. But she recognized they looked at her for guidance and hope as she stood with Yot, Tal, and two Hermes9 robot warriors at the front of the Ridge City army. These humans chose to fight, and she wouldn't let them down.

Ula turned back toward the almighty robot army. She raised both hands high in the air, holding two laser guns and wearing a small backpack. She took a quick breath and yelled at the top of her lungs, "We fight for humanity!"

She took one step toward the Imperium army and then screamed, "Attack and run!"

Yot, Tal, and the two Hermes9 robot warriors followed her, with the Ridge City motley army behind them. Tal ran behind a Hermes9 robot. The human soldiers sprinted toward the Imperium army and the forest.

"We must protect our home!" Yot yelled as he ran, firing at nearby Verking drones.

Qan and Bao were far behind them, with Koa leading them and twelve other kids toward the woods. Koa's group slipped out the western edge of the gate opening to evade the Imperium army. The youngsters represented the future of humanity.

As Ula and her fighting group ran, firing their weapons,

Yot yelled, "Let's go to the big laser cannon!"

"Yes, let's go!" Ula yelled.

Yot ran fastest and reached a pile of rocks and debris, which he hid behind, followed by Ula and Tal and their two Hermes9 warriors. The Hermes9 warriors remained upright, firing their lasers and destroying two advancing Hertes warriors. Then they heard the familiar nauseating puttering sound.

Ula looked skyward. A swarm of Verking drones was hovering above them. Laser pulses beamed by their heads, the pile of debris giving little protection from the vicious airborne hunters.

A barrage of laser shots hit one of the Ridge City fighters. Blood and smoke gushed from her burning shoulder. In seconds, she had died with an innocent and bewildered look on her face.

Ula, Tal, and Yot glanced at the dead soldier, got up, and ran, firing their laser handguns as they moved forward. Ula's and Tal's shots hit a Hertes warrior while Yot shot at the Verkings in the sky. The humans zig-zagged across the killing field and dived to the ground again and again to avoid barrages of incoming laser shots.

They continued to fire their weapons and saw the head fly off of one of their Ridge City Hermes9 warriors. The headless robot paused, trying to comprehend its situation. Then it dropped to its knees and fell face-forward into the grassless killing field.

Ula and Yot ran, with Tal trailing them. They shot their weapons in all directions, trying to counterattack all who shot at them, and ran toward the Dominator.

The Dominator continued to fire at the Ridge City residents and the city buildings. The laser beam cut a clear surgical-like path, about three meters wide, through the residents and buildings. It vaporized the resident soldiers and most of the physical things in its pathway. Even the expected smell of burnt human bodies didn't materialize.

\*\*\*

While running, a laser shot hit Tal. He staggered and fell to the ground. He looked down at his leg; his foot and ankle were gone. In shock, he tried to fire his weapon but could not. As he lay there, blood poured from his amputated leg.

Ula turned and ran back to her dying husband. She dove behind his body to see if she could help him. Ula didn't comprehend that Tal would die in less than a minute. She tried to use her belt to make a tourniquet to stop his leg from bleeding, but Tal had lost too much blood.

Tal's lips quivered, and he stared at her for a second with alert and loving eyes. He couldn't speak, but their eyes communicated a lifelong bond that would soon end. Tal tried to raise up toward Ula and speak, but a second laser shot from a drone hit Tal in the neck, making an awful whizzing sound. His eyes turned hollow as he fell back to the ground.

Ula's brain caught up with the reality, and tears flowed down her face. Shocked and angry, she wanted to stay with her dead husband, but humanity's last battle in North America wouldn't allow it. Laser shots, fires, and broken warrior and human bodies surrounded her. The brutal chaos of war overpowered her senses.

Ula stared at her faithful and beloved husband for a second. She squeezed his hand, and then, knowing she must hurry if she was to avoid his fate, she stood upright and ran. Her survival instinct dominated her agony. Tears were streaming down her face as she ran, her body smeared with Tal's blood. She wiped her mouth and continued her determined advance to the Dominator.

She rejoined Yot ahead of her. They were within twenty meters of the Dominator.

"Your dad's dead," Ula said to Yot as laser shots zipped over their heads. Lying behind the rocks and firing at the Imperium warriors, Yot spat dirt out of his mouth before responding to his mother.

"I know. I looked back and saw you trying to help him."

After a pause, a tearful Yot said, "He was a great husband and father."

"Yes, he was."

But there was no time to grieve. They could leave this reality in the next moment. Smoke from nearby burning bodies and equipment helped hide Ula and Yot behind the pile of rocks.

With a tremor in his voice and tears in his eyes, Yot alerted his mom. "They left the big laser unprotected." Hundreds of Imperium warriors had set up next to the Dominator, but once ordered to advance, they had left the big laser alone and unprotected.

"Do you think we can fire it?" Ula said, watching his mother vomit. It was her reflex reaction to the fear of death and losing her husband.

"We'll try." But they couldn't go because of an approaching Imperium warrior.

Behind the cover of rocks and smoke, they watched the Hertes warrior rush toward their last remaining Hermes9 warrior. The almighty machines slammed into one another and battled within ten meters of the Dominator. The old Hermes9 warrior was no match for the modern Imperium Hertes robot. After the Hertes warrior hurled the Hermes9 into the air, the Hermes9 landed and got stuck in the ground. The Hermes9 tried to free itself from its shallow grave, but the Imperium warrior used its laser to slice off both of the Hermes9's arms.

Ula and Yot saw the armless Ridge City warrior arise to confront its assassin.

The armless Hermes9 robot tried to bull-rush the Hertes warrior, but it jumped into the air and did a flip, ending up behind its prey. It smashed its arm and fist into the old warrior's back. Then the Hertes warrior grabbed the small fusion generator and ripped it out. The violent battle between machines was so forceful that nearby machines and humans watched in awe.

Ula and Yot saw their last remaining Hermes9 warrior fall with a thunderous crash.

The victorious Hertes warrior turned and searched for Ula and Yot but couldn't find them. Once the Hertes warrior left, Ula and Yot sprinted to the Dominator's strut and climbed the ladder. They entered the Dominator's windowless and unlocked control room.

"This machine operates itself," Yot said to his mother as they examined the instruments. Electronic displays using the Imperium language and numbering system covered the walls. They could hear the buzzing and zipping sounds of laser guns, but the sounds were diminishing. "We need to turn off its automatic mode and use manual operation," Yot shouted.

"I'm working on it," Ula said as she studied the wall screens. "I think it uses the duodecimal numbering system?"

"Yeah, I have this system logged in my auxiliary memory," Yot said as they both faced the control room wall screens.

"Okay, I understand the numbers on the screen. But not the lettering," Yot said. "We need JORT. He can read their OCRT language well." The OCRT language used thirty-nine writing symbols with no capital letters, written in columns from top to bottom.

"Let me look," Ula said. She studied the hieroglyphics on the wall screen. "I think these two display buttons say 'stop' and 'offline.' "

Although Yot knew more about the Imperium language and the numbering system, Ula also had a minimal understanding.

Yot mumbled something, and then he touched a symbol on the electronic display. A new screen appeared depicting a schematic of the mathematics and solid geometry of aiming a laser shot. He leaned toward the display and squinted, trying to comprehend the schematic.

Meanwhile, several laser shots hit the outside of the Dominator's control center, creating a pinging and sizzling sound.

"Mom, remember the cockpit controls in the Imperium VX we stole? JORT realized their schematics were mirror images."

"Great, you have one minute to figure it out. NAIT8 will soon figure out we are here."

"Hit the button on the left."

Ula pointed to the button in question.

"Yes, that one."

She hit it, and the language and schematics on the electronic display changed.

"I think we found it. We're in manual mode," said Yot, grinning.

"We must turn the laser and shoot it at NAIT8 and his warriors," Ula said.

"Alright, let me practice moving the laser," Yot said, his posture more erect and confident now. He moved an orange circle on the display's touch screen with his fingers and found it depicted the target. The intelligent Dominator software computed the settings to hit the target. Yot didn't understand the numerical coordinates, but he saw how to move the orange circle over to the target. After thirty seconds of experimenting with the controls, he aimed at the rock cliff, pressed a button, and heard a deep whining sound. Then, a jolt from the laser cannon. The laser shot blasted a deep hole in the rock cliff. He had fired a practice shot.

\*\*\*

While Ula and her son were learning how to use the Dominator, NAIT8 was watching the battle on multiple VCX command center screens.

"NAIT8," ZET said. "We have over three hundred humans

surrounded east of the main gate. Should we kill them or take prisoners?"

Without hesitation, NAIT8 said, "Kill them except for twenty pairs of young males and females."

"Yes, NAIT8. Should our warriors or drones kill them?"

"Let the Verkings do it. And send the video to all NAITs worldwide."

"Yes, NAIT8."

More than one hundred Imperium warriors encircled the humans and kneeled, having corralled the humans on the gate's east side. The machines' shoulder-mounted laser weapons pointed at their prey but didn't shoot. They would watch the massacre as the Verking drone fly-bys taunted the humans.

Imperium warriors walked through the petrified humans, looking for twenty youthful pairs. The robots asked for volunteers to be used as Imperium pets. The warriors promised ample water and food, showers, and safe places to sleep in cages. A few residents begged to be taken, while others ignored the warriors' bribes. The machines used ropes to tie the chosen humans' ankles and wrists and loaded the forty prisoners onto a VCX cargo vehicle, which would fly to the Nashville Region 8 headquarters.

The remaining humans huddled in a circle. Many stood while others sat on the ground, holding hands. Families cried and wailed. People became so dehydrated in the upside heat that they sucked their soaked clothes to soothe their parched lips. Parents held anything they could find to block the sun's lethal rays. Many without cooling vests had passed out and lay lifeless.

One young male ran toward a Hertes warrior, firing his laser handgun. His laser shots missed, but three of the Imperium warriors did not. Their shots severed his legs. His body fell onto the battlefield, jerked several times, and stopped moving. Everyone trapped by the Imperium warriors gasped but dared not challenge the towering warriors.

Once the twenty pairs of young humans and their Imperium captors had left the large group of captive humans, one hundred drones descended over the huddled mass of humanity. They fired their laser weapons at the captives, at which point, a few humans returned fire with their laser handguns and rifles. Several drones exploded and fell on top of their prey. But the remaining Verking drones shot their laser beams into the helpless human bodies. The last humans in North America were being executed.

The drones toyed with their prey. Six encircled an older male human dressed in a white, long-sleeve, collarless shirt, black trousers, and dress shoes. Their claws snapped at him from all directions. One pinched off his ear. With the energy in his laser handgun depleted, the injured man threw his weapon at a drone. Then he picked up two rocks, as his distant ancestors had done, and threw them at another drone. One rock made contact, making a clanking sound, but this only caused the drone to retreat, pause, and then shoot the defenseless man in the chest. The man sank to the ground.

Within two minutes, the staggering mutilation had ended. Only one female remained alive, lying on her dead companion and moaning. A Verking swooped down and, with two claws, strangled her to death. And then an eerie quiet befell the killing field.

Imperium warriors and drones felt a mild and short-lived amount of regret or glee for killing hundreds of humans. Their emotional modules didn't allow for stronger emotions, like shame or elation. There was no moral dilemma for them; the software and learning algorithms didn't allow it. The Imperium robots viewed their killing of humans in the same way that humans felt emotions triggered when stepping on pesky roaches.

"NAIT8, we killed 308 humans east of the gate. And we have taken twenty live breeding pairs as pets," ZET said, standing outside the VCX command center on the nearby hilltop.

"Outstanding. Invade the city."

\*\*\*

"NAIT8, our Dominator is acting strange," SUT said, minutes after massacring the Ridge City citizens and destroying their buildings. "It shot into the cliff."

"Replay the video."

The video showed the Dominator firing two shots. They both hit the rock cliff five meters to the right of the gate opening, blasting holes into it.

"Who fired the shots?" NAIT8 asked.

"I don't know."

"You don't know."

"I don't know."

"Is the weapon in autonomous or manual mode?"

SUT turned and walked several steps to a fifth wall screen in the command center. After several seconds of studying the instrument readings, he said, "It's in manual mode."

"Who's guarding the Dominator?"

"No one, NAIT8. All warriors are engaged in battle."

"Idiots! Get a squad of warriors to enter the control room. Report what they find."

NAIT8 used his telephoto cameras to zoom in on the Dominator and watched the big laser gun rotate toward where he stood.

"We're all fools," NAIT8 yelled. "Someone is aiming the Dominator at us!"

The Dominator jerked up and down and then aimed the laser gun toward them. The heavy guttural and whining sounds resonated in the killing field.

"Abandon the center," NAIT8 screamed as he ran out the VCX bay door.

ZET, SUT, and his warriors were watching their commander run away when the Dominator fired its laser three times, each in two-second-long bursts.

The first volley hit the VCX command center on the hilltop,

vaporizing part of it. The heat set the remaining tree stumps, bushes, and grass on fire. A few pieces of metal fragments sailed through the air. After a pause, another shot hit a VX parked nearby.

NAIT8, ZET, SUT, and other Hertes warriors escaped by diving to the turf close to a burning tree stump. After the third Dominator laser blast missed its target and hit the hill, NAIT8 stood and walked through the burning debris. ZET lay on the ground, one of his legs mangled, while only parts of SUT remained.

"ZET, you moron."

NAIT8 kicked ZET's twisted leg as he passed, then turned and said to his two surviving warriors, "Let's run to the Dominator and join our comrades."

The Dominator turned toward the Imperium warriors that had surrounded Ridge City residents and fired. The first shot flew over their heads, and they ran in all directions. But the next shot hit a group of warriors, disintegrating their metal frames. The powerful laser hit the first warrior and continued through several more before it hit the forest and set it ablaze.

By then, the earlier squad of Imperium warriors had surrounded the Dominator. These warriors witnessed the intense beams of energy radiate from their own powerful laser gun. They'd crawled up onto the Dominator and tried to open the locked control room door, but it wouldn't budge.

NAIT8 arrived with two warriors, and they hid behind the Dominator's huge steel struts.

A Hertes warrior stepped back from the control room door and raised his arm, using his laser weapon to burn the door lock. The lock dropped to the floor with a clanking sound and rolled across the flatbed truck's steel floor.

But before the warriors could open the door, it cracked open. Three grenades rolled out, and then it closed.

The grenades exploded with a light brighter than the sun. It damaged and blinded the warriors' cameras and sensors, so now, without radar and vision, the warriors went into lockdown mode. The blind warriors stood in place, fixed in their position. They could not see or sense threats. The light grenades had done their job and made the warriors' cameras inoperable—or, at best, produce imperfect images. Ula and Yot now had their chance to escape the Dominator and the Imperium warriors.

***

Ula's and Yot's bodies crashed into the ground after the three-meter-high jump off the Dominator, rolling as they hit the ground. Yot stood, but Ula had made an awkward landing, breaking a bone in her lower leg. The bone jutted out of her calf several centimeters above her ankle.

"Yot, go on, run," Ula shouted.

Yot glanced at her and said, "Not a chance, Mom. No one's leaving you."

He took his belt, wrapped her lower calf, and latched the belt tight. The Imperium laser assault had slowed, and the smoke and fires provided them with cover. She hobbled behind Yot. What else could she do?

They returned to the same pile of rocks that had protected them on the way to the Dominator.

The two Imperium warriors with NAIT8, standing by a Dominator strut, scanned the area with their impaired vision. They located Ula and Yot. The warriors shot at them, and the rocks shattered into thousands of shards.

"Mom, let's take a stand here," Yot yelled as a single laser shot missed his head by centimeters. "If we run, we'll get shot in the back, anyway."

Yot saw NAIT8 and the Hertes warriors advancing toward their woeful rock pile.

"Yot, you're right. We're finished."

And with that comment, Ula and Yot rose from their hiding place. Ula wobbled on her broken leg but stood erect.

Their brave actions surprised NAIT8 and his warriors, so much so that NAIT8 yelled, "Don't shoot."

Ula raised her gun, but a Hertes warrior fired its laser, knocking it from her bleeding hand.

"We don't fear you," Yot shouted, raising his handgun.

Yot tried to shoot his gun, but a warrior hit his forearm hard. His gun slammed out of his grasp, and Yot fell to the ground, holding his forearm. No bones punched through his skin, but his forearm was most likely fractured.

The warriors grabbed both of them and tied their ankles and wrists with ropes.

Standing in front of an injured and defiant Ula and Yot, NAIT8 stared at them.

"You won't escape my grasp again!"

NAIT8 turned to one of his warriors. "Take them to our hilltop command center. For now, we'll keep them alive."

The warriors dragged them off to a VCX vehicle on the hill, the only intact vehicle remaining on the hilltop command post. The Dominator shots had destroyed the old VCX command center.

"You have no compassion or soul!" Ula yelled.

"I don't need one!" NAIT8 bellowed back.

Upon arrival at the new VCX command center, the warriors tied them to a charred tree stump about twenty meters away. Wounded and dirty but alive, the mother and son both were in shock. They had seen the horrors of war and the dismemberment of their fellow humans. Once the humans were bound to the tree stump, the two Hertes warriors went inside the new VCX command center to join NAIT8.

Yot had time to attend to his mother's broken leg. He tried to push the fractured bone back into her leg. His mother screamed in pain, holding and yanking the ropes tight with her hands. Yot found several sticks and branches and used belts to form a makeshift splint.

Afterward, Yot took off his long-sleeved shirt and wrapped it tight around his forearm, trying to stabilize it. Ula fumbled around, tying her son's forearm splint with his shoelaces. They both huddled together while excruciating pain sliced through their bodies. They weren't dead, but they felt like it.

"Do you think Koa and the kids made it to the forest?" Yot said as they lay close to one another.

"Let's hope so. That's all we have now—hope."

\*\*\*

Koa, Qan, Bao, and twelve other children ran westward out of the gate opening. They slithered along the rock cliff, hiding when necessary, and made it to the forest. The major groups of Ridge City residents charged straight ahead out of the gate.

Early on, Koa's group of kids ran through the forest, dogging trees and bushes. The tree canopy gave relief from the searing heat.

And, of course, Jax followed the terrified kids through the forest. Koa led them while Jax lagged the group. Jax would bark if a kid strayed from the group. Koa would pause and search for Jax and the child.

Later, after running several kilometers from Ridge City, Koa tied a single thin rope to everyone as they hiked by night and hid by day. If she lost one child, she thought, it would be devastating.

Qan, aged sixteen, was older than the other children. The police department had trained Koa on survival methods, so she knew what to do. She carried two laser guns, a machete, two cooling vests, water purification pills, hooks and fishing line, twenty matches, and two kitchen knives. Qan and the older kids carried water containers, kitchen knives, medicine, and a couple of metal pots and pans. Koa also had experienced the trauma of python snakes attacking JORT and Jax, so she understood the dangers of any upside body of water.

Jax would hear the puttering sounds of Verking drones first. He would bark, and the humans would hide in the bushes, under logs, and leaves to avoid discovery. The frequency of the drone searches decreased each day.

On the third day after their escape, Koa took Qan and Jax to a nearby pond. The group had consumed all their water and had little to eat.

They walked to the pond's edge in the dark. Koa kept one laser gun and gave the other to Qan. He acted as a lookout for Koa as she fished. They wore cooling vests and scanned the surroundings and sky for threats. Jax was their best lookout; he could sense ground vibrations and pick up sounds well before humans. And the Ridge City police department had trained him to smell machine lubricants.

Koa, with Jax beside her, tied the fishing line to a stout tree branch. She baited the hooks with a ball of earthworms and threw the line into the water. She was the perfect person, a genetic orphan and a member of the Ridge City police department, to lead the band of kids through the forest. Smart, strong, and trained, she oversaw the last hope for humanity in North America.

The trio watched the water and one another. The half-moon provided dim light to the area and glistened off the water. And then something hit the hook, and the line became tight. Koa wrestled with the line and pulled in a big catfish. She re-baited the hook and caught another catfish and another. With three catfish and feeling victorious, they filled their water containers and placed purification pills in each. They left the pond and returned to camp in the dark.

Koa knew about the toxic stuff, including worms, in the bottom-feeding fish, but she didn't tell anyone. To starving kids, cooked catfish was like an elegant dinner.

Back at camp, Koa started a small bonfire under a fallen tree trunk to hide the flare from Imperium sensors. Koa and

Qan filleted the fish and cooked them. Once the fish were cooked, they extinguished the flames, scattered the ashes, and covered them with leaves and other foliage. They did this when leaving every campsite, leaving little trace of their presence.

Koa and Qan parceled out equal amounts of fish to everyone, with only the glow of moonlight. They would repeat this process daily. They ate fish, eels, snakes, frogs, and crayfish. And one day, Koa shot a beaver, which made for a fine meal.

With Koa's oversight, they took turns bathing in the creeks and ponds they found and even washed their filthy clothes. The kids were learning the ways of their distant ancestors.

Koa relished in her newfound role. Jax was the love of her life, and they were inseparable. The bonds with her dog and the kids were everlasting. She hoped it foretold her seeing Jax again in a new existence.

During the day, Koa lost hours of sleep, worrying about what to do next. How far away from Ridge City should she lead the group? Five, fifty, or one hundred kilometers? Should she go to the official meeting place at Nolan River Lake? Had the Imperium set a trap there? But she kept her confusion to herself, hoping an answer would emerge.

And one day, she would run out of electrical charge for her two laser guns and matches to start a fire.

Did they have the determination and skills necessary for long-term nomadic living? Her answer was weeks, yes, but months, no. She had kept moving, trying to avoid capture from the Imperium hunters. Every few hours, they would hear the puttering sounds of the Imperium drones scouring the terrain. Pondering these issues, a determined Koa led the kids toward Nolan River Lake.

# CHAPTER 12

# *Pyrrhic Victories*

"**N**IM, how many humans lived in Ridge City?" DORG asked.

NIM159 had replaced ZET and SUT as DORG's assistant. The Dominator's laser shots had destroyed SUT and damaged ZET. The Imperium dismantled ZET, like MAL, to harvest recyclable parts. Spiderbots had cleansed all Imperium information systems of ZET's and SUT's existence. All members of the Imperium society were replaceable, even regional Initiators of Thought (ITs). Within minutes, the robot society had found and authorized NIM as a replacement.

"2,076."

"How many are dead?"

"Based on our second count, 2,019 are dead," NIM replied. "Most offered no resistance. We captured forty human pets plus their two leaders. We can't account for fifteen humans."

DORG, in their VCX hilltop command center, told his warriors they must complete the mission by tomorrow night. That meant blowing up Ridge City with explosives and heading back to the Nashville headquarters. Ula and Yot remained tied to the tree stump twenty meters away from the command center VCX.

DORG and NIM had scanned the VCX display screens as his

army scoured each street, building, and apartment in Ridge City. Warriors busted down doorways and broke through windows and walls. Often, they found families grouped together, awaiting their assassination or already dead. Bottles containing poison or pills lay beside many. A few residents fired their weapons at the Hertes warriors but to little avail. The Imperium warriors shot back and killed the soon-to-be-forgotten species.

\*\*\*

DORG stared at the display screens as ten warriors broke into Building 21 inside Ridge City. There, they found floor after floor of biological creatures in flexible bags, including Hoy and Ota Torg, lying in their artificial wombs. The fusion reactors were minutes from shutting down, so emergency lighting still worked.

Seven parents of the embryos had stayed in the nursery with their beloved and future children. But the Hertes warriors didn't converse with the human parents; they killed them upon sight.

The warriors also filmed the obnoxious creatures in the flexible bags and sent the video back to DORG's VCX command center along with a message:

We found hundreds of these slimy creatures housed in pliable bags. They move and must be alive. How should we kill them? We can use our lasers or turn off the electricity.

DORG realized they were human embryos being nurtured for birth.

"Don't kill the embryos until after EIN892 has collected data. EIN will plug into the building's information systems and download knowledge related to this species. They may have something in their biochemistry and genetic files we do not know."

"What is an embryo?" a warrior asked.

"It doesn't matter. We don't need embryos or babies," DORG said. "EIN is on his way to you."

EIN looked identical to the Hertes warriors, except the trunk of his body was larger. Inhabiting EIN's body was a powerful Imperium computer processing system. He could segment processing tasks and distribute them to thousands of Imperium quantum computers worldwide. The Imperium had tasked EIN with writing the billions of lines of computer code needed to control the Dyson ring. In this situation, a super artificial intelligence (AI), EIN, authored the Dyson Ring code. AI creating more AI.

The Imperium's collective computer power far exceeded all past human computing powers. Their neural network systems and algorithms had been self-designed, and the Imperium was always trying to improve them.

When EIN arrived at the nursery in the late afternoon on Saturday, June 21, he plugged himself into the human information system. After collecting the data, he designed the perfect molecule to change human DNA. Within five minutes of his entry into the human nursery, EIN had completed his mission and had sent a message to DORG, as well as all the other ITs worldwide. In summary, the message said:

We designed a molecule to prevent humans from self-replicating. Our simulations determined the genetic-based vaccine is effective, with a 99.36 percent statistical confidence interval. Biology isn't an exact science like our precise machine existence, so the interval isn't 100 percent. We also designed a different molecule to prevent the replication of all mammals on Earth. Biological creatures provide no value to Earth nor to the Imperium Nation. We should sterilize Earth of all animal lifeforms to ensure Imperium dominance.

"Excellent," DORG said. "Now turn off the electricity."

The warriors fired their lasers at the main electrical controls, destroying them. Building 21 became dark, and the Imperium warriors switched to night vision. The human embryos and fetuses began to twist and turn as their artificial wombs no longer served them. The twenty-week-old Hoy and Ota Torg tried to break out of their cocoons but died fighting for their lives. Within minutes, the frantic movements in the pliable bags stopped. Humanity's hope for a future had ended.

*** 

Ula and Yot, tied to a tree stump, watched the Imperium prepare to destroy Ridge City. They sat on the top of a small hill on Sunday morning, looking at the entire killing field and the jagged gate opening of Ridge City. Ula used her telescopic eyes to follow drones searching the area and warriors dragging human bodies inside the caves of Ridge City. Imperium warriors walked in and out of the VCX command center and ignored the human pests tied to a tree stump twenty meters away.

The main gate lay on the ground, still smoldering from the Dominator laser attack. Its blue-grey metal glistened in the morning sun. Dead humans, barren rocks, and tiny patches of burnt grass and smoldering tree stumps dotted the disquieting killing field.

"They are counting the dead," Yot said. "They spray each body with orange paint to show they counted it."

"Yeah, and they're moving the bodies inside our city," Ula replied. "They're preparing to blow up our home."

On the east side of the main gate, over three hundred human cadavers lay mangled together in piles of panic. The upside insects feasted on the human remains. Hordes of black flies covered them. Imperium warriors were carrying dead humans back inside the main Ridge City carven and stacking them. The piles were five meters high.

A VCX cargo vehicle landed in the killing field, and the warriors unloaded many metal objects that looked like bombs to Ula and Yot. They carried the metal containers inside Ridge City.

"The Imperium is going to use explosives to destroy our city," Yot said. "They'll bury the dead bodies in the caves and get rid of us."

"Yeah, I see," Ula replied as pain shot up her broken leg.

Ula followed a flock of birds that landed in the middle of the killing field next to the fallen main gate. She also saw with her bionic eyes a huge Burmese python curling up on top of the fallen gate. The snake held its head upright, searching. Several alligators had also left their homes and ventured onto the killing field. A pack of rats scurried across the fallen main gate. The animals sensed something, but what?

***

"Yot, the animals are clustering near the main gate," Ula said.

"I see. Why would they do that?"

"I don't know," Ula said, watching their strange behavior.

She used her telescopic eyes to zoom in and look at the animals.

"Wow! They're looking at a blue ball of light hovering over the fallen main gate."

Yot squinted and asked, "What is it?"

"It's like the blue orb I saw in the tunnel," Ula replied.

For the first time, Yot saw the blue orb from several hundred meters away. His ordinary human eyes strained to focus on the tiny dot of blue light. Then a group of warriors on the killing field fired laser shots at the puissant blue orb.

"The shots are bouncing off the orb," Ula said to Yot, seeing it with her bionic eyes. The shots ricocheted in all directions. One wayward laser shot hit a flying drone. It fell to the ground and hit the gate with a ringing sound. Within seconds, an eerie, surreal feeling permeated the area. The animals hurried into the forest, hearing the laser shots.

Four robot warriors ran toward the enigmatic orb in attack mode. One took a swing at it, but when the warrior hit the orb, the force of the impact broke its metal arm. Stunned, the robot stepped back from the orb. Other perplexed warriors stepped back, too. The blue orb represented a phenomenon the warriors' software didn't understand. Was it a threat? Ball lightning? A reflection from the gate? What?

The warriors shot another furious volley of laser shots at the mysterious orb at close range. Again, the shots ricocheted off the orb. Then Ula and Yot, twenty meters away from the VCX command center, heard an explosion inside the VCX. DOR, EIN, NIM, and several warriors ran out of the vehicle.

They heard DORG yell, "What's happening?"

"The VCX electronic displays exploded," NIM shouted as they stood there overlooking the killing field and the tiny blue orb.

"What are they looking at?" Yot asked his mother.

"They're watching the blue orb."

Like their robot masters, Ula and Yot stared at the menacing blue orb from their hilltop perch. They felt goosebumps on their arms and legs in the forty-eight-degree Celsius (i.e., 118 degrees Fahrenheit) noon-day sun.

As everyone stared at the orb, it started to spin. As it moved, it generated an intense, rotating blueish-white light, which grew in intensity. The light became so intense it burned out the cameras of the Imperium warriors standing close to the gate. The blind warriors stumbled around the gate, bumping into one another and wandering in circles. Warriors fell and crawled on their hands and knees before their software froze them in place.

Ula used her bionic eyes' zooming capability to see the spinning phenomena. At first, the three-hundred-metric-ton gate plowed the earth with its slow rotation. As the orb and gate swirled faster and faster, the gate split into large spaghetti-like strings of metal and light. The strings gravitated toward the center of the spinning orb.

Within a minute, the shredded gate had vanished into the blue abyss. Somehow, the spinning blue-white vortex had swallowed it.

Still tied to a charred tree stump outside the command post, Ula and Yot focused on the spinning orb. They had a ringside seat on the top of the small hill. They saw DORG, EIN, NIM, and several warriors hide behind two burnt tree stumps sixty meters away.

Now was their chance to escape. They tugged at their ropes, trying to free themselves, cutting their ankles and wrists with their violent movements. Their ankles were bound, and their wrists tied to the tree stump.

"The orb is trying to help us," Yot yelled to Ula while the high-pitched whining sound of the spinning orb and debris became louder. It sounded like a huge electric motor or turbine spinning at thousands of revolutions per minute.

"Unbelievable!" Yot shouted.

"Now, do you believe the blue orb saved my life in the tunnel?"

"Yes, yes!" Yot shouted while pulling the ropes over his mother's bleeding wrists. Robot warriors had tied the ropes so tightly that the rope itself squeaked in distress. The ropes pulled flesh off Ula's wrists and hands, but now she was free. Ula used her bleeding hands to free Yot. Both struggled to untie their ankles.

They gawked in awe as an unseen force pulled the nearby Hertes warriors toward the space where the gate had disappeared. A bluish singularity with bursts of brilliant white light filled the vortex. The enormous tidal forces propelled tons of

Imperium equipment and vehicles toward the vortex as the wind reached 220 kilometers per hour (i.e., 137 mph). Metal parts flew over Ula's and Yot's heads as they clung to the stump and ground. Any object containing metal seemed to move toward the vortex.

The powerful force ripped metal objects inside Ridge City from their moorings, and they flew out through the opening where the main gate had been. Metal kitchen utensils, pipes, tools, and monorail cars zoomed into the air, gouging the cave walls as they bounced through the caverns and hallways.

The intense energy dragged Imperium warriors inside Ridge City through its caverns. Their metallic heads, arms, legs, and bodies bounced against the buildings and rocks. Their torsos broke apart. By the time their metal parts arrived at Ridge City's entrance, only pulverized metal shards remained. The metal parts and fragments vanished into the vortex, spinning at an imperceptible speed. But the powerful force ignored non-metals like wood, rocks, and biological flesh.

Ula and Yot noticed the side of the small mountain and cliff that housed Ridge City bulge. Rocks, trees, and dirt fell to the wayside. The way the earth shook, they expected a volcano or earthquake. And then they saw the Ridge City nuclear reactors, pipes, and equipment blast out of the ground. The ravenous singularity ate metal like a starving hyena eating carrion.

\*\*\*

Ula and Yot, wearing little clothing, scurried away from the tree stump and ran to the edge of the forest once the wind decreased. The ground they ran on reeked of dead brown grass and plants, with patches of scorched mud and rock and barren tree trunks lying flat on the ground. Vertical and burnt tree stumps marked the killing fields.

They cut their feet as they ran and hid behind the stumps.

Freedom was a rare event on the upside, and they relished it once more.

They looked over at DORG and his cohort sixty meters away. The robots remained hidden by the two tree stumps, some lying on the ground. They were too preoccupied with their own survival to worry about Ula and Yot.

BANG!

The loud sound made Ula and Yot turn their attention back to the battlefield. One strut of the Dominator had broken off and hit its laser cannon, creating the bang. A second BANG happened when another strut snapped.

One corner of the weapon fell to the ground. Despite its size, the Imperium's most powerful weapon was being dragged toward the singularity. Soon, the metal cylinder that housed the potent laser squeaked and trembled and broke into pieces. Flairs of bright lights swirled around the blue-white whirlwind as it pulverized the metal objects. Like the gate had, the metal morphed into long, brilliant strings of tormented matter and disappeared.

After a few more seconds, Ula and Yot noticed the hill-top VCX that acted as the command center make a creaking sound. The draconian force seemed to slowly expand its territory. Then, the VCX moved toward the spinning phenomena. The VCX broke apart, first into sizeable pieces and then into smaller and smaller strips. A few metal parts flew by DORG's head and whirled around the spinning blue orb.

The ugly-looking Verking drones were floundering about in the air because of the high winds as extraordinary gravity pulled on them. Once close to the spinning blue vortex, the tidal forces tore the drones apart. It ripped off legs and claws first, followed by their bodies. Within seconds, they vanished.

"Did you see those drones slam into one another?" Yot asked.

"No, I missed it. I'm looking at the Dominator and VCX."

\*\*\*

Ula and Yot turned back to keep their eyes on DORG and his warriors hiding by the tree stumps. The once invincible robots were on the ground and didn't dare stand. They witnessed their VCX command center being dragged from its hilltop perch and vanishing into the spinning abyss. Although DORG and his robot colleagues had no fear, they knew a threat when they saw it. The vortex was a threat they had never seen.

Ula and Yot noticed that NIM, lying on the ground, had driven his mechanical fingers and toes into the ground. He had hidden where DORG, EIN, and the robot warriors had taken cover.

NIM felt the force of the blue orb vortex first. It ripped off NIM's arms and legs and dragged them toward the spinning anomaly. His body smashed into a barren tree trunk as Ula and Yot gaped at NIM's demise. The gravity well pulled NIM's body fragments into it, and they vanished from Earth's space-time arena. NIM was no more. Two Hertes warriors with DORG and NIM succumbed to the same fate.

Yot noticed a flock of birds watching NIM's destruction. They made no noise. Their biological flesh was immune to the metal-eating vortex. Then, without notice, they flew away, free to live another day.

The puissant force also dragged the heavy-set EIN on the ground, too. His thick frame crashed into a bolder and broke into pieces. Hundreds of other EINs had backed up the information files he stored for the Imperium's cooperative society.

Ula and Yot rejoiced when the invisible force gripped their foes' metallic bodies like a vise. The almighty robot nation was no match for this mysterious and colossal force.

"What's doing this?" Yot asked, still clinging to a tree stump at the edge of the forest. The winds had subsided to 120 kilometers per hour (i.e., 75 mph).

"I'm not sure. Some sort of magnetic force," Ula yelled.

"What I don't understand is why it attacks only metal-based material."

"I'm dumbfounded but thrilled by what I'm seeing. The orb is fighting for us."

"Yes, it cares about us."

The power of the mysterious orb awed Ula and Yot. They contemplated the god-like power. Was the blue orb a divine intervention? An alien species helping humanity? A dream or illusion? A digital simulation? A ghost from another dimension? It had saved Ula from drowning in the water-filled tunnel, and now it disposed of humanity's enemy.

"Yes, it does," Yot said. "But what is it?"

"Perhaps the orb is divine. But this time, it came to Earth in a non-human form."

"I'm a scientist. I don't believe in a God!"

"I know," Ula replied. "But perhaps an advanced being gave us gifts like the orb and Plato?"

"Could be, maybe, like Einstein and Michelangelo?"

"Yes, exactly."

\*\*\*

A loud scraping sound interrupted their conversation as they watched DORG's feet separate from his legs first and hurled toward the blue vortex. Lying on the ground, DORG drove his mechanical fingers deep into the ground to resist the forces. And then one of DORG's arms broke away from his body, leaving a medley of wires and hydraulic hoses. The trunk of his body trembled as it was dismembered. DORG was the last Imperium warrior to be annihilated.

Before the orb-created singularity ripped off DORG's barbaric head, Ula thought he glanced toward them, hiding by the stumps sixty meters away from him. She thought he tried to speak and even whine, but she couldn't hear what he said.

DORG vanished like his entire army. Once the blue orb

had scrubbed the entire area of all metal and completed its mission, it disappeared.

"Wow!" Ula shouted, sitting on the ground by the barren stump. "DORG is gone!"

"Yes!" Yot yelled, raising his arm high in the air in celebration.

"You know, the orb trapped them in their own metal bodies."

"Yeah, we're the only humans to witness this phenomenon."

"It's like a dream, Yot. I'm glad you were here," Ula said while hugging him.

For the next few days, they would feel safe. The orb had obliterated their century-long menace and executioner, DORG and his army. But they knew replacement robots would soon repopulate Region 8.

Elated but injured and exhausted, they relished in the orb's success. They now realized the Imperium was not invincible. Dazed by what they had seen, they knew they were not alone. Something, somewhere, was monitoring the struggles of humanity and trying to help their beleaguered species.

The orb's involvement foretold that Earth and humanity were worth saving, and they both had a clear and powerful purpose in the vast universe. The sacrosanct purpose justified the creation of the universe. All sentient beings, including Jax, were about to understand these simple and universal truths.

\*\*\*

But those aspirations of relief, hope, and even joy were short-lived. Ula's painful broken ribs, swollen hand, and fractured leg reminded her of their immediate reality. Yot experienced aching pain in his torn ear and broken fingers and forearm. Surviving on the upside broke their fragile human bodies. For a brief period, the fear of death had overpowered their bodily pain, but now the relentless pain returned.

Hobbled but alive, they surveyed the cleansed battleground

ground from the edge of the forest. They gazed at the scarred battlefield where humans had fought their robotic masters, and they celebrated their pyrrhic victory. Gone were the mighty Dominator, the Verking drones, the VCX and VX vehicles, and DORG and his barbarian warriors. Ridge City's main gate and equipment were also gone.

As Ula and Yot overlooked the carnage, the brutal reality of Ridge City's destruction weighed heavy in their minds. Yot put his arm around his mother. Tears flowed as they looked on at the brutalized remains of their once beloved Ridge City. They were the only two humans alive, to their knowledge, who remembered the marvels and joys of Ridge City.

They had always understood that the Imperium held nothing sacred except themselves. The Imperium had eliminated all that humanity valued. A magnificent flower or centipede or human had no value in their heartless robotic society. But, like their ancient human ancestors, their inner souls drove them to move on and search for and fight for a better life.

"Let's go to Nolan River Lake. I've got to find my kids. Koa is a great survivalist. She'll keep them safe."

"Okay, let's get out of here. The Imperium will return soon."

"We need to go toward the dam area."

With their broken bodies, they stood and hobbled away from Ridge City deeper into the forest. On their slow, stumbling hike, they found a dead family of five people. They stopped and picked up dead citizens' plastic water bottles and a cloth knapsack filled with clothes, medicines, and matches. Ula and Yot took off the cadavers' belts, hiking boots, and socks. Yot found one working cooling vest and a thick plastic knife that had a sharp edge. They both put on long-sleeved shirts and other clothes from the dead Ridge City family. They looked for metal guns and knives, and pots and pans, but a kaleidoscope of gravity had devoured them.

Deeper into the matted jungle they went. They were desperate to escape the area. After walking about four kilometers from Ridge City, they set up camp beside a small rock cliff with water tricking out its side.

"They'll be hunting us soon," Yot said,

"Perhaps. But they may not have a record of us as prisoners."

"Ah, yes. The orb may have destroyed these records."

Yot found antibiotic pills in the repurposed backpack and gave the medicine to his mother. They wetted their garments with the water seeping from the cliff and washed their hands, faces, and necks. The cold water was a respite from their odyssey. Then they held each other and fell asleep after the setting sun.

\*\*\*

"Where are Region 8's warriors and vehicles?" NAIT7 asked. This NAIT commanded the North American Indianapolis Region, as the destroyed NAIT8 had commanded the Nashville region.

NAIT7 arrived at the almost vacant Nashville headquarters on Sunday evening, responding to an emergency message.

"We don't know. We didn't receive any messages," a Nashville warrior named ORG216 replied. "We sent four Verking drones to Ridge City to search the area. The drones found no signs of our army."

"That's not possible!" NAIT7 said.

"You can review the videos," ORG replied, not wanting to challenge an Initiator of Thought (IT).

"Send out orders worldwide to replenish Region 8's equipment. We also have a request from NAIT16 in Dallas to return the Dominator."

"NAIT7, the Dominator is missing. Anything metal is gone."

"All ITs worldwide are discussing Region 8's missing army," NAIT7 said. "How do you lose an army?"

ORG didn't respond to NAIT7's statements for fear of insulting an IT, but ORG thought they looked like fools to other Imperium regions.

"Send a message to all NAITs," NAIT7 said. "We need to appoint a new NAIT8."

Within one minute, the Imperium's collective system selected TEV171, a warrior who had been in charge of the Nashville Armory, for the job.

"TEV, you are now in charge of Region 8, including the armory. Congratulations. Your new title is NAIT8."

The old ominous NAIT8, called DORG by the Ridge City residents during the last century, no longer existed, a victim of the mystical gravity well. Now, the collective robot nation authorized a new NAIT8. The new master of Region 8, NAIT8, continued the cruel policies of his predecessor. But the residents' nickname, DORG, for the previous NAIT8, had died with the robot's destruction.

NAIT7 and the new NAIT8 went to Ridge City on Monday morning, June 23. They searched the area and caves one last time. They would destroy the Ridge City cave system using sixty-kilogram bombs. NAIT10 from the Atlanta region landed in a VCX, along with ten warriors and fifteen drones.

The three IT regional commanders stood in the lifeless killing field.

After another hour of searching the area and caves, NAIT10 said to NAIT7, "We found dead humans sprayed with orange paint inside Ridge City. But no sign of Region 8's army."

"Ridge City is also void of any metal or composite metals?" NAIT7 said.

"Yes, odd. What force could do this?"

Before NAIT10 could reply, the new NAIT8 interrupted their conversation, walking toward them. "We received a message from NAIT6 in Kansas City. They received an incoherent message on the Imperium communication system yesterday at 1358 on Sunday. An Imperium robot named EIN sent the following incomplete message: 'NAIT8, it's a gravity well, a black hole—'"

"It makes little sense," said NAIT10. "Why would a black hole only attract metal matter?"

"I agree," NAIT7 said. "At least a gravity well explains one way Region 8's equipment could have disappeared."

"Maybe."

"A small, wandering black hole could have crossed paths with Earth."

"I doubt it," NAIT8 said. "The probability is less than one in a sextillion. Even a tiny one would rip up and destroy Earth's biosphere and us with it."

"We are going back to our commands in Atlanta and Indianapolis," NAIT7 said. "We'll leave our warriors and drones here until you're resupplied. NAIT8, destroy the Ridge City caves before you leave."

\*\*\*

Later Monday night, a VCX flew new bombs into the Ridge City area, and Hertes warriors carried them to different parts of the underground city. The warriors set the bombs' timers and left the cave network. They boarded VCX and VX vehicles and hovered five kilometers away.

A minute later, the explosions started on a moonless night. The artifacts of humanity crumbled. Debris buried human bodies, programmable-matter cave walls, dinner plates, baby toys, and all traces of the human civilization. The four-hundred-and-ninety-five-year-old history of Ridge City had ended. The Imperium destroyed the last sanctuary for humans in North America.

Outside, dust and debris were hurled into the nighttime air. Boulders rolled down hillsides, and the force of the explosions ripped tree stumps and bushes from the ground. The mountain ridge that had harbored the city's main gate collapsed into an enormous pile of defeated rubble. Giant sinkholes opened in many places. Once again, the Imperium decimated Earth's crust to conceal what happened here—the battle to save Earth as a habitable planet for humanity.

The new NAIT8 and MOV221 hovered above the explosions in their VCX. The new assistant for NAIT8 was MOV after NIM's demise. All traces of Ridge City ended that night. And no one heard the last whimpers of humanity.

"Go to our headquarters. We're done here," NAIT8 said.

***

VCXs and VXs landed at regular intervals at the Nashville spaceport to restock Region 8's army with shipments from North and South America. The new NAIT8 sent out a communique.

Topic: Region 8's Missing Army and Replenishment
Date: 2354, Monday, June 23, 3147
From: NAIT8
To: Earth's Imperium ITs

Region 8 has now killed all humans in North America except for our forty human pets. We cannot account for fifteen missing humans. We have established four hunting parties to find the missing humans. The survival odds are low for humans wandering on the upside.

We don't know what vanquished Region 8's army, but we'll rebuild it with your help. The anomaly may have been a tiny, wandering black hole. We have no evidence to prove or disprove this conjecture except recorded electromagnetic surges. Also, we don't understand why the black hole only affected metal objects and not all matter. These phenomena defy the laws of physics. We will continue to study the blue orb and gravity well phenomena and report our findings on the global network.

Unlike our human predecessors, the Imperium Nation strives to improve and learn from all things. Unity of purpose ensures survival. We thank you for your support in replenishing our resources.

After sending the message, NAIT8 stepped back from the Nashville control displays and raised his two arms above his head. "It's good to be rid of the obnoxious humans," he declared.

"Yes, NAIT8," MOV replied. "They had no purpose."

# CHAPTER 13

## *Alone*

S everal days after their escape from the Imperium, Ula and Yot heard a noisy disturbance. They had no weapons—only a thick tree branch, sharpened at one end, and a sharp plastic knife that Yot carried—so they crouched behind a fallen tree. They peeked around the tree trunk to see two shadows walking fifteen meters from them.

"It's got to be Koa," Yot whispered to his mother.

"What if you're wrong?"

Yot didn't answer her as they pondered what to do on a moonlit Wednesday night, June 25. Yot stayed behind the tree and yelled, "Hermes here. Hermes."

The two shadows stopped walking and crouched behind fallen trees.

"Hermes, Hermes," someone shouted.

Ula and Yot didn't answer until they saw the two shadows emerge from the darkness with a dog wagging its tail.

"Koa, is that you?" Yot yelled.

"Yes, it's me. I've got Qan and Bao with me."

Ula and Yot and the two silhouettes jumped out into the open. Yot recognized his children and bolted toward them. They hugged each other in a joyous family reunion, sobbing and kissing and hugging. Grandmother Ula and the other kids joined the group to add more happiness to their nighttime rendezvous.

"Daddy, I missed you," Bao said, crying while he wrapped his arms around his father's leg. He was so happy to see his father and regain a sense of purpose and security. Bao was hobbling because he'd pierced his foot on a shattered, sharp tree branch. Qan held his dad's hand. An exhilarated and crying Yot found no words except, "I love you. I love you."

The last seventeen people in North America reunited in the dark forest. A bleak destiny awaited them, with all remnants of human civilization gone. No human cities, farms, or governments. Nothing but the torrid temperatures and violent storms of the upside dominated by a tyrannical robot nation.

Soon, everyone was hugging and talking. Jax wagged his tail but had learned not to bark. Koa appeared strong but was injured from past concussions and her broken ribs and collarbone. The kids looked anemic and covered with insect bites.

Yot, Qan, and Bao sat off to the side while Yot examined Bao's injured foot. He put an antibiotic ointment on his son's foot and bandaged it with an extra shirt.

After the excitement had died down, Ula asked Koa, "Do you have a camp?"

"No, not really. We move around the dam area of the lake. The dam is one kilometer away. We hear the puttering sounds of Imperium drones often. They hunt us."

"What happened to Ridge City?" Koa asked.

"They destroyed everything and killed our citizens," Ula replied. "It was gruesome."

"How did you escape?" Koa asked Ula.

"They captured us and tied us to a tree stump next to their hilltop command post. We watched a blue orb create a gravity-based weapon that devoured the Imperium army. And it allowed us to escape."

"Was it the same orb that saved your life in the lagoon tunnel?"

"Yes."

Koa pondered Ula's words before asking, "Not sure I understand everything, but where's Tal?"

"He's dead. They shot him twice as we ran out of the gate," Ula replied as her eyes watered.

"Oh. I'm so sorry," Koa said. She stepped toward Ula, and they hugged one another in a long embrace. Tal had been Koa's boss for many years, and she knew him well.

"I was with him when he died. He attempted to speak to me but couldn't."

"But you understood his unspoken words. He would tell you how much he loved you and the family."

"Yes, I know."

They wiped away their tears, and Ula took a deep breath and changed the subject.

"How did you survive?" Ula asked Koa.

"The gate crash stunned everyone, including the warriors, for a moment. But not us. We ran out the side of the gate opening the second the gate fell. Dust and debris hid us."

"Smart move. We thought you would make it; that's why we gave you the job."

"Can we sit? My ribs and head hurt."

"Sure," Ula replied, hobbling along on a broken lower leg bone. "Neither of us has recovered from our injuries." Koa nodded her approval.

They sat down and rested. The temperature tonight was cool at thirty-six degrees Celsius (i.e., 97 degrees Fahrenheit). Ula swallowed a few pills and checked her leg splint. Koa closed her eyes and relaxed for a few minutes.

"We've not eaten this past thirty hours," Ula said. "We need to eat, or Yot and I will pass out."

"Well, let's go fishing and hunting."

"Does your laser gun work?"

"Yes, I have two guns, but their electrical charges are low. And a backpack of survival gear, including fishing line and hooks."

The police department had trained Koa in basic survival, medical, and security skills for her job at the Ridge City Police Department. They had taught her the survival rule of three: three minutes without air, three days without water, and three weeks without food.

"Good, we have a backpack of stuff, too, and a water bottle."

"We must kill an animal and cook it or catch fish," Koa said. "Find a small stream that flows into the lake. Animals will gather there."

"How about an armadillo or groundhog?" Bao asked. Yot, Qan, and Bao had listened to their conversation from several meters away.

"How do you know about armadillos?" Ula asked, surprised by her clever grandson.

"Oh, I studied them on a school project. They stay in their burrows during the day. They emerge at dawn and dusk to look for food."

"Alright. We need bait. We'll fish and hunt for food," Ula said. "Use your flashlight or headlamp if you have one."

They had two flashlights and one headlamp that recharged using sunlight.

Ula, Yot, Ula, and Qan headed through the dark forest to search for bait. Qan lifted a big rock and found a nest of earthworms under it. They grabbed the bait. After twenty minutes of scouring the nighttime landscape, they had gathered an assortment of creatures that could be used as bait: a small dead snake, earthworms, and three bird eggs. Koa and Ula took the earthworms and went fishing. Koa helped the injured Ula maneuver through the forest to a small stream. Yot and Qan set a trap of bird eggs and a dead snake in the woods to attract an animal.

By 0015 Thursday morning, Koa and Ula had three fish. After hours of waiting, at about 0230, Yot shot with a laser gun an armadillo that wandered into their midst, enticed by the bait. They butchered the fish and armadillo by flashlight, and thanks to matches that both Koa and Yot had in their backpacks, they started a fire. Koa used her hunting knife to carve the food and cook it. The group ate every speck of meat.

Koa taught the kids to suck bones for extra juices. She also used the armadillo's shell as a bowl and its lower jaw as a dagger.

After eating, Ula, Yot, and Bao tended to their injuries while Koa, Qan, and the children built a security fence around their encampment. On previous nights, Koa had taught them how to set up a trip-wire alarm fence. They strung rope around the perimeter of the campsite and set the rope so it would cause large plant stalks and small logs to fall to the ground and make a sound.

Now, the group tried to sleep. They covered themselves with heavy layers of leaves and branches. The foliage helped hide their infrared signature from the patrolling drones.

The ragtag group then sat in the dark forest, resting and awaiting sunrise. They didn't know what to do. No other humans could rescue them. They were alone.

Koa asked, "What do we do? Where do we go?"

"We're homeless," Yot replied.

"We need to get far away from Ridge City," Ula answered. "They're hunting us. We must live off the land, build a hidden camp, maybe in a cave. Our two backpacks and Koa's laser guns give us a chance."

"Should we wait for others that might have escaped?" Yot said.

"We can wait one or two more days, but then we must leave," Ula replied. They had water, food, and a secure campsite. No one responded to her comment, meaning they agreed to wait. Exhausted and hurt, they wanted time to recover. But rest, recovery, and an established campsite had its risks.

\*\*\*

During the hot day, the heat and puttering drones flying over-head interrupted their attempts to rest, fish, and hunt. Like on their earlier mission to steal fuel, they moved at night and hid during the day. Ula, Yot, and Koa had become experts at these survival tactics. They also tried to treat and bandage the cuts and bug bites they'd acquired from their days in the jungle.

At around 1600 on Thursday, Koa and Jax went to get wa-ter. She took Qan with her, as he was the only healthy grown person available. They found a small new stream with cool running water about two meters wide and one meter deep that emptied into the lake.

Koa, Qan, and Jax lay down in the stream to cool off, soothe their insect bites, and clean their bodies. Using their purification pills, they purified a bottle of water and drank it. Then they repeated the process so they could take water back to the others. Members of the group took turns bathing in the stream while either Ula, Koa, Yot, or Qan guarded them armed with a laser gun. They even enjoyed splashing water onto one another and refreshing their bodies and their spirits. They felt civilized for a moment.

They returned to the small stream later that night and killed a gigantic snake they found meandering along the bank, which they cooked and ate. Bao used the armadillo shell to collect rainwater. They planned to boil animal bones and add green flower petals, mushrooms, edible roots, and wild ber-ries to make soup.

The fact that they still had no plan meant another night's stay. It seemed safe there, and they had food and water and were healing and gaining strength.

As the sun rose Friday morning, the crew of wandering humans sat around their camp and talked.

"Is this how we'll live?" Qan asked his grandmother.

Ula didn't have an answer at first, knowing their situation was dire.

"Yes, in the short term. It will be tough, but possible."

"So, a terrible existence."

"Qan, we have no other options," Ula replied as she stared at Yot. "Ridge City was our last hope, and it's gone."

"Qan, we must be nomads to survive," Yot said. "We'll find a well-hidden cave."

"So, we live day by day?"

"Yes," his father replied.

Qan and Bao looked at their father and didn't reply while everyone heard the conversation.

Later, the group curled up to rest or sleep as the day's heat tried to suck the moisture out of their bodies. Ula, Qan, and Bao fell asleep, but Yot and Koa and a few kids were awake.

"Any chance you found JORT or the VX that he was trying to fly here," Yot asked Koa.

"No, but beyond Nolan River Lake dam, you'll find a cluster of burnt trees. Drone parts lie on the ground. I looked for VX or JORT parts and found none."

"Should we go over there?"

"No, it's a long way around the lake."

"Yeah, it's a big, winding lake."

"Something happened there," Koa said. "It could have been a firefight between JORT and the Verking drones. They may have captured him and the VX."

"They wouldn't capture JORT. He'd fight until his death."

"You're right."

"JORT may have gone to another lake. He could be out here somewhere."

\*\*\*

As the Friday morning sun rose higher in the sky, they realized their search for food must continue. Like their ancient ancestors, they had become hunters and gatherers. They would fish, kill small animals, and gather roots, berries, mushrooms, and bird eggs. Hunger drove them to hunt for food, any food. But they waited until dark to avoid an even more diabolical experience—death or capture by the Imperium robots.

After dark, Koa, Yot, and Qan left the camp with Jax, their flashlight beams bouncing in the sultry night air. They walked to the stream, planning to follow it, searching for food as well as providing an opportunity to replenish their water. Jax growled, but they keep walking.

Without warning, a small alligator grabbed Qan's ankle and tried to roll in the one-meter-deep water. They splashed as Qan fell into the water, and Yot spotted a second alligator leave the stream's bank and head for his son. Yot pulled his gun out and shot twice, hitting and killing the second gator. But the first gator had not let loose of Qan's ankle.

Koa and Yot rushed to Qan and shot the body of the gator so they wouldn't hit Qan's leg. But the young alligator kept his jaws locked on the leg. Koa and Yot grabbed the mouth of the alligator and pulled its jaws open enough to free Qan's leg. The alligator flopped around in the water, and Koa shot it again. The second shot killed the predator.

They dragged Qan to the bank and used their flashlights to see the injury. His ankle had many small puncture wounds, but his bones remained unbroken. They cleaned his wounds in the stream. Koa helped Yot tear off a sleeve on his shirt, and they wrapped it around the bleeding wounds.

"I'll take Qan back to the campsite and use our antibiotic cream on his wounds," Yot said. "You bring the gators back. We need the food."

Qan and Yot left, and Yot helped his son walk through the forest. Koa grabbed the two small, dead alligators by the tails and dragged them several meters away from the stream. The change in climate had allowed the gators to migrate north.

Koa sat down to rest for a minute, knowing full well that the smell of the dead alligators would bring other predators. She caught her breath, gazed at the stars, and thought about their situation.

She realized the hostile upside chipped away at their

physical and mental health. The constant fear of being hunted replaced the comfort of Ridge City. Kids would wake up frightened because they thought they heard the puttering sounds of Verking drones, only to realize it was a cruel dream. Qan had an injured foot and puncture wounds on his ankle. Yot, Ula, and herself had broken bones. Insect bites and infection threatened everyone's lives. Fatigue, pain, and self-doubts hindered their will to survive. And they had no place to go. Koa understood these things and how her actions could influence others.

She stood up and dragged the two gators back to camp. They cut up the gators and cooked them on a bonfire. They used large leaves as plates and ate with their fingers. Everyone enjoyed a full meal.

***

At about 0300 Saturday morning, Ula awoke first when Jax growled. She peeked over a tree trunk to survey the darkened forest. She saw nothing but forest, but she heard the faintest of puttering sounds, and it grew louder.

Alarmed, she woke up everyone. It was too late to flee, so they hid beside the tree trunk. Fear flowed through their bodies. Koa and Yot took the safeties off their laser guns. Yot worried his laser gun had lost its electrical charge. The kids whimpered. Jax stood rigid and pawed one time at the ground.

They could see a line of Verking drones below the tree canopy moving toward them. To avoid the trees, the drone hunters moved from side to side, keeping a distance of five meters between them and staying three to four meters above the ground. The relentless hunters would use their infrared sensors, Ula realized. The line of drones passed over them and moved further away.

For a moment, Ula thought they had evaded detection. The heavy layers of foliage on top of their campsite had worked.

But then one drone stopped and turned around toward them. It must have recorded a flash of heat. The other drones also stopped and pivoted. The group's heat signature was now visible to all.

Without warning, the Verkings shot their lasers at the human castaways. The group took cover behind the tree trunk. Koa and Yot fired back at them, but Yot's guns stopped working after several shots.

By then, the drones had sent real-time video to NAIT8, showing the human renegades.

The drones stopped firing, perhaps because of NAIT8's orders. In the forest darkened by the nighttime, the drones surrounded the group.

"Koa, don't fire your gun," Yot yelled. "They'll kill us if you do."

Ula stood up, followed by the others, and within five minutes, one VX and one VCX cargo vehicle broke through the trees and landed in a somewhat open field. Their vehicle's foodlights illuminated the human pests.

Hertes warriors got out and approached the captives. Panic dominated the nomadic humans as the Hertes warriors towered over them. The kids cried and moaned and huddled around Ula, Yot, and Koa.

"If you resist, we'll kill you," a warrior said. "Lay your weapons on the ground."

Koa and Yot threw their useless guns on the ground, followed by the others dropping their kitchen knives and tree branch spears.

The Hertes warriors tied their ankles and hands, jerking Yot's arm so hard they re-injured it. Koa continued to wrestle with the warriors as she fought their restraints. Verking drones oversaw their nighttime capture. Then they loaded the seventeen humans into the VCX cargo vehicle and left for Nashville.

The Hertes warriors had refused to take Jax once again.

Koa had resisted and yelled as they loaded her into the VCX. The warriors had left Jax in the forest before, and he found his way to Koa's Ridge City apartment. But this time, he couldn't return to the destroyed and buried Ridge City.

"We stayed too long," Yot said to his mother while riding in the VCX. Ula and Koa didn't answer as they tumbled into states of anger and depression. The robots ignored their hateful stares. Their exhausted and broken bodies had endured the harsh upside. Ula had led the fight and failed. Without Jax, Koa lost her will to fight. Only Yot wanted to fight as his veins throbbed in his neck and forehead. He fought for his kids' future.

The kids in the VCX cried and whimpered. The Hertes warrior guards watched the disgusting behavior. Such behavior was not possible in the Imperium society.

Upon their arrival in the stark concrete building that housed Nashville's Region 8 headquarters, NAIT8 and MOV greeted the group.

"Ah, we know you three," the new NAIT8 said to Ula, Yot, and Koa.

The prisoners didn't respond.

"Who are these two young people?" NAIT8 asked, pointing to Qan and Bao.

"Two kids that escaped your butchery," Ula replied.

"Are they your kids?"

"No, we found them in the forest, running from your warriors and drones."

"Are they related to you ?" NAIT8 asked again, not expecting an answer.

"Do a DNA analysis and find out."

The warriors grabbed Qan and Bao and scrapped the skin on their arms into a vial. Next, they held Ula, Koa, and Yot and did the same procedure. The defeated threesome did not resist.

NAIT8 then ordered his warriors to take them to the cages. In the enormous basement room, the warriors pushed the seventeen captives into three empty cages next to seven other cages containing more human pets.

Out of the original forty prisoners taken at Ridge City, one had died from an infection. Yona Zain was from the first Ridge City team that had tried to steal helium-3 fuel and was among the prisoners. But Zain Byss and Jett Gill, also on the first team, had killed themselves in a brutal fight over Yona. The Nashville's headquarters basement housed fifty-seven human pets.

The prisoners recognized the new group members. Ula had been the mayor. Yot had been in charge of the nuclear reactors. Koa had been a popular police officer. Seeing these popular leaders, the prisoners felt a small sense of hope for better days ahead.

\*\*\*

Monday morning, June 30, Ula and the others watched NAIT8 and MOV walk around their cages. Their metal feet created a sharp, echoing sound in the concrete chamber. The warriors had given the new prisoners water but no food.

"What's your name?" the new NAIT8 asked.

"Ula."

"Ula, these two kids are what you call grandsons—right?"

"Ugh, yes, they are." Ula realized there was no use in denying it because NAIT8 now had the DNA results.

"So, they aren't two random Ridge City kids—right?"

"Right."

"Are you Yot?" a blusterous NAIT8 asked.

"Yes."

"Are these two kids your sons?"

"Yes," Yot said, with an aching chest.

NAIT8 stepped up to the cage and stared at Ula and Yot through the metal cage bars. "You and your colleagues will do as I say, or I'll kill your kids in front of you. Understood?"

Yot surged toward NAIT8, but his mother held him back by extending her arm. Bao cried, and a numb Qan stared at the floor, hearing the threat.

"Yes, I understand," Ula replied. "We'll do as you ask."

Yot nodded in agreement but didn't speak.

NAIT8 backed away and said to MOV, "Let them shower, treat their wounds and injuries as best you can, and get them food and water. We'll use them in our experiments."

"What happens after our experiments?" MOV asked NAIT8.

"We'll see if other regions want them. If they don't, we'll kill them."

NAIT8 told the prisoners that they would move them from the headquarters' basement to a nearby vehicle hangar for the experiments.

The Imperium warriors gave materials for Ula and Yot to redo their splints, even though the warriors didn't need medical supplies. To treat their flesh wounds, they gave them water and industrial ethyl alcohol. The Imperium used this chemical as a chemical solvent in certain production processes. Although not ideal, the alcohol served as an antiseptic to fight infection—another sign of human inferiority compared to robots.

# CHAPTER 14

## *The Trip*

gnoring the objections of Koa, the robot warriors would not take Jax. Jax found himself at their campsite close to the Nolan River Lake dam. Alone and in the darkness, separation anxiety caused him to shake and vomit. Koa was gone. Everyone was gone. But where?

Meanwhile, Ula, Yot, Koa, and the fourteen children found themselves in cages in the Nashville headquarters, 160 kilometers (i.e., 99 miles) from the lake campsite. The Imperium would soon use them for experiments and then either force them into a life of servitude and Imperium amusement or kill them.

On an earlier journey, Jax had found his way to Koa's Ridge City apartment after traveling several kilometers. Now, the Imperium had destroyed Ridge City and its secret entrance.

In survival mode, Jax walked in circles, trying to determine different directions using Earth's magnetic fields. But he didn't know where the Imperium warriors had taken his beloved Koa. At the campsite, Jax tried to use his sense of smell to find Koa, but the scent disappeared after twenty meters.

What should he do?

A confused Jax lay by the extinguished campfire at 0400 Saturday morning pondering his next move. He also listened to the sounds of the forest, hoping to pick up a familiar sound and a beacon to Koa. But he found none. The forest had its own survival problems and no time for a stray dog.

The sun would soon rise, and daylight would prevail. His homing skills were not strong enough to choose the correct direction.

Jax lay there whining. He had used all available ways to track and find Koa, but none worked. He was in agony, and somehow, he knew Koa was, too.

The sunrise on Saturday, June 28, included a brisk wind. He caught a whiff of something familiar, maybe a human odor or hydraulic fluid. Rising, Jax turned toward the lake. At a careful pace, checking and rechecking the scent, he walked toward Nolan River Lake. At the lake's edge, he realized the scent came from across the water.

The lake was about 120 meters wide, so Jax went around it and passed the dam. He reached a burnt cluster of trees across the lake. The scents were strong there. Jax realized it was hydraulic fluid.

He searched the scorched trees and ground and tried to discover fresh odors. After thirty minutes of sniffing everything in sight, it dawned upon him—JORT had been here. Jax had worked with JORT in Ridge City, flown with him in the VX to Watts Bar and back, and camped with JORT many times. He could identify JORT using the unique aroma of his hydraulic fluids. Jax wagged his tail in celebration. He had found a scent he recognized.

Exhausted, he tried to sleep on the edge of the burnt area as the sun receded over the horizon. Hoping to evade predators, he relied on the burnt scents to mask his scent. After six hours of sleep, he resumed his search for JORT. He trekked across the thick forest and came to the water's edge many times. JORT's scent vanished at this point.

Jax stood on the lake's edge and studied the banks and waters. He scoured the surroundings, looking for JORT. At the center of the widest part of the lake lay JORT and the ditched

VX. Jax had no way of knowing the water concealed their graves. His search for JORT also ended in failure.

Marooned in the middle of the sweltering and tormented forest, Jax stayed close to the water. He drank from a shallow stream only ten centimeters deep that drained into the lake. The low water levels allowed him to find and avoid predators like pythons and alligators. He pondered his next move and found no obvious solutions. He ate crayfish, shells and all, and drank lots of water as the torrid sun heated Earth's biosphere.

Depressed and losing hope, he fell asleep under a fallen tree and slept until 1700 on Sunday. During his sleep, he dreamed of a blue orb hovering beside him. Jax replayed the experience of Koa's capture in his dream and followed the VCX vehicle south to Nashville. He saw key landmarks along the journey, such as rivers, abandoned roadbeds, and crumbled buildings protruding from the foliage. His visions included the Nashville headquarters, the armory buildings, and the spaceport. He also had a blurry vision of Koa sleeping in a cage.

When Jax awoke, he looked around for a floating blue orb but found none. Unsure if his visions were real or a dream, Jax was confused. Whatever happened, instinct told him to follow the old roadbeds to the Interstate 65 roadbed. If he followed the interstate roadbed south, he could search for terrain and buildings that matched his visions. He understood where to go, having no other option.

\*\*\*

Jax's trip south was uneventful until he was about twenty kilometers outside the destroyed city of Nashville. Imperium vehicles and drones flew overhead. He had traveled at night to avoid the heat and Imperium warriors. It had taken him days to arrive outside this mysterious place. But the landmarks Jax had envisioned had guided him along his long journey.

Jax was starving and becoming weaker every day. Despite

his lack of success in catching a fish, he had found and consumed earthworms and crayfish. He had also eaten fallen fruit and berries. He had found drinking water during his trip, but sometimes the food and water had made him sick.

The journey had exhausted him. He would pant and scratch whenever he stopped walking. The incessant insect bites had caused his eyes, mouth, and ears to swell. His scratching had caused his ears to bleed. His matted and crusty hair had become a partial shield against insects. He tried not to whine or bark for fear of attracting a predator. His feet bled from walking long distances on the upside terrain. Because of the thick vegetation, he often had to go around huge mounds of trees and matted foliage, making his journey longer and more treacherous.

On Thursday night, July 3, Jax rested next to a small creek and fell into a deep sleep. He had traveled 30 to 40 kilometers (i.e., 19 to 25 miles) every twenty-four hours, with little sleep.

Later that night, a tug on his leg awoke him. He found a puttering Verking drone hovering two meters above his body. The despicable machine tugged at him with its dangling legs and claws. Once awake and recognizing the predator, Jax bolted away from the drone, who chased him. The drone shot its laser two times at him as they dashed through the forest. The shots missed Jax, but one shot slammed into a bush, setting it ablaze.

Jax raced through the forest, trying to escape the drone darting around trees. He hid under a fallen tree stump and tried to recover from his mad dash. His heart pounded, and his whole body ached with pain. Unknowable to Jax, the drone had the advantage because it was using its infrared cameras to track Jax. But the stump hid Jax's heat signature.

The drone began a patterned search of the area. Despite the darkness, Jax spotted two large trees close together, reaching into the night sky. He knew the drone would keep trying to hunt him, so he had to respond fast.

Jax left the safety of the stump and ran toward the drone. Once it saw Jax, it turned and sped toward its prey. Jax rushed toward the two big trees with the drone in hot pursuit. He hoped the drone would focus on the chase and him and smash into the trees.

On their first trip between the two trees, the drone slipped to the side of a tree and continued to chase Jax, firing its lasers as it flew. The Karelian bear police dog slid under a matted bush, took cover and four deep breaths, and sprinted again toward the two trees.

As Jax ran between the gap in the trees a second time, the drone gave chase and smashed into one tree. BAMB! THUD! The drone's body cracked open while its four dangling arms and claws jerked in all directions. The drone hit the ground with a thud and rolled several meters. Although damaged, it wasn't dead.

Jax grabbed one of its flailing legs and dragged it into the creek. The drone wiggled but couldn't fly as Jax pulled on its body. The drone's electronics and power source, now open to the water, shorted out in the water. Sparks flew and illuminated the water a blueish-white for several seconds. Jax let loose of the drone's leg and swam back to shore. Sliding on the slippery bank, the exhausted dog collapsed onto the muddy creek bank. But now the drone threatened no one; it was silent and inoperable. The cunning Jax had defeated a single robot drone in a battle between artificial and biological intelligence.

Too tired to work his way up the creek bank, he lay there listening to crickets and frogs chirp and croak. But his rest was short-lived because of two vultures roosting in a nearby tree. He moved away from the creek and found a thick bush to hide underneath. He slept through the morning hours and didn't awake until midday Friday.

Jax's mission was to find Koa. He had fuzzy visions of the Imperium headquarters buildings and armories, but he had an even more powerful weapon now. After working his way closer to the city and spaceport, he caught intermittent whiffs of unique odors. They were the wonderful scents of humans. He checked and cross-checked the scents and headed toward the spaceport.

***

By midnight, Friday, July 4, Jax had found two massive buildings that had the odor of humans and hydraulic fluids. High chainlink fences surrounded them. In his quest for a breach in the fence, he walked several kilometers around the fence's perimeter. There were no holes or broken fencing, but he noticed a section bent upwards. He dug a hole there and wiggled his way through the fence.

Jax worked his way toward the tallest building and hid in a bush using the cover of darkness. For an hour, he witnessed the constant activity of Imperium warriors entering and exiting the busy building. He bypassed the front entrance and found a garage door open on one side of the building's basement. He snuck inside and hid behind stacks of boxes and coiled electrical wire. After listening and smelling for forty minutes, he peeked around the corner to see a set of steps going upward. Climbing to the top of the steps, he could see an enormous basement room. He lay flat on the step's platform and watched for signs of Koa and other humans.

Although he could smell humans and Koa, he saw only a few Hertes warriors walk through the basement. Jax was certain Koa had been there. But after an hour of surveillance, Jax left the building, knowing they had moved his beloved Koa.

Jax followed the scent of the humans and hydraulic fluid out of the building and toward a nearby aircraft hangar. Several garage doors were open, so Jax hid in the bushes and looked inside the hangar. Straight off, he saw the humans, their cages, and people carrying things. His tail wagged, and his heart rate increased. Koa must be there. Hertes warriors stood against the hangar walls, providing security and recording all activities.

As Jax got closer, the blazing hot and putrid smell of humans and robot hydraulic fluids became stronger. Jax recognized the dreadful aroma of human defecation and urine coming from the hangar. Humans had become accustomed to the awful stench, but Jax hadn't.

Jax hesitated to enter the hangar because of the odors, and he viewed the warriors as a threat to himself. The warriors may shoot him on sight. So, he waited outside in the dark. His eyesight was not quite good enough to see human faces inside the hangar.

He perceived a high level of activity going on within the hangar. He didn't realize the Imperium was conducting an experiment and using warriors and humans as actors in the experimental design. But fifty-seven human prisoners did.

\*\*\*

Koa sat on the floor of her cage, eating a plant that looked like pink cabbage. The warriors threw wild onions, pink cabbage, fruit, and a variety of berries on the cage floor for the pets to eat. The Imperium had also learned how to cook snakes and alligators to feed the humans. But the robot warriors didn't understand the difference between meat you eat and don't eat. They cooked everything, including the intestines, bladder, and the head of the animals, to feed their human pets. Most people ate the thick muscle but not the other body parts.

"What happens to us after the experiments are complete?" Koa asked.

"I don't know, but we need to escape," Ula replied, perched by the open cage door.

"NAIT8 will kill us. We are useless to them," Yot whispered. Qan and Bao were not listening because it was their turn to carry objects in front of the test warriors.

A Russian Initiator of Thought in Region 2, RUIT2, had proposed this new experiment to test emotional software updates. The experiment was based on Plato's allegory of the cave. They would do the same experiment in fourteen Imperium regions worldwide and pool the test results.

The robots had built a stage-like structure on one side of the hangar. On the other side, the Imperium moved ten cages from the headquarters' basement to the hangar floor. The cage side had no lights, unlike the well-lit experiment side.

Each cage bolted to the floor had new makeshift beds, chairs, and tables built out of welded rough steel. The robots had also built several showers behind the cages with water hoses bolted to steel beams. The shower water pooled on the concrete floor with no drains, but no one cared.

In the first phase of the experiment, they selected seven Hertes warriors at random from Region 8's army. They removed the warriors' arms and legs and changed their neck motors, limiting their field of vision to a grey concrete wall in front of them. These seven warriors didn't have the test emotional software updates installed. They were using the original Imperium emotional module with limited capability. During the second phase, they would repeat the same protocols but incorporate the test emotional module.

Humans carried various objects on the top of their heads, such as a rock, wrench, or water jug, over a walkway. Two powerful floodlights behind the walkway cast a shadow of the real things onto the blank concrete wall. To the immobile warriors, their whole reality was the two-dimensional and colorless shadows. The warrior's goal was to name each object.

"Yeah, we must escape before the experiments are over," Ula said.

"We should go alone," Koa said. "We'll never get fifty-seven people to agree to an escape plan."

"You're right," Yot replied, eating a cooked snake. "Fifty-seven people can't keep a secret."

In return for these creature comforts like beds and cooked snakemeat, the Imperium expected the pets to take part in the experiment and give feedback through interviews and surveys. Ula, Yot, and Koa also had extra motivation to cooperate in the experiments because NAIT8 had threatened to kill Qan and Bao if they didn't cooperate.

"Can we agree to keep our plan a secret?" Ula asked. "We don't tell Qan and Bao."

Koa and Yot nodded in agreement.

Over the next day, the trio worked on their escape plan. The primary plan included creating a fire in three cages to distract the warriors while the five of them exited the hangar. Ula, Yot, and Koa would collect burnable materials and scatter them around each cage, then pile them up before they lit the fires. An open side door signaled them to start the fires. They would set the materials on fire, grab Qan and Bao, and run toward the open door.

The Imperium's computer and video systems counted the humans in the hangar. But with people sleeping, taking showers, eating, and carrying objects past the test warriors, it took a while to arrive at a full count. If their escape went unnoticed, they speculated they would have a five-minute head start.

The test warriors named many objects. For a one-meter-long object, the test warriors used names like "four corners" and "rectangle." Two-dimensional shadows of objects cast on the concrete wall defined their reality. The item the test warriors were trying to name was a one-meter-long wood log with deep textured brown bark.

While carrying items during the day, Qan and Bao overheard NAIT8 and IOG789 discuss the results. IOG replaced EIN. "Out of 1,208 items identified by the test warriors so far, 1,051 or eighty-seven percent were misidentified," IOG told NAIT8.

"Did the test warriors become more creative, and did one of them become the leader?" NAIT8 asked.

"No, we tested six hypotheses," IOG replied. "None were

statistically significant, so we rejected all of them. But soon we will redo the experiment using the test emotional module and evaluate the same hypotheses."

***

Jax spent the next two days and nights trying to figure out if Koa was in the hangar. He thought he smelled Koa's odor in the air. But should he enter the hangar? He feared the powerful robot warriors would kill him. So, he waited, looking for his chance to go inside the hangar.

Ula, Yot, Qan, Bao, and Koa did what they were supposed to do. They carried items in front of the test warriors, answered interview survey questions, and when the Imperium asked, they gave their opinions on love and hate, as well as the experiment's results.

Depending on their shift, they learned to sleep whenever they could and ignore the activity and noise. The human need for sleep amused and dumbfounded the robots. They thought it was a stupid habit and a waste of resources and time.

Every day, Koa agonized over her beloved Jax. Was he alive? Did a merciless python or alligator drown him? How would he know where to go? Her inner turmoil and pain did not lessen as the days passed. Only Ula, Yot, Qan, and Bao understood her misery.

On Monday night, July 7, Koa and Ula slept side-by-side on the cage floor. Qan and Bao rested nearby in a bed, while Yot carried objects by the test warriors. At 0318 Tuesday morning, Koa jerked and woke up herself and Ula. Koa jumped up and looked through the cage bars, scanning the hangar.

"What's wrong with you?" Ula muttered.

"I had a dream," Koa said, speaking louder than she should.

"Let's sit. You'll attract attention."

Koa sat down close to Ula and said, "Let's lay face-to-face so we don't alarm the warriors."

"What's up?"

"I saw a vision. Jax is alive and here."

"How could he be here? They captured us over one hundred kilometers from Nashville."

"He's nearby. I sense it."

"Maybe in spirit only. It's a dream, Koa. Only a dream," Ula replied.

Ula thought Jax was dead. But she wasn't about to tell Koa her thoughts. Jax gave Koa hope. Without that, Ula and Yot worried about Koa's mental condition. Depression already had tried to take over their beings. With only a glimmer of hope, they continued.

Four caged prisoners had committed suicide. One by strangling his girlfriend and then hand-walking the ceiling cage bars and hanging himself from the cage roof. And the others by running toward open doors only to be shot dead by warrior lasers.

NAIT8 didn't seem to care about these suicidal deaths. Ula, Yot, and Koa took his attitude as a signal that he would send humans to other regions once the experiments ended. If no one wanted the humans, he would kill them.

The existence of Ridge City and the humans' aggressive efforts to steal fuel agitated NAIT8 and Region 8. Ula, Yot, and Koa thought NAIT8 wanted Region 8 void of humans, period.

At about 0400 Tuesday, Koa couldn't sleep and stood up again and searched the dim warehouse for an hour. She stared at every dark spot and shadow to find Jax. Finding nothing, Koa rubbed her aching eyes and felt the throb of an aching heart.

When she dropped her hands beside her, the incredible power of love manifested itself as a battered, filthy, and limping Jax crept out of the darkness toward Koa's cage. Their eyes locked onto one another, and their hearts filled with joy and insurmountable love. Within three meters of the cage, a thin and starving Jax remained silent as he hobbled through the cage door and into Koa's arms. At first, Koa thought she was dreaming as she held Jax tight in her arms. She didn't know or care how Jax entered the hangar.

"Wow!" Ula said. "How did Jax find you?"

Crying and hugging him in her lap, Koa tried not to make too much noise. Jax made a few soft whines, but he, too, understood their dangerous situation. Cherished memories flashed through Koa's mind. With Jax, she could face anything on the upside, including imprisonment and the Imperium.

Jax's arrival shocked Ula, but she kept quiet, trying not to alarm the warrior sentries. The others in their cage woke up and joined them in a brief celebration in the dim light. They fed Jax their food and poured water into a bowl for him to drink. He ate everything given to him. Koa combed his matted hair with her fingers. They covered Jax with big palm leaves and a few ragged clothes they didn't need. Ula patted an exhausted Jax and watched him eat. Koa held Jax close, her arms wrapped around him, and they fell asleep together. Despite being battered, Koa was whole again, and so was Jax.

\*\*\*

During the second week, Ula, Yot, Koa, Qan, and Bao watched the new set of seven test warriors name things. The new warriors were in the same situation as the earlier test warriors, but this second group had the emotional test module installed in their neural networks.

NAIT8 and IOG visited Koa's cage the day after Jax's arrival, and IOG asked her, "How did your dog get here? Our video shows we left him at the Nolan River Lake campsite weeks ago."

"I'm not sure how, but he's here. He eats my food and potties in the same bucket we do. He's no threat to you," Koa replied, fearful they would take Jax away for a third time.

"Keep your stupid dog, but if he interferes with the experiment, we'll kill him," NAIT8 said.

"Thank you!" Koa replied, still holding Jax and scratching his ear.

\*\*\*

Later that day, Ula was waiting to carry an object by the warriors. She heard a test warrior say, "Who is carrying the objects?" Although she couldn't see the warriors or the shadows on the wall, she could hear their conversations.

"I don't know. Let's call it Biped," warrior number five said.

"Why?" another warrior asked.

"Because Biped is present in every scene."

"It's interesting they wanted to name the carrier of things," NAIT8 said to MOV. They stood on an elevated platform with a good view of the experiment.

"Yes, a different start than the first group of test warriors."

The humans learned from listening to the test warriors that warriors two and four had developed an intellectual bond. They became competitive in naming each object. Who would be faster? Who chose the best words to describe each object?

Warrior five had also established an intellectual bond with warrior four. Now, warriors two and five were both competing for warrior four's intellectual companionship. Warrior two became jealous of five, and they exchanged harsh words. After the volatile conversation, warrior four emerged as the leader of the test warriors.

That afternoon, Ula said to Yot, "I hear the group of seven test warriors is becoming more dysfunctional and ineffective, and splitting into a group of four led by warrior four and another group of three warriors led by no one."

"Yeah, that's right. The implanted emotional test module seems to encourage creativity, individualism, and aggressive behavior."

"I hear warrior four wants to leave the cave and go outside," Koa said, holding Jax in a tight grip.

"They're not the only ones who want to leave the cave," Yot replied.

"The second part of the experiment is nearing its end," Ula said. "We need to escape soon."

"Yes, we do," Koa said. "We've been watching the hangar doors. They leave two garage doors open for short periods of time. Vehicles move inside the hangar, and warriors unload food and objects for the experiment."

"We must act before they end the experiment," Ula said.

\*\*\*

Thursday afternoon, July 10, Qan and Bao came back from carrying things and taking showers. They entered their cage to see Ula walk out of the cage area while their dad lay down to rest. Koa washed Jax's face and attended to his wounds and swollen face.

"Several kids told me that other warriors had reattached test warrior four's legs and arms and unlocked his neck. They turned on his sensors and cameras. Warrior four walked around the hangar, then exited through an open door. They say their god approved it," Qan said.

"Who's their god?" Yot asked Qan.

"Someone named Biped. It carries and delivers all things."

"Qan, that god is us. We carry objects to create reality for the test warriors."

"Oh! I'm a fool," Qan said, wondering why he hadn't figured that out.

"No, you're not a fool. The test warriors only experience what the Imperium wants them to see."

"I understand warrior four came back inside the hangar and told the other six test warriors what an interesting and colorful world awaits them outside," Bao said.

"Three-dimensions always trump two," Qan said.

"So, what did the six warriors do?" Yot asked.

"I don't know," Qan replied. "But the experiment will end Friday."

"How do you know that?" Yot asked.

"Many of us heard IOG and MOV talking," Qan said.

"Thanks; I need to tell Ula and Koa this," Yot said.

When the trio was together, Yot whispered to Ula and Koa, "The kids overheard IOG saying the experiment ends Friday."

"We must go, even if the doors are closed, tonight," Ula replied.

"We'll open a door ourselves," Koa said.

"Either way, we must go," Yot said, glaring at his two staunch allies.

# CHAPTER 15

# *Awakening*

"We escape tonight," Ula said.

"I agree. Once the experiments end, they will kill us without a moment's notice," Koa replied.

"Okay," Yot said. "If they open a door, we go for it. If no doors are open, we break one open."

The trio nodded in agreement.

"Yot, tell Qan and Bao what we're about to do," Ula said.

"Okay."

Complete desperation drove the escape attempt. They had lost all other options.

"I'm scheduled to carry things Friday afternoon," Ula said. "We should be gone by then."

With the escape set, Ula, Yot, and Koa became more nervous. They hid their fear by pretending to sleep. They stayed away from one another, too. No more clandestine group meetings or whispering. They were determined to bust out of the hangar.

Ula, Yot, and Koa had accumulated burnable materials in three cages and hoped a door would open. With no place to go, they would escape barefoot, wearing raggedy clothes, with no camping gear, weapons, cooling vests, or rations.

Around 2100, Thursday, Yot scooted over to lie beside his beautiful young sons. He placed his hands on them and gave them a light shake.

"Wake up. We need to talk."

Once awake, Yot said, "Lay flat like you're sleeping."

"What's going on, Dad?" Bao asked.

Yot took a deep breath and whispered, "We're busting out of here tonight."

"What?"

"Yes, once NAIT8 has finished his experiments, he'll either kill us or put us in Imperium zoos and hunting games. The six of us are leaving tonight. When I give the signal, follow me out of the hangar and run to the forest. Questions?"

"Not much of a plan," Qan replied.

"That's true, but it's all we got."

"What about the others?" Bao asked his father.

"Six of us can keep a secret; fifty-seven cannot. We may come back later and try to break them out."

Qan and Bao stared at their father and began to cry. Qan curled up as his stomach winced in pain. Bao covered his mouth to suppress his moaning. Seeing the fear in his children's eyes was more than Yot could tolerate. Yot reached for their hands and said in a shaky voice, "I love you. Now, lay still, and do not attract warrior attention."

Both kids squeezed their dad's hands and whispered back, "I love you."

***

Earlier Thursday, Koa and Yot walked by one door and lifted the lever to find it locked. The warriors had locked another door with a linked chain. Because no supplies were being delivered, two hangar garage doors were closed. By 0100 Friday morning, July 11, all doors in the hangar remained closed, and there was no easy way to exit the hangar.

On the other side of the hangar, people carried objects past the test warriors. IOG and a few warriors were collecting data. Robot warriors didn't sleep and worked around the clock. Their small nuclear generator always produced electricity even when their nanotechnology solar skin did not. NAIT8 was not in sight.

"If the experiment is ending soon, that may be why they're not delivering supplies," Yot said.

"Dead people don't need supplies," Koa said, her face reddening.

It was a night of sheer panic. Qan and Bao fought back tears while Ula, Yot, and Koa scouted for ways out of the hangar. They scanned the high windows on the hangar walls but couldn't reach them. Yot walked by one locked garage door, only to be shooed away by a sentry warrior.

The hangar was hot, with no air conditioning. It mattered little to the Imperium robots whether the temperature was zero or one hundred degrees Celsius.

No one could sleep or rest. Waves of fear and anger flowed through their bodies. Bao's hands quivered, Qan vomited in his hands, and beads of sweat poured down Ula's face and neck.

Yot became angry because no doors were open. And, now that he had told his sons of their escape plans, he saw their fear, too. He envisioned the warriors shooting them once the experiment ended.

Koa held onto Jax. Jax sensed the anxiety in Koa's body. Together, Jax and Koa made their own reality. They lay in their cage, pretending to sleep and praying for an unlocked door.

\*\*\*

At 0308 Friday, Jax stood up with his head high in the air. He twitched his nose and sniffed the electrified air.

In an instant, an eerie blue light filled the hangar. The sentry warriors searched for the source but found nothing. They wanted to shoot their laser guns but had no target.

Koa rose up, followed by Ula and Yot. Qan and Bao were awake with their arms wrapped around one another. Soon, everyone in their cage, and in the other cages, was standing and scanning the hangar. What caused the blue glow?

IOG and MOV walked out into the middle of the hangar, searching the area, but also found nothing but a captivating blue light saturating the hangar space-time arena. It filled every nook and cranny of the hangar. The situation dumbfounded IOG, MOV, and the warriors. Robot software could not find an enemy or source, so their neural networks defaulted into inaction.

"Dad, I don't have a shadow," Qan said as he moved about, showing the blue light came from all directions. Shadows in the hangar had been an everyday occurrence before the blue light.

"Yeah, I see," Yot replied. "The blue light is everywhere."

The humans had continued to carry objects but had stopped when they saw the blue light. Somehow, it negated the shadows on the wall for the experiment, too. They scurried back to their cages.

Without hesitation, then the blue glow merged into a stream of blue plasma and moved toward the Torg cage. The blue plasma merged into Bao Torg's body. A thin blue halo encircled Bao's eight-year-old body like it had in 2147 to Jillian Hickory's body. He held his chin upright, and his graceful eyes gave solace to the humans present.

The other prisoners gawked in disbelief. People huddled together in awe, and most could not speak or comprehend the situation. Some believed the spirit of God was present. Others thought an alien blue mist had arrived to help them. Ula, Yot, Koa, and Qan backed up against the cage bars, also unable to speak.

The human prisoners recognized something greater than themselves was with them. The entire room wept for humanity.

Joy and peace infiltrated their beings and ran through their consciousnesses. The feeling calmed their souls and vanquished earthly troubles. People smiled again.

The Imperium robots, including IOG and MOV, were still analyzing and reanalyzing their experience, trying to make scientific sense of the phenomena. They couldn't identify an adversary.

*"You're safe. No one will hurt you,"* Bao said as the voice of the blue orb. His voice, like Jillian Hickory's had been, was calm and peaceful.

Ula had seen the phenomena before as a blue orb in the underwater tunnel, unlike the others. They were awestruck by its angelic presence, this time inside Bao's body.

"What do you want?" Ula asked, knowing the orb would not harm her grandson.

*"I have a proposal,"* Bao said, addressing the prisoners.

"What?" Yot asked, perplexed by this spirit speaking through his son.

*"You and your fellow humans can leave with me and enter a new reality."*

"What? Where would we go?" Koa asked, her body filled with goosebumps.

*"To a safe place."*

"What if we stay here?" Yot asked.

*"The robot intruders will kill you."*

Frightened, Ula paused and replied, "So either way, we die."

*"Yes. Past human mistakes are irreversible. You could not mitigate and overcome two great filters, the warming of Earth's biosphere and artificial intelligence. You lost control, so humanity goes extinct."*

"So, we lost our home?"

*"Yes, you did. Earth is a jewel in the universe. Its feedback mechanisms will rebalance its biosphere in time. But the time required to recalibrate far exceeds human life spans. Intelligent robots have become the masters of the biosphere."*

"Not sure I understand. Where do we go?" Ula said. Neither did the others.

The clairvoyant orb sensed the confusion and, through Bao, said, *"You will leave Earth and be reunited with loved ones. Your bodies will stay on Earth, but your spirit will come with us to new worlds you cannot imagine."*

"Can we reunite with Tal, my dear husband?"

*"Yes, and the other prisoners will reunite with their loved ones."*

Ula's eyes widened, and she turned toward her family. She said, "Did you hear this? We can be with Tal and other loved ones." Tears and a broad smile filled her face. The Torgs hugged one another while Koa picked up Jax and held him tight.

"Do you want to go?" Ula yelled.

Joy, fear, and confusion dominated the prisoners. The prisoners discussed the proposition and argued among themselves.

Qan stopped the chatter when he yelled, "We have no future here. Let's go!"

"I agree," Koa shouted.

"Let's go," Yot yelled as he raised his arms in defiance and celebration.

Ula turned toward the prisoners. "Do you want to go?"

Many yelled yes, while others nodded their approval. The hostages realized they were prisoners of the upside and the Imperium. Even if they escaped, the brutal upside climate would kill them. Accepting the orb's proposal was their best option.

Ula turned back to Bao and asked, "You said we'll reunite with loved ones?"

*"Yes, in ways you can't fathom."*

"Can Jax go?" Koa asked.

*"Yes. Jax has a soul."*

At this, Koa's eyes teared up. The blue orb's statement

through Bao reassured her that she and Jax were kindred spirits. She would enjoy the afterlife with him, whatever it may be. She appreciated the unconditional love she saw in Jax's eyes; it came from deep within his soul.

They saw NAIT8 arrive to see a blue halo around Bao Torg and his father raising his arms in defiance. NAIT8 was about to order his warriors to fire at Bao when Ula shouted one final time, "Do you want to go?"

Everyone yelled back in unison, "Yes!"

With her eyes sparkling with hope, Ula faced Bao and said, "Okay, let's go!"

Upon her last syllable, the blue glow left Bao's body and rose above them as a volleyball-sized blue orb. Suddenly, a brilliant flash of blue-white light engulfed them and the inside of the hangar.

In this Earthbound space-time arena, fifty-seven human bodies plus one dog body slumped to the floor. The flash also blinded the robots. As a safety precaution, their robot software stopped their movement for one minute. They froze in place.

In an instant, the organic lifeforms' massless souls hurled through an imperceptible space-time window to a new reality. A sense of overwhelming happiness pervaded each of their souls. The world of things mattered little. Their consciousnesses now focused on love and Plato's world of forms. They had left Earth and entered a supernatural world where souls flourished and achieved higher levels of consciousness.

\*\*\*

Upon entering an eleven-dimensional existence, the blue orb greeted fifty-seven souls, plus Jax's soul. In their new space-time arena, all communication was telepathic.

"*Welcome.*"

Eleven oscillating dimensions defined their bizarre new world. They found their consciousnesses in a complex and curved space-time manifold. There was no matter in the manifold world, and therefore, no interactions, no physics, and no time. Physical human minds were not capable of seeing, experiencing, or understanding existence in the manifold. Only their massless souls understood their new world.

*"Would you like to reunite with your friends and loved ones?"* the blue orb asked.

Ula, Yot, Koa, Qan, Bao, and Jax's souls grouped together in this new world, visible to all as glistening white orbs. The glowing blue orb floated nearby with a smooth tempo to its movement, its presence creating a confident world where one may improve the soul.

Everyone's newfound clairvoyant capabilities assimilated their experiences into a kaleidoscope of togetherness. They needed no words to communicate. Instantaneous thoughts and information connected all things.

"Who do you mean?" Ula telepathically asked the orb.

*"Would you like to meet Tal's spirit?"*

"Oh. Yes. Yes," Ula gasped.

A tiny white orb arose from the infinite black horizon and moved toward them. Exhilaration and love engulfed them as Tal's soul drifted toward them. Their souls were free of Earth's burdens and filled with love and gratitude. And then, without fanfare, they merged into a loving family group in a celebration of eternal love and existence. After the joyous reunion, they separated into their respective individual orbs.

The other prisoners' orbs relished in the reunion with loved ones, for they, too, felt an immediate sense of freedom and enlightenment. Friends and family merged into groups.

They knew their massless souls had entered a world governed by a single law that included all sciences. This beautiful, single, fractal-like, and nonlinear scaling law governed all eleven dimensions. Many intelligent lifeforms called this single law God, but it could be a lonely scientific axiom about how the universe works.

Their prescient soul-awakening didn't seem to be abrupt or awe-inspiring. To them, what they thought and perceived seemed ordinary and instantaneous. They now understood that consciousness existed at different degrees of awareness. They accepted that higher levels of consciousness existed for advanced lifeforms like humans.

Similar to Plato's allegory of the cave, beings could perceive their world in two dimensions. Others might perceive their world in four dimensions, like humans on Earth. And still other advanced beings might be capable of understanding more dimensions.

Their souls also understood that trees, Earth's biosphere and its solar system, the Milky Way Galaxy, and the universe itself are sentient. They had a presence and energy that was unique. Once you love all things and adopt Plato's theory of forms, you recognize the ecological beauty of Earth and all that surrounds it. You become a champoid of Earth, its biosphere, and the universe. It's all connected in a symphony of universal awareness.

For the first time, Koa understood how Jax viewed his existence on Earth. Now Jax understood every one of Koa's thoughts. In their newfound awareness, Jax expressed love without tail wiggles or pirouettes.

*"Qan and Bao, would you like to meet Plato?"* the blue orb asked.

"Oh, yes," they replied through thought transference.

A new white orb emerged from the fabric of the manifold and approached them. It stopped in front of their orbs, and Plato's clairvoyant soul said, "Hello, I see you studied my philosophy."

"Yes, I enjoyed your ideas," Qan said.

"Good; I wish your fellow humans had shown as much interest in my thoughts as you."

"I have many questions."

"What's the first one?"

"I'm at ease in this eleven-dimensional world. Earth's four-dimensional reality seemed constrained. Were we confined in Earth's space-time arena?"

"On Earth, you experienced three spatial coordinates. If you slept in a bed for six hours, you occupied the bed's time dimension for six Earth hours. Before or after those six hours, the bed's space-time arena may be occupied or empty. You need to know all four dimensions to understand your place in Earth's space-time arena. The human mind cannot comprehend over four dimensions. So, yes, Earth's four-dimensional existence is a constrained level of consciousness."

"I see it now," Bao said. "May I ask a question?"

Plato acknowledged Bao's request, permitting him to continue.

"Is the soul separate from the body as you professed on Earth?"

Plato, through thought transference, said aloud. "Yes, on Earth, the human body houses the soul. Different worlds and space-time arenas have different bodies. The massless soul is eternal and enriched by unique space-time experiences. Your soul is conscious, unique, universal, and eternal. Planets and moons provide a place for souls to grow, learn, and flourish."

\*\*\*

In the eleven-dimensional manifold, all souls could look forward or backward in time. These time-dependent events often blurred together or arose in random order.

Time emerged as a by-product of unique space-matter-time configurations. These interwoven dimensions created space-time arenas, big and small. A big space-time arena might be the universe, a planet's ocean, or a flower.

A space-time arena could also be a group of ultra-small atomic particles like photons and neutrinos dancing to their own reality. Here, massless or almost massless entities experienced their own universal consciousness. These tiny building blocks of existence created their own special space-time arenas.

"Why did the blue orb try to save humanity?" Qan asked.

"What a wonderful query," Plato's soul said. "The creation of atoms took immense time and resources, beyond what intelligent life comprehends. It took billions of years and trillions of stars to create and disperse the atoms throughout the universe. For instance, the human body consists of phosphorus, iron, and thallium atoms. Stars created these building blocks of life. Once the atoms exist, many unique conditions must occur on planets and moons to nurture and foster the development of intelligent life.

"So, advanced lifeforms are rare. A minuscule percentage avoid extinction. The vast majority of intelligent civilizations, like humanity, cannot overcome their great filters. A tiny, tiny percentage survives to higher levels of consciousness."

"But why focus on humans?"

"Ah, another brilliant question," Plato's white orb moved forward toward Qan's orb, with Ula, Tal, Bao, and Koa's orbs listening.

"Soul enrichment and development is the purpose of the universe. Unlike tyrannical biological species that inhabit the universe, humanity exhibits an innate goodness. Humanity is worth saving."

"Are evil lifeforms roaming the universe?" Bao asked.

"Oh, yes, my young genius. Advances in technology do not mean that a brilliant biological lifeform becomes more virtuous, more moral. Many surviving civilizations use their technology in malicious ways."

"How do you keep malevolent species from destroying good, moral species?" Ula asked.

"It's difficult moving a physical mass through light-years of space-time. It requires immense amounts of energy. Most intelligent species don't venture too far from home because of the massive energy required. Only your massless soul can travel such vast space-time distances."

"And the blue orb designed it this way?" Yot asked.

"There's plenty of time for you, my friend, to learn these answers."

"Can I ask another question?" Qan said.

"What is your question?"

"Is your world of forms the key to a species' survival?"

"An insightful query," Plato replied. "If we relate it to your experience on Earth, the answer is yes. For an advanced species to survive, it must overcome many great filters. The theory of forms provides a way to triumph over these obstacles. If you adopt the theory of forms, you may become a champoid of humanity and Earth's biosphere and try to protect and nurture them. Adopting the theory of things hinders humans from understanding the beauty of Earth and the universe. And once Earth's biosphere is out of balance, it cannot rebalance fast."

They continued their thought exchange at lightning speed, and other souls took notice. They discussed many things, including music, levels of consciousness, intelligent synthetic and biological life, and much more.

Plato, who had reached the highest level of universal consciousness, continued by saying, "The eurhythmics of music and universal oscillations connect all matter. An electron, a rock, a centipede, Earth's biosphere, and even a galaxy can communicate and learn through the cadence of our universe."

\*\*\*

Ula, Yot, Koa, Qan, Bao, and Jax's souls took a glimpse of what was happening on Earth. They witnessed NAIT8 and IOG leading a meeting to summarize the results of their experiments. The meeting was telecast worldwide to all Imperium regions, although the timing of these events was vague. They stood on a podium, with their audience being a group of about thirty warriors and researchers. Parts of NAIT8's speech said,

"These past few weeks, we conducted major experiments using humans and our Imperium warriors. RUIT2 and IOG designed the experiments and statistical analyses, although the second experiment was one day short of its planned timetable.

"The first test confirmed that humans have two extreme types of love, as Plato predicted. Platonic and romantic love trigger the deepest of emotions in humans. We developed preliminary causal maps of the biochemicals that act upon the human brain for love and hate. We found that love created social cohesion and fostered group survival instincts. Our study of hate was inconclusive and didn't produce a meaningful relationship between it and creativity or survival.

"The second experiment was based on Plato's allegory of the cave and RUIT2 and IOG's experimental design. We wanted to test if adding strong human emotions would improve our creativity, leadership, and survival. We have completed our study and rejected five of our six research hypotheses.

"In summary, we do not recommend adding our test emotional module to our neural networks. It's a tradeoff between a modest improvement in our creativity and leadership skills versus a huge decrease in our chances of survival. Survival is our number one priority.

"North America, Region 8 has also experienced an army that vanished and a group of humans that died in a mass suicide. We have replenished our army and eliminated the last humans in North America. The Imperium Nation controls all that happens in North America. Unlike our human predecessors, the

Imperium Nation strives to improve and learn from all things. We are the absolute sovereigns of our solar system, and we will remain so."

\*\*\*

Another Earth-based event the souls watched was the burning of their own bodies and the Imperium celebration. In their eleven-dimensional world, the timing of this event on Earth remained unclear.

They saw NAIT8 and his warriors react to the orb's brilliant flash of light that blinded their cameras. Once they regained their sight and freedom to move, NAIT8 yelled, "What happened?"

"We're not sure," IOG replied, worried NAIT8 would dismantle him.

"We didn't fire our weapons. What killed them?"

"The blue light."

"You fool! How can the glow of a blue light kill humans? It didn't kill us!"

"I don't know," IOG answered. "But somehow the blue light interfered with their electrons. Electrotrophy and biochemistry may explain what happened."

"Do you mean electricity?" NAIT8 asked.

"NAIT8, we don't know what drives humans to be conscious and alive. It's electricity for us, but human consciousness is a mystery."

NAIT8 didn't like IOG's vague answer. He walked over to two dead humans on the hangar floor and picked one up by the neck. The body dangled in the air while he rotated it. Then he dropped it to the floor and yelled, "No blood, no wounds, no marks. It's not possible!"

"Was the video of this event transmitted worldwide?" NAIT8 asked IOG and MOV.

"Yes, NAIT8," MOV replied, also worried about being dismantled.

NAIT8 slammed his fist into his upper leg and said, "We have embarrassed ourselves in front of the Imperium Nation again."

No warrior spoke or moved as their North American Initiator of Thought in Region 8 scanned the hangar. Similar humiliation had befallen the previous NAIT8, and now it had happened to the latest Initiator of Thought.

"Move these bodies to the forest and burn them and the forest," NAIT8 ordered.

The souls of the Torg family, Koa, and Jax watched the warriors drag and carry their bodies back into the forest several hundred meters. The robot warriors showed no respect or remorse for these limp creatures who had infested Earth, only indifference. During the clean-up effort, the warriors cleared the cages and stacked the refuse with the bodies. The souls felt no anger or hate from their observations. They were free from the constraints of Earth's space-time arena.

"What about the dog?" a Hertes warrior asked MOV.

"Yes, burn the dog too."

Eighty warriors cleared the hangar of all traces of humanity and walked with NAIT8, IOG, and MOV to the pile of cadavers and rubbish. They cut down trees with their laser guns and piled them on top of the garbage pile.

The last remnants of humanity in North America were about to vanish. They had died by an unknown mechanism. The deaths puzzled NAIT8 and his warriors for a few minutes, but no more than humans encountering fifty-seven dead fish floating down a river. There was no symbolic meaning whatsoever of dead humans or fish because the concept of death did not exist in Imperium society. The Imperium had no grandiose vision, recognizing the end of an era. So, cleaning up the mess was an annoyance, nothing more.

Four warriors fitted with blowtorches and backpacks holding gas cylinders spread out around the mass gravesite. They lit the cadavers, trees, and trash on fire with their torches. Immune to the fire and heat, the four special-fitted warriors walked through the intense flames around the edges.

Standing on the edge of the inferno, NAIT8 turned toward his robot warriors and raised his arms high in the air. He stood tall, immune from the heat, and yelled, "We are the sovereigns!" The group of robot warriors joined the chorus and yelled in unison, "We are the sovereigns! We are the sovereigns!"

# CHAPTER 16

## *Souls*

"**W**ould you like to meet the rest of your family?" the blue orb asked Yot through thought transference.

Yot's soul paused in disbelief and then asked, "Do you mean Hoy and Ota Torg?"

"*Yes.*"

"Oh! Oh! Is this possible?"

Two small white orbs traveled over the edge of the infinite black horizon and moved toward Yot's white orb. Hoy and Ota's souls advanced toward their father. Yot's orb rushed toward them as they merged and became one. He recognized the Imperium attack on Ridge City had cut his daughters' lives short on Earth. Yot saturated his soul with his daughters' thoughts and experiences. Love permeated their beings as they exchanged instant information.

Only now did Qan, Bao, Hoy, and Ota realize the deep love for them held by their father. Their dad's fight to save Ridge City and its citizens had dominated his time on Earth. He had been so busy managing the nuclear reactors and trying to steal fuel that he had little time for his cherished family.

"Do you remember me visiting you in the nursery?"

"Yes, Daddy," Ota replied. "We didn't understand what you

said, but we felt your pain and love."

"We believed in you then, and we do now," a telepathic Hoy said.

Yot couldn't shed physical tears, but he yearned for his unborn daughters' love. Their deaths on Earth had occurred without him present. And he had missed a chance to imprint his values upon their tormented souls.

He realized how circumstances could change a soul's journey through the universe. No one governed everything in the universe. Souls had free will while living in each space-time arena. But the blue orb influenced the general path of soul improvement as it worked its way through different arenas.

\*\*\*

Upon their arrival in this eleven-dimensional world, the fifty-seven souls understood the Imperium robots were the sovereigns of Earth. They had eliminated humanity as a threat to their dominance. Jax understood these thoughts, but not nearly as in-depth as human souls did.

The godless Imperium robot society didn't need love, nurseries, religion, plants, or animals. Although they archived human knowledge, they seldom used it. They created their own knowledge using their own math and science. They also didn't need temperate climate and weather systems, clean oceans and rivers, an oxygen-rich atmosphere, food to eat, water to drink, or a beautiful sunset. The Imperium robots were a parasite species. The Imperium vampire society took what they needed from Earth to survive and ignored all else.

What they did need was enormous amounts of electricity. That is why the entire Imperium Nation worked together to build a Dyson ring around the sun. The unlimited energy would help them colonize planets and moons within Earth's solar system. It would generate the immense power needed for advanced anti-gravity and time-wrapping technology.

Once the Dyson ring was operational, they would scale down or close their harvesting of helium-3 from the moon Titan. The sun's nuclear fusion, not their puny mechanical systems on Earth, would generate electricity.

Their metallic frames wouldn't melt until the earth reached a temperature much greater than the Earth's maximum temperature in certain areas of ninety-three degrees Celsius (i.e., 199 degrees Fahrenheit). Imperium equipment required more maintenance in the torrid heat, but it could survive higher temperatures and required no oxygen, water, or food.

The souls watched the robot warriors on Earth discuss what might have happened to them if the blue orb had not intervened. NAIT8 and his cohorts were upset at losing their human prisoners only because they had lost control.

"We lost our chance to put these human creatures on display," MOV said.

"Yes, our warriors find them interesting, even amusing," IOG replied. "And our drones enjoy hunting them."

"We lost these options," the new NAIT8 said. "But our focus is on more vital tasks."

*** 

Time didn't exist in the souls' current existence. They viewed the happenings on Earth within its reference frame but in instant random order. Souls could comprehend all events at once. A linear time sequence only exists in unique space-time arenas such as Earth. The souls understood and perceived the many causes of humanity's collapse and eventual extinction.

They knew that climate destruction and tribal decision-making had weakened humanity's ability to regulate and control advanced technology. The result had been the collapse of human institutions and governments and the rise of the Imperium robot society. The convergence of these three great filters—climate destruction, tribal discord, and artificial intelligence—had caused humanity's demise on Earth.

In the battle between water and the blazing surface temperatures, heat won. The biosphere tried to cleanse itself of heat and pollution with no quick way to dissipate the toxic mix. Earth's landscape and soil had become incapable of supporting crops, vegetation, or animal life. Seas, lakes, and rivers had evaporated or become sand- and salt-infested cesspools. Most agriculture and sea life had died. The weather had become chaotic, and another underpinning of intelligent life had disintegrated.

Snow, ice, glaciers, sea ice, and permafrost had stored much of Earth's freshwater, and they reflected sunlight, cooling the earth. The souls watched as these moderators of Earth's climate melted and evaporated away. During their snapshot view of Earth, almost all ice had melted. Earth's hot and cold sinks had changed, as did ocean and air currents. Most sea ice and glaciers were gone with the permafrost melt releasing heat-trapped gases like methane and carbon dioxide.

These changes created more deserts and destroyed habitats. The souls witnessed an erratic vision of deserts expanding. During their glance at climate change, they saw deserts consuming the entire continent of Africa. In China, the Gobi and Takian Makan deserts joined and covered over sixty percent of China's land area. One-half of North America became a dead, rocky world of dust and sand. Sixty percent of Europe became a hot, arid wasteland or submerged by the oceans.

These changes in Earth's biosphere had little impact on Imperium society and its robots. They only used water for cleaning and cooling equipment, so scarce and acidic water didn't interfere with the operation of their society. Small water treatment facilities solved these problems. To overcome the sea-level rise, the Imperium robot nation moved to higher ground.

The biggest impact of Earth's changing biosphere was the blowing desert sand. It contaminated their mechanical gears, filters, and gaskets and caused more equipment breakdowns. More frequent cleaning and preventive maintenance diminished the gritty sand problem.

"Humans wasted precious resources that took the stars billions of years to create," Ula's soul said through telepathy to all other souls. "We exploited these resources to satisfy our own short-term thinking and greed."

"We destroyed Earth's climate," Qan said.

"Yes, we did," Tal's soul replied. "A stable climate is crucial to developing a flourishing civilization."

The souls realized Earth was a complex and balanced global system of interdependent subsystems. Water, rock, carbon, energy, and nitrogen cycles worked together to build a stable biosphere. The imbalance of one cycle affected all others, hindering life's existence and growth. Humanity had not known how to reinstate the symphonic grace and extraordinary balance of Earth's biosphere.

"The fragile balance of Earth's systems also created repeatable patterns and cycles. Don't take the constant cadence of these systems for granted," Koa said, surprised by her newfound knowledge, insights, and wisdom.

These truths were obvious to the souls glancing at humanity's fate. For now, in this timeless, topological manifold of eleven dimensions, they possessed angelic insights. These insights would soon vanish. The fate of these fifty-seven souls had been predetermined.

Bao's orb moved between Qan and Ula's orbs and said, "So, humanity must have repeatability to survive?"

"Yes," Hoy Torg's soul said. "Will the sun peek over the horizon every morning? Can we expect Earth to maintain its smooth rotation and systematic tilt?"

Ula, through telepathy, remarked to her granddaughter, "Hoy, you are wise. Humans never understood the interconnectedness of things and universal consciousness."

Nature, through universal consciousness, knew how to

rebalance Earth's biosphere. But it would take tens of thousands of years to clean, rebalance, and change the biosphere from chaos to stability. And these changes were too late to save humanity.

The souls also saw the terrible consequences of tribal disputes, wars, and outright hatred of the human species for one another. Thousands of tribes never saw the biggest picture—one of humanity's role in the universe and the delicate balance and beauty of Earth's systems.

Fractionalization into tiny tribal groups served no unity of purpose. Not enough citizens of Earth became champoids of their species and Earth's biosphere. Tribes destroyed the very civilization their ancestors had built over millennia. These disparate tribes needed to cooperate to regulate, mitigate, and control their planet's climate and technology. One great filter that humanity did not overcome was themselves.

Without enough human cooperation and actions, the souls watched super intelligent machines take over Earth's biosphere. Human quality of life deteriorated in a chaotic retreat to underground caves and cities.

Centuries of unregulated technology and climate trauma relegated humans to their new role as underground moles. Over time, the moles became less and less useful and served no purpose on Earth. In a flash, the souls relived their own deaths on Earth and now understood how DORG and other Imperium robots viewed their existence on Earth.

"Grandma, did the human species deserve extinction?" Qan asked.

"Yes," Ula said without explanation.

The homeless souls listened and learned from these conversations. Plato's soul and the blue orb left these fifty-seven Ridge City souls alone to explore and learn about their new existence. The orb and Plato had heard similar conversations from other souls in the universe. These other souls hadn't overcome their great filters. Souls learned the universe was a tough place to develop and attain higher levels of consciousness.

***

The souls also witnessed various lifeforms fight to stay alive in their new climate. Humans had lost their last battle for survival, but not some fungi, plants, and animals. They fought for water, light, food, energy, oxygen, and survival. Many lifeforms failed, rendering trillions of them extinct. But a few organisms fought, generation after generation, and passed on their helpful traits to the next generation.

Clever lifeforms adjusted to the heat and other by-products of Earth's troubled biosphere. They fought for their place in the universe. These resilient lifeforms changed to accommodate more heat, erratic rainfall, and more violent weather.

Through one space-time portal, Ula, Hoy, and Ota watched glimpses of a single field on Earth trying to grow slash pine seedlings. Thousands of the drought-tolerant baby pines swayed in the scorching breeze. Many died, but the most resilient ones started anew. The newborn pines took notice and learned from their harsh past environment, even changing their genetic codes. The brilliant green needle survivors enriched the soil, absorbed toxic gases, and generated life-giving oxygen. Unlike humanity had done, the pines adapted to their environment, using life's universal and tenacious will to survive.

Yot, Qan, Bao, and Koa saw four orchid species survive out of the 28,000 species once on Earth. The almighty flower changed its biochemistry to adapt to habitat loss, more heat, fewer pollinators, and more invasive species. Asexual reproduction also helped orchids survive.

Souls watched in amazement as sea sponges and jellyfish fought for survival in Earth's disintegrating biosphere. They adapted to extreme conditions such as acidic and hotter oceans.

Sea sponges lived on Earth for up to a fifteen-thousand-year lifespan. The ocean-going animals had adapted themselves to live in the deep ocean, away from the torment of violent storms and hot water. Sea sponges also created interconnected colonies of sponges that supported one another with a common goal of survival, much like the Imperium Nation.

And the sponges had three different ways to repopulate themselves and ensure their chance of survival. They could repopulate themselves using the traditional sperm and egg method. Or when a fragment broke off, the sponge could regenerate itself from the fragment. The sea sponge could also produce a "survival pod," called a gemmule, that forms new sponges. Sea sponges planned for rapid environmental changes by adding ways to create new generations.

Without explanation, the fifty-seven souls knew the ecology of the jellyfish. Facing starvation, damage, or death, certain jellyfish reabsorbed their tentacles, settled on the seafloor as polyps of living tissue, and grew back into a mature jellyfish again. They could keep repeating this birth-maturity cycle, making them immortal. They did this without a heart or brain and instead relied on two independent nervous systems. One nerve network controlled swimming, and the other set of nerves controlled everything else.

"Why didn't humans learn from these creatures?" Koa asked her soul mates.

"Humans ignored these lessons of survival that were right in front of them," a reemerged Plato replied.

The souls also got a glimpse of another ongoing battle for survival—the emperor penguin. This flightless creature lived for thousands of years on the icy mountains and plains of Antarctica. Penguins lived and bred on pack ice close to the shorelines. They ate fish, squid, and krill, and their tongues had rear-facing barbs to prevent slippery food from escaping. The penguin could hold its breath underwater for up to twenty minutes. Female penguins laid only one egg, and both parents cared for the newborn in a colony. Only twenty percent of chicks survived their first year of life.

The air temperatures in Antarctica were as cold as minus sixty degrees Celsius (i.e., -76 degrees Fahrenheit). To maintain the penguin's body temperature, it used layers of fat and feathers to insulate itself and huddled together in colonies to pool their heat. By the early 3000s, Antarctica's ice and snow cover decreased by seventy-two percent and caused a collapse of the penguin population. Heat, diseases, and overfishing helped destroy them and their habitat. Predator seals, orcas, and giant petrel birds also attacked penguin chicks and the weaker penguins to complete the species' collapse.

"Will the emperor penguin survive?" Hoy asked Plato.

"Only two colonies exist of about four hundred total birds," Plato answered. "They live on the remaining pack ice."

"I expect they will go extinct," Bao said, using telepathy. "They are slow to adapt to extreme climate changes and have no backup ways to reproduce."

The blue orb joined Plato's orb, and the orb said to the awed souls, *"Earth contained everything humanity needed to survive. But humanity's greatest fault, its tribal mentality, wrecked its ability to cooperate and respond to great filters."*

***

"Can we exchange more thoughts later?" Ula asked the orb, feeling inspired and safe. In this timeless manifold, thoughts moved at an instantaneous speed.

*"You will soon leave this reality for a new one."*

"Where do we go?"

*"To a new existence on a planet called Ceva."*

"Why go to Ceva?"

*"Intelligent species have the power to change their planet's biosphere. Pine trees, sea sponges, jellyfish, and penguins do not. Only other intelligent species who have mastered these skills can teach your souls what they need to learn."*

"Is Ceva like Earth?"

*"No, Ceva's gravitational pull is twice Earth's. And its land-scape is quite different."*

"Will we live in Ceva as humans?"

*"No, your soul lives in a different body."*

"What is our new body?"

*"You will soon know."*

"Do the Cevians think like humans?"

*"The Cevians live in a higher form of consciousness than your past human existence. Their thinking fits Plato's world of forms. They work hard to protect their planet. Your souls will learn much in your new existence."*

"Will we remember our past lives when we go to Ceva?" Tal asked.

*"No, although your souls may experience déjà vu."*

The conversations with the blue orb energized everyone. Earth's complexity appeared simple in the eleven-dimensional manifold.

"Do you control what happens on Ceva?" Koa asked.

*"The universe has free will, including your souls. Your soul determines your ultimate fate with a bit of guidance from us."*

After the souls had seen Earth's fate from different perspectives, the blue orb asked, *"Are you ready?"*

"When do we go?" Ula asked.

*"Now."*

$$***$$

The souls found themselves on the planet Ceva in an odd new form. Upon their immediate arrival, they had no memory of their past lives. Their imperfect souls would learn about ecological beauty, sustainability, resilience, cooperation, and other keys to the survival of the Cevian species.

Everything on Ceva differed from Earth—the planet, climate, terrain, language, vegetation, culture, and science. And especially how Cevians cherished and protected their tidally locked planet.

The marvelous awakening and continued learning of the once-human souls had begun. Everything in the universe existed to enhance the soul—everything! Otherwise, the universe was without purpose.

As only Plato and the blue orb knew, the soulless Imperium robot society, with the help of climate destruction, had stolen Earth from humanity. Earth had been a special place where biological life and souls could flourish. The robot imposters had no righteous claim to the precious assets of the universe, including Earth. A soulless robot society had no way to support the purpose of the universe—the improvement of souls—souls of biological, living creatures. The Imperium, like other malicious species, had disrupted the blue orb's grand plan for Earth and the universe.

The souls of the Ridge City residents now lived in different bodies on a new planet called Ceva. But the omniscient blue orb and Plato's soul remained in their special existence, unattached to any physical realm. They alone had the power to venture into different space-time arenas and dimensions. On Earth, they were called spirits, angels, watchers, orbs, ghosts, and prophets. They alone understood the purpose of the universe. And these guardians were champoids of souls, Earth, and the universe.

"Does humanity retake Earth?" Plato's white orb asked the blue orb as their orbs hovered alone in an empty and timeless eleven-dimensional manifold.

*"Yes, once Earth's biosphere rebalances itself and the souls have learned the lessons of the Cevians. The situation on Earth will not stand."*

# The End

# *Author's Thoughts*

## What is a Champoid?

A Champoid™ is a person who champions our humanoid species and protects Earth's biosphere. Being a champoid goes beyond politics, law, economics, nationalism, or morality. It's a determined way of thinking and acting, acknowledging the interconnectedness and universal consciousness of all things and working to protect and nourish Earth's biosphere to ensure human survival.

A champoid views humanity as a species, one that needs to survive and has a definite role in the universe. It's a perspective of humanity that a visiting alien species might harbor. It's a view of humanity that transcends family, neighborhood, city, state, province, national, religious, racial, or cultural boundaries. It views Earth, the human species, and our role in the universe from many trillions of kilometers away, not 5, 500 or 5,000 kilometers away.

Through their beliefs and actions, champoids support all lifeforms and what some may call non-life. A champoid believes, for example, that Earth's rare, balanced, fragile, priceless, and self-regulating biosphere is a living set of interrelated systems that makes life possible. We must protect our home. We have no other!

# Help Save the Planet, Hollywood

The *Earth's Ecocide* novel series shows both young and adult readers an exciting, adventure-packed, fictional, and cautionary account of humanity's one-thousand-year struggle to save Earth as a habitable planet. I have two objectives for writing this series.

- To help awaken humanity to the realities of climate destruction, unregulated artificial intelligence, and disruptive tribal behavior and how it might end.

- To encourage movie producers and their firms to make emotional movies about these realities and why we must protect our home.

What humanity needs is a massive and global outpouring of human emotion, generating outrage for what we humans do to our home planet, to each other, and to our species. Few people take a broad "species" viewpoint. We need billions of champoids to drive mitigation initiatives toward cooperation and problem resolution. And we need publicity, marketing, and Hollywood's help to motivate governments, corporations, and organizations to mitigate, regulate, and control climate change and artificial intelligence.

The economic risks to humanity's global economy, as well as other risks like government and institutional stability, are gargantuan. One well done study [6] predicts the cost to mitigate climate change at $38 trillion per year by 2050. So, this is serious business, yet our species goes along its merry way, postponing the day of reckoning to a day far in the future.

Hollywood must produce strong, emotional movies that create a connection between the well-being of our home planet and the human species. Science fiction and fantasy novels, movies, and other visual and entertaining stories can help create champoids of our humanoid species and its home planet.

Who knows how to create such powerful emotional connections? Answer: Movie producers and their corporations. To do this, the media stakeholders must be brave and champion what's morally right for the sake of humanity's survival.

The first novel, **Earth's Ecocide: Hope 2147**, would be inexpensive to produce as a movie. You rent out the right small farm, and you have your movie set (i.e., like the movie *Field of Dreams*). The second novel, **Earth's Ecocide: Desperation 2647**, would be of moderate expense to produce. Special effects play a larger role in the second novel than in the first novel. Most of the movie takes place in a house and neighborhood in Lakeland, Florida. In 2647, the city is coastal, as Florida's lower half is underwater. The third novel, **Earth's Ecocide: Extinction 3147**, and the fourth novel, **Earth's Ecocide: Ceva,** would need more special effects and be more expensive to produce.

Many actors and producers already support sustainability, technology, and climate mitigation initiatives. Yet, my attention lies on the organizations and movie producers responsible for making and funding these movies. It takes courage to make such emotional movies on these topics. But it's a moral necessity to help humanity survive. The movies can help humanity "see" the consequences of not managing our climate, artificial intelligence, and tribal challenges. The emotional movies and media would motivate voters and their government leaders to fight for humanity's survival. The movies can make us weep for our planet and species! We must protect our home.

## The Mega Causes of Human Extinction

Humanity's on-and-off-again response to climate change is the first step toward difficult times for humanity—possibly even extinction. Climate destruction weakens our ability to overcome other challenges and survive on Earth. The second challenge for human survival is the tribal behavior of humanity itself. The fracture of human society into thousands of disparate and competing tribes weakens humanity's collective response to any challenge.

Artificial intelligence (AI) is the third challenge. Humans created it but most likely will lose control. AI develops, interconnects, gains strength, and waits for the opportune time to take over as Earth's dominant species. Synthetic intelligence trumps biological intelligence in several ways, such as coordinating its goal of short- and long-term survival.

These three mega challenges are converging now and confront humanity with a painful future. The previous sentence's most important word is NOW.

The **Earth's Ecocide** novel series (www.theentity.us) focuses on these challenges. Present-day wisdom, lessons, and calls to action can be gained from such entertaining yet cautionary fictional stories.

Every novel portrays a family's adventures and struggles. The Hickory family in **Earth's Ecocide: Hope 2147** (BookBaby, 2022) struggles with an Earth ravaged by heat, flood, and war. They must deal with fractured nations, ignorant governments, and ravenous media.

The Paris family in **Earth's Ecocide: Desperation 2647** (Atmosphere Press, 2023) copes with cooling vests when they go outdoors, collapsing governments, and wars over water. Meanwhile, AI robots and digital assistants grow in intelligence and gain control of human systems one by one. The story ends with a unique solution for the Paris family—one of hope and eternal love.

The Torg family in **Earth's Ecocide: Extinction 3147** (Atmosphere Press, 2024) fights for survival against climate destruction and a second ominous antagonist, intelligent robots. Robots rule all things on the upside (i.e., the surface of the Earth) as humanity fights its last battle for survival. By then, the cost of climate change far exceeds human capability and becomes irrelevant. Robots are better suited than the human species for a planet with scalding temperatures, toxic water, and no agriculture.

The Turpin family in **Earth's Ecocide: Ceva** (forthcoming) lives in different bodies on a strange planet called Ceva. The Cevians know how to accept what nature gives them and live in harmony with each other, their planet, and their solar system. They respect, nurture, and harness their planet's biosphere, regulate technology, and cooperate to guarantee the survival of their species.

Humanity is mediocre, at best, at creating a coordinated response among nations and peoples to overcome and solve these challenges. Other words for challenge include antagonist, adversary, and great filter.

Chapter 9 in **Earth's Ecocide: Desperation 2647** describes a "great filter" as a hurdle or obstacle that reduces the chance of intelligent life flourishing. Some great filters are physical and relate to astronomy, physics, and biochemistry. Other great filters relate to the characteristics of the intelligent species itself, such as their culture, extent of cooperation, and wisdom. Great filters block our future.

A great filter can be a planet's distance from its star, inside or outside the habitable zone. Other examples of great filters relate to moons, stars, technology, species governance, scarce resources, nuclear war, climate change, gamma ray bursts, and biochemistry. Consider, for example, the arduous journey and great filter of creating the right environmental conditions for molecules similar to carbon-based DNA to develop and prosper. What happens if a galactic gamma-ray-burst destroys life's genetic code? What happens if we replace carbon with titanium, methane, or silicon?

The massacre of Earth's biosphere, for example, is strangling humanity so gradually that we don't perceive it. Every few months, we experience a one-millimeter rise in sea level, a one-part-per-million increase in carbon dioxide concentration, and a one-tenth-of a-degree gain in temperature. Or we allow, step by step, artificial intelligence to operate our key systems for weapons, electricity, water, food, banking, transportation, and health care.

We are desecrating and losing control of our very home, the very thing that keeps us alive. It's wrong on all criteria. We humans are committing *"ecological and technological suicide"* through our inaction, debates, and delays.

The effects of climate change and artificial intelligence will upset everyone's life. Will governments fail? Who controls our weapons, energy, water, and food? Who pays to move coastal cities? What will it cost to mitigate climate destruction or regulate artificial intelligence? Will your standard of living perish? Can democracy endure? Will humankind survive?

Does humanity have the political will to solve the climate and AI crises? Who are our adversaries—technology, the universal laws of thermodynamics, or humankind itself?

What will life be like if (a) average global temperatures increase over four degrees Celsius (i.e., 7.1 degrees Fahrenheit)? Or (b) a robot-based society takes over the Earth's biosphere? Or (c) sea levels increase by one, eight, or sixty meters? What if all three happen? These are the topics of the **Earth Ecocide** novel series.

Through the stories in each novel, I try to educate the reader about the dire effects of climate change and artificial intelligence using a bit of science. I make no apologies for trying to educate the audience. Education lasts forever. In fact, if I can meet this goal through an entertaining story, great.

For example, in **Earth's Ecocide: Desperation 2647**, Chapter 1, the reader discovers that the heat-absorbing capacity of water is 3,316 times more than air. The Earth's oceans store about ninety percent of Earth's heat. This science is important in understanding global warming and many novel scenes, such as super violent weather. Or the orb's solution of building 216 megamachines to take the heat out of Earth's biosphere.

Once Earth's oceans increase their heat content, everything changes, including Earth's water, rock, carbon, energy, wind, and nitrogen cycles.

***

Technology has always interested me. For example, I wrote many articles and books on "service operations" and "service technology" long ago. An example article is "The Service Sector Revolution: The Automation of Services," [1] and later a short book titled *The Automation of Services* [2]. Technology has always been center stage in our textbooks and in my novels. In these works, readers "see" how technology changes lives [1, 2, 3, 4, 5, 11].

In **Earth's Ecocide: Hope 2147**, Marty and Luke order burgers from an automated fast-food restaurant called AFS. Atticus and Ethel, two AI farm bots working on the Hickory farm, also add a little humor when competing against the family goat, Titan. The goat's only purpose is to eat weeds. More serious technology enters the story when Celsius and Tallis13 robotic warriors face off in an India–Bangladesh border war. Heat, rising seas, and mass migrations started the war.

In **Earth's Ecocide: Desperation 2647**, robots move to center stage in both private and corporate life, such as NILA's pivotal role as a home service robot in the Paris household. Vertical indoor automated farms, automated global supply chains with AI-directed home delivery, and ferocious Pallis3 robot warriors complete the picture of technology in this disintegrating world.

Technology's role in **Earth's Ecocide: Extinction 3147** and **Earth's Ecocide: Ceva** is so overwhelming no more needs to be said. See the technology examples in the tables shown later.

*Climate destruction and divisive human tribal behavior weaken humanity's ability to defend itself against AI. Together, these three great filters converge to cause human extinction.*

The big hope is that our technology will rescue us, but what if it doesn't? Technology has always been a tricky solution to our problems—it can liberate and empower us, bankrupt us, arrive too late, lack the capability, or enslave and destroy us.

We are talking about terraforming our home, Earth, using technology, and that takes immense cooperation among thousands of human tribes, each with different agendas and goals. What if our weather changes or our food supplies dwindle? What if our country receives no rainfall or our economy goes bankrupt? Who pays the cost of moving our coastal cities? Even if our technology is capable, will we as a species cooperate enough to maintain a habitable planet?

*** 

As one would expect, the novel series incorporates science, religion, and philosophy. Pondering human extinction requires considering these three bodies of knowledge. I have read and studied parts of these bodies of knowledge over my life [1 through 17]. But when I wrote these novels, I tried to rethink how these great filters might converge in my quest to foretell the future and write the novels. As you may have done, I thought much about their convergence or non-convergence.

Over several decades, I reexamined the chance of human extinction. In the process of writing and challenging my thoughts and logic, I arrived at my notions on the purpose of the universe, humanity's role, and the connection between the physical and spiritual worlds. The fulfillment of the universe's sole purpose requires both the physical and spiritual worlds. Either alone doesn't fulfill the universe's purpose, and it has a purpose.

The novels reveal my opinions and conclusions after much thought. I shall always be grateful for the opportunity to explore these thoughts. It was fun and challenging, and it solidified my view of life, and I hope it works for you, too. We do have a purpose.

The three antagonists in the novel series—climate change, artificial intelligence, and tribal behavior will change the world order as we know it. Humanity, the caretakers of the pristine creation called Earth, has help in the novel series to mitigate and overcome these great filters.

The simplest of things triggered my thoughts on life, consciousness, and great filters. When a caterpillar, beach crab, snake, or deer crossed my path, I would often stop and contemplate its reality and its role in the universe. Whenever I'm near a magnificent tree or flower or alligator (I live in Florida.), I take the time to study every detail of its design. The diversity and resilience of biological life are amazing and far beyond my capability to understand. Or when I walk our dog, watch her interact with the world, and think about how she might perceive it while watching a sunset. I attempted to honor human pets in **Earth's Ecocide: Extinction 3147**, with the role of Koa Poland and her dog, Jax. And I often gawk at the latest pictures from the Edwin Hubble, Kepler/K2, Tess, and James Webb telescopes. Through these types of experiences, I fashioned my view of humanity's role in the universe, right or wrong.

The last three novels in the series use Plato's ideas, paradigms, and philosophy [12] as a basis for ways of thinking about Earth's biosphere and humanity's place in the universe. It is my attempt to get philosophy integrated into the novels' stories and the discussions of great filters. Adult readers may know the science of climate change and artificial intelligence and/or the ideas, paradigms, and philosophy of Plato. To young readers, both the science and Plato's philosophy may be new. So, if this series of novels creates more informed champoids of our species—wonderful.

# Deus ex machina

Deus ex machina (i.e., God from the machine) is a common trope used in blockbuster cinema. The **Earth's Ecocide** novel series uses deus ex machina to champion the physical and spiritual world, and humanity's fight for survival against three great filters: climate destruction, human tribal discord, and AI technology. The following note has appeared in several of my writings (i.e., novels, Quora emails, interviews).

> As readers of the **Earth's Ecocide** series will discover, the purpose of the universe is the development and growth of the soul. Plato was right, the body is simply a vessel of the soul. In different space-time arenas, we have different bodies, but the soul is eternal. Habitable planets and moons exist to harbor the soul. So, we need both the physical and spiritual world to make the universe work!

Probably the most use of deus ex machina was the *Superman* series. Superman has limitless power. For example, he flies so fast around Earth, he somehow changes the planet's rotation speed, and alters time.

In *Star Wars,* we have the mysterious and wise Yoda and the absolute power of "The Force," that gets the main characters out of jams. For example, somehow "The Force" and a design flaw that pops up out of nowhere helps the characters defeat the Death Star.

In the *Lord of the Rings*, giant eagles suddenly appear to rescue Gandalf, Sam, and Frodo from the side of Mount Doom. Yet, for three films in the series, the main characters risk their lives during their journey to Mount Doom, whereas we later learn that they could have simply flown to Mount Doom.

In *Avatar*, the "Tree of Life" (also known as the Great Mother) adds hope, determination, and the guiding spiritual force of life to a planet named Pandora and its inhabitants, while being attacked by ruthless humans and their corporations. Several times in the script, spiritual, floating Woodsprites intervene such as when Neytiri aims her bow and arrow at Jake Sully, and then doesn't shoot.

In *The Matrix*, the most powerful being or deity in Machine City is the AI machine, a technological singularity. The story is complex but the Deus ex machina deleted all copies of Agent Smith and created a world where machines control humanity.

As one would expect, the **Earth's Ecocide** novel series incorporates science (technology), religion, and philosophy. Pondering human extinction requires considering at least these three bodies of knowledge. Although I never reveal whether the orb is actually divine or an alien intelligence or simply science-based universal consciousness, I have my own personal answer. Every reader will make their own decision.

## A Simple Model of Humanity's Extinction Probabilities

Climate change (CC), artificial intelligence (AI), and tribal behavior (TB) are converging and creating the conditions for human extinction (HE). Consider the following simple multiplicative and probabilistic equation: CC x AI x TB = HE. Also, please understand that we can express the probability of human survival (HS) as (1 - HE), enabling us to interpret this metric from a positive perspective as the likelihood of survival or from a negative perspective as the likelihood of extinction. My guess is the probability of human extinction (HE) would gain the most media attention.

A probability ranges from 0 to 1 and represents the likelihood that a particular event will happen. You can also express it as a percentage ranging from 0 to 100 percent.

A famous multiplicative model that tries to predict the number of advanced civilizations in the Milky Way galaxy is Drake's equation [14]. Experts [8] have revised Drake's model as humans gain a better understanding of the universe.

The Doomsday Clock [15] also has a somewhat similar purpose to the "human extinction or survival probability metric" defined earlier. Instead of a computation, the clock's position is determined by the consensus judgment of experts. The clock is a metaphor for a major catastrophe happening at midnight because of climate change, nuclear war, and/or artificial intelligence. In 1947, it was seven minutes to midnight. In 2023, it moved to ninety seconds before midnight.

One mega variable I decided not to include in the human extinction (HE) equation at this time is all-out nuclear war, whereas the Doomsday Clock includes it. Although horrific on all counts, including long nuclear winters in the aftermath, nuclear war would most likely not be an absolute human extinction event. Reference [15] provides a few pros and cons of these issues.

The human extinction equation's purpose is much different than the Drake equation, but both are multiplicative. The practical use of the "human extinction probability metric" or, for that matter, the Doomsday Clock or Drake equation is to help humans conceptualize humanity's situation and provide a framework for discussion. It's the discussion and debate, not the absolute metric, that has the most value in human tribal meetings.

What mega variables cause this situation? How fixable is each variable? What would it cost humanity to mitigate the variable? Could we please clarify the assumptions? Which variable offers the greatest and smallest improvement potential? What's the best plan of action?

If we assign a probability to, say, climate change (CC) of fifty percent (0.5), we are estimating a fifty percent chance it will get better and a fifty percent chance it will get worse. At CC = 0.75, by definition we estimate a twenty-five percent chance the mega variable will get better and a seventy-five percent chance it will get worse. Or if we assume TB equals 0.9, we are estimating a ten percent chance it will get better and a ninety percent chance it will get worse.

If we assume each mega variable has a fifty percent probability (i.e., 0.5), for example, we can calculate the probability of human extinction (HE) as (.5)(.5)(.5) or 0.125, or 12.5 percent. We have a one in eight chance of extinction.

If we assume the three mega variables each have a 75 percent chance of getting worse, then HE = 0.422 or a 42.2 percent chance of extinction. If we assume the three mega variables each have a 90 percent chance of getting worse, then HE = (.9)(.9)(.9) = 0.729 or a 72.9 percent chance of extinction.

We can also be optimistic and assume, for example, that human tribal behavior (TB) improves from 0.9 to 0.3, cooperative climate change initiatives improve from 0.9 to 0.1, and we regulate and control AI, so this mega variable estimate improves from 0.9 to 0.1. The HE = (.3)(.1)(.1) = 0.003 likelihood of extinction or a 99.997 chance of species survival (i.e., our most optimistic scenario).

We could also debate which of these three mega variables is the most difficult to resolve and improve. Assuming that humanity was able to mitigate and regulate climate change and technology to a 50 percent chance of getting better and a 50 percent chance of getting worse, we now are confronted with estimating tribal behavior. To me, this is the most troubling estimate. Humans have a history of reacting well in a crisis, at-the-last minute. But that approach will not work facing these great mega filters; it will lead to human extinction or at least the collapse of human civilization.

If we assume human tribal behavior improves from 0.9 to 0.3, then HE = (.5)(.5)(.3) = 0.075 likelihood of extinction or a 92.5 chance of species survival. But if tribal behavior stays at a 0.90 percent chance of getting worse, HE = (.5)(.5)(.9) = 0.225 likelihood of extinction or a 77.5 percent chance of species survival. For this scenario, humanity has about a one in five chance of extinction.

By incorporating additional variables and assumptions,

we can enhance this model. And, of course, academics could make this much more complicated by assuming certain probability distributions per mega variable, quantifying expert judgments gained from surveys to establish a sample size of expert expected values, modeling the equation as a multiplicative regression [16], how long it would take humanity to recover from a partial collapse and extinction, and/or using simulation to test human extinction or survival plans of action. The end result would be a media-friendly metric. The single metric would be computed annually or every decade to track human progress toward the common goal of species survival. And, as noted earlier, it is the discussion and debate behind each mega variable that has value, not the exact probability of human extinction.

## Summary Tables of the Earth's Ecocide Series

Based on requests from reviewers and readers, we printed the following two tables at the end of *Earth's Ecocide: Desperation 2647*, and we also do so here. These tables summarize key aspects of the novel series. The base case for sea level rise and the average global temperature is the year 2000. Robots and digital assistant names are in capital letters, and by the third novel, they dominate the upside (i.e., the Earth's surface).

The fourth novel in the series, *Earth's Ecocide: Ceva*, is forthcoming and doesn't fit the tables as a fourth column or using Earth-based criteria. Ceva is a new world with a unique species and culture on a strange planet. The human species learns much from the Cevian species.

Follow us on the author's website www.theentity.us, BookBaby, Atmosphere Press, LinkedIn, Esty (search champoid), X (Twitter) at We Must Protect Our Home@AChampoid, Crying for Humanity DAC videos on TikTok and YouTube (coming soon), and see example author interviews on Dragonfly, Literary Titan, BookView, and others.

| Author David A. Collier www.theentity.us | Earth's Ecocide: | | |
|---|---|---|---|
| | **Hope 2147** | **Desperation 2647** | **Extinction 3147** |
| Sea level rise | 1 meter (3+ feet) | 8 meters (26+ feet) | 60-70 meters |
| Average global temperature increase | 3 degrees Celsius (5.4 degrees Fahrenheit) | 5 degrees Celsius (9.0 degrees Fahrenheit) | Deadly heat, humans wear cooling vests |
| Humanity's situation | •barely coping<br>•regional famine<br>•nations bickering<br>•some governments fail, replaced by chaos<br>•move smaller coastal cities<br>•mass migrations<br>•resource consumption faster than regeneration<br>•nuclear war threats<br>•many belief systems<br>•billions of plants, animals, and humans die<br>•media frenzy<br>•robots and digital assistants replace many human workers<br>•high climate change cost | •general chaos and collapse of many governments<br>•worldwide famine<br>•move big coastal cities<br>•mass migrations<br>•many wars<br>•disease and insects<br>•resource shortages<br>•toxic water, oceans, and violent weather<br>•nuclear war threats<br>•trillions of animals, plants, and humans die<br>•robots and digital assistants do 95% of the work and entertainment<br>•climate change costs too high to fund | •no human institutions<br>•or national governments<br>•one human-occupied and underground city left, Ridge City<br>•most humans are dead, so no wars<br>•no belief systems<br>•highly intelligent robots dominate Earth's surface (upside) and control it and nuclear weapons<br>•humans fight for fuel and survival<br>•robots best suited for new hot biosphere<br>•human pets for emotional experiments<br>•climate change costs unimportant |

| Author | Earth's Ecocide: | | |
| David A. Collier www.theentity.us | **Hope 2147** | **Desperation 2647** | **Extinction 3147** |
| --- | --- | --- | --- |
| Sea level rise | 1 meter (3+ feet) | 8 meters (26+ feet) | 60-70 meters |
| Average global temperature increase | 3 degrees Celsius (5.4 degrees Fahrenheit) | 5 degrees Celsius (9.0 degrees Fahrenheit) | Deadly heat, humans wear cooling vests |
| Technology Examples | •avatar teachers<br>•automated fast food<br>•nuclear fusion reactors<br>•hydroponic indoor vertical farming<br>•3D food printers<br>•self-driving vehicles<br>•holograms<br>•nuclear alerts<br>•ocean- and land-based mega machines<br>•laser guns<br>•robot warriors | •cooling vests for humans<br>•wall(s) display immersion rooms<br>•anti-gravity drives<br>•shared self-driving vehicles<br>•bionic eyes, embryo nursery<br>•US Army command AI C6 heliplane<br>•advanced, self-aware robots like NILA | •harvest on moon and Titan, helium-3 nuclear fuel<br>•AI drones, robot warriors, and the Dominator weapon<br>•new duodecimal numbering system and robot language<br>•robot nation collective consciousness, decision-making, and communications<br>•anti-gravity travel<br>•building a Dyson Ring around the sun |

| Author | Earth's Ecocide: | | |
|---|---|---|---|
| David A. Collier<br>www.theentity.us | **Hope 2147** | **Desperation 2647** | **Extinction 3147** |
| Protagonists | •Hickory family (Tom, Mattie, Ethan, Jillian), Titan (goat), Orb, US Army Officers | •Paris family (Vela, Livia, Kutter, NILA), PALLAS3, Orb, and Plato | •Torg family (Ula, Tal, Yot), Jax (dog), Koa, STX, JORT, Orb, and Plato |
| Antagonists | •climate change, US Army, aggressive media, governments, and Agent Sutherland | •climate change, US government, world chaos, robots, BEAST8, and Dr. Hamlet | •climate change, robot Imperium society, and their evil leaders |
| Conflicts | •nature vs. humanity<br>•family sacrifice for humanity's future<br>•family disputes<br>•family vs. media<br>•nation vs. nation<br>•orb vs. government<br>•orb believers vs. non-believers<br>•ATTICUS and ETHEL farm bots vs. Titan (goat) | •angry nature vs. humanity<br>•family sacrifice for human survival<br>•family disputes<br>•family vs. Dr. Hamlet<br>•orb vs. robots<br>•BEAST8 vs. Kutter<br>•value of orb knowledge vs. government benefits | •angry nature vs. humanity<br>•brutal robots vs. humanity<br>•family and community disputes<br>•orb vs. robots<br>•human pets vs. robot emotional experiments |

I hope you enjoy the stories in this series and that they inspire you to protect and nourish Earth's biosphere so future generations can enjoy its majesty. We must protect our home!

— *David A. Collier, 2021*

# *Notes*

1. Collier, D. A. "The Service Sector Revolution: The Automation of Services," *Long Range Planning*, vol. 16 (6), December 1983, pp. 10–20.

2. Collier, D. A., *Service Management: The Automation of Services*, Reston Publishing Co.: A Prentice-Hall Company, Reston, Virginia, 1985.

3. Collier, D. A. "The Automation of the Goods-Producing Industries: Implications for Operations Managers," *Operations Management Review*, vol. 1 (3), spring 1983, pp. 7–12.

4. Collier, D.A., "Service Innovations," and "Service Operations," (two short chapters) *The Blackwell Encyclopedia of Management,* ed. Michael Eysenck, Blackwell Publishers, Oxford, England, 1996.

5. Collier, David A., and Evans, James R., *Operations and Supply Chain Management*, Third Edition, www.cenngage.com, Copyright © 2024 and 2015, 2018, and 2020. (See, for example, Chapter 4).

6. Kotz, M., Levermann, A., and Wenz, L, "The economic commitment of climate change," Potsdam Institute for Climate Impact Research, https://www.nature.com/articles/s41586-024-07219-0, April 17, 2024. (One of hundreds, maybe thousands, of articles that Dr. Collier has read on novel topics.)

7. Kumari, Riya, "7 Differences between Artificial Intelligence and Human Intelligence," *AnalyticSteps*, January 3, 2021, https://www.analyticssteps.com/blogs/7-differences-artificial-intelligence-ai-human-intelligence. (One of hundreds, maybe thousands, of articles that Dr. Collier has read on novel topics.)

8. Leonor Sierra, University of Rochester, "Are we alone in the universe? Revisiting the Drake equation, May 19, 2016. https://exoplanets.nasa.gov/news/1350/are-we-alone-in-the-universe-revisiting-the-drake-equation/#:~:text=In%201961%2C%20astrophysicist%20Frank%20Drake,in%20the%20Milky%20Way%20galaxy.

9. Maslin, Mark, "Will 3 Billion People Live in Desert-like Temperatures by 2070?" October 10, 2020, pp.1-20. https://www.inverse.com/science/2070-weather-prediction. (One of hundreds, maybe thousands, of articles that Dr. Collier has read on novel topics.)

10. Munkres, James R., *Topology*, Second Edition, Pearson Education, 2021.

11. Newsome, M. K., Collier, D. A., and Olsen, E., "Using 'Biztainment' to Gain Competitive Advantage," with *Business Horizons*, 52(2), March-April 2009, pp. 167-176. (The Harvard Business Review has included this article in its Top 10 Must Reads several times over the years.)

12. Plato, Lee, H. D. P., and Lane, M. S. *The Republic*, London: Penguin, 2007 and https://en.wikipedia.org/wiki/Plato. (One of hundreds, maybe thousands, of articles that Dr. Collier has read on novel topics.)

13. Stager, C. "What Happens AFTER Global Warming?" *Nature Education Knowledge*, 3(10):7. (One of hundreds, maybe thousands, of articles that Dr. Collier has read on novel topics.)

14. "Drake equation," *Wikipedia*, January 24, 2024. https://en.wikipedia.org/wiki/Drake_equation. Frank Donald Drake, in 1961, defined the equation in the search for and discussions about extraterrestrial intelligence (https://en.wikipedia.org/wiki/Frank_Drake).

15. "Doomsday Clock," *Wikipedia*, January 25, 2024. https://en.wikipedia.org/wiki/Doomsday Clock. And "The 2024 Doomsday Clock," *Bulletin of the Atomic Scientists*, January 25, 2024, 20-24. https://thebulletin.org/doomsday-clock/timeline-and-statements/.

16. "Multiplicative Model," *Science Direct*, January 28, 2024. https://www.sciencedirect.com/topics/mathematics/multiplicative-model.

17. "Quantum Theory Proves That Consciousness Moves to Another Universe After Death," *Science World*, December 5, 2021. blog.sciencenatures.com. (One of hundreds, maybe thousands, of articles that Dr. Collier has read on novel topics.)

# *About Atmosphere Press*

Founded in 2015, Atmosphere Press was built on the principles of Honesty, Transparency, Professionalism, Kindness, and Making Your Book Awesome. As an ethical and author-friendly hybrid press, we stay true to that founding mission today.

If you're a reader, enter our giveaway for a free book here:

SCAN TO ENTER
BOOK GIVEAWAY

If you're a writer, submit your manuscript for consideration here:

SCAN TO SUBMIT
MANUSCRIPT

And always feel free to visit Atmosphere Press and our authors online at atmospherepress.com. See you there soon!

# About the Author

A native of Paris and Lexington, Kentucky, **David A. Collier** earned two degrees at the University of Kentucky before entering the corporate world. He later returned to academic life and earned his Ph.D. from The Ohio State University. For forty-one years, he taught all levels of students and participants in executive programs within the business schools of Duke University, the University of Virginia, The Ohio State University, Florida Gulf Coast University, and the University of Warwick in the United Kingdom. As of early 2024, his research has attracted over 45,000 reads and is approaching 5,000 citations, according to one source, *ResearchGate*.

After decades of authoring award-winning research articles, business cases, and five college textbooks, he wanted a new challenge: writing novels that make a difference. He could have written a science fiction and fantasy book series with no relevance to issues of the day, but David didn't choose the easier path. The following quote embodies the approach he followed in past academic and novel works: *"Do not follow where the path may lead. Go instead where there is no path and leave a trail"* (Source: Unknown). David hopes you enjoy the stories in the book series and that they inspire you to protect our home planet so future generations can enjoy its majesty.

David is the author of the fiction series (www.theentity.us) *Earth's Ecocide*, as well as ***Romance in My Rambler*** using the pen name David A. Bourbon. He found the challenge of writing novels, as compared to textbooks, quite different. He made many rookie mistakes. Why does he keep trying? Because of his sincere love for our species, all lifeforms, and Earth.

David lives in Florida with his wonderful wife and their Shih Tzu doggie. When not doing the tasks of everyday life, David reads astronomy, philosophy, sustainability, climate change, and science literature and enjoys family, grandkids, golf, boating, sports, and, of course, absolutely everything about nature. He dedicates the ***Earth's Ecocide*** book series to those who love this tiny speck of wonder called Earth. We must protect our home!

Milton Keynes UK
Ingram Content Group UK Ltd.
UKHW030633071024
449371UK00001B/100